IN CASE OF REAL TROUBLE

''Mr. Garrett?'' It came from my right, in the shadows next to a dumpster. ''Hi, I'm Larry Bonner. I've been waiting for you.''

He extended a hand but I didn't take it. ''I don't think I know you.''

He smiled and dropped his hand to his side. I kept my eye on it, but he kept it there. I stayed on the balls of my feet, my knees slightly flexed, ready to move fast if I needed to. ''No, sir, you don't,'' he said. ''I've been sent to offer you a job.''

I watched his eyes. If he was getting ready to make his move, he was very good at concealing it. I looked past him, over his shoulder, watching the shadows. Then, without turning my head, I looked to both sides. Street eyes, the cops call it. In the neighborhood where I worked, you needed them.

''This is an emergency. A serious emergency,'' he went on. ''We'd like you to consider starting right away.''

''Who's we?''

''Can we go inside and talk?''

''Not until I frisk you.''

The February Trouble

by

Neil Albert

A SIGNET BOOK

SIGNET
Published by the Penguin Group
Penguin Books USA Inc., 375 Hudson Street,
New York, New York 10014, U.S.A.
Penguin Books Ltd, 27 Wrights Lane,
London W8 5TZ, England
Penguin Books Australia Ltd, Ringwood,
Victoria, Australia
Penguin Books Canada Ltd, 10 Alcorn Avenue,
Toronto, Ontario, Canada M4V 3B2
Penguin Books (N.Z.) Ltd, 182–190 Wairau Road,
Auckland 10, New Zealand

Penguin Books Ltd, Registered Offices:
Harmondsworth, Middlesex, England

Published by Signet, an imprint of Dutton Signet, a division of Penguin Books USA Inc. This is an authorized reprint of a hardcover edition published by Walker Publishing Company, Inc.

First Signet Printing, February, 1994
10 9 8 7 6 5 4 3 2 1

Printed in the United States of America

To

Ross Macdonald

1915–1983

None Better

The author wishes to express his deep appreciation to his agents, The Schlessinger-Van Dyck Agency of Philadelphia, for their continued loyalty, confidence, and support. Their efforts on his behalf are very much appreciated.

1

Monday, 6:00 A.M.

I like the time just before dawn, just when the sky starts to lighten. I always have.

When I was a kid I used to get up when it was still dark and watch. I thought, back then, it wasn't just the sun starting to shine on the same old things—each time the sun came up, the world was created all over again. I waited to see if it would turn out to be the same as the day before.

Much later, after Nam and the ambush and the hospitals, after I was off the medication, I'd drink all night and wait to see if things might come out different, just once, but they never did. My squad never came back and every morning the scars were still there.

Later still, the summer after my divorce, I was up at dawn again. I wasn't drinking much by then, just sitting in the backyard in a lawn chair, thinking and waiting. Hoping that one of those dawns, things would be different, that I would be able to go into the bedrooms and see the kids that had never been born. Once, while I was prowling the hallways, I thought I saw them, a couple of little blonde girls snuggled in bunk beds in a vacant room. After that I never looked again.

"Mr. Garrett?" It came from my right, in the shadows next to a dumpster. It was a man's voice, a young man's, cheerful and energetic. And even though it was pleasant, I took two steps back and put down my briefcase to free up my hand. He stepped forward and stood with me under the streetlight. Whoever he was, or whatever his business, he looked glad to see me. Late twenties, well dressed, clean shaven, and bundled against the cold. Not many people who worked around my office looked much like him. At that hour of the morning the neighborhood mostly busied itself with panhandling, boosting cars, and small-time hustling. It was too early for the big local industries, hooking and drugs, and this fellow didn't look like part of either one.

"That's me."

He stood close, and I moved back again to keep some distance.

"Hi. I'm Larry. Larry Bonner. I've been waiting for you."

He extended a hand but I didn't take it. "I don't think I know you."

He smiled and dropped his hand to his side. I kept my eye on it, but he kept it there. I stayed on the balls of my feet, my knees slightly flexed, ready to move fast if I needed to. "No, sir, you don't. I've been sent to offer you a job."

I watched his eyes. If he was getting ready to make his move, he was very good at concealing it. I played for time and said the first thing that came into my head. "I just got back from vacation. Actually, I'm still on vacation till tomorrow."

I looked past him, over his shoulder, watching the shadows. Then, without turning my head, I looked to both sides. Street eyes, the cops call it, always in motion, always watching as much of what's going on around you as you can. In the neighborhood where I worked, you needed them.

"This is an emergency. A serious emergency. We'd like you to consider starting right away."

"Who's we?"

"Can we go inside and talk?"

"Not until I frisk you."

He seemed startled. "Sure, no problem."

"Turn around. Open your coat and extend your arms out to the sides."

First, I checked behind me. There was nothing but broken sidewalks, abandoned cars, and the dark bulk of row houses and storefronts. The streetlights glinted on dirty snow and broken glass in the street. I patted him down, front and back, all the way to the ankles.

I checked the pockets of his jacket. There was no gun, of course; he wouldn't have let me search him if there was. Mainly I was interested in how he reacted to being touched, and he passed the test. He was jumpy and ill at ease, and partly off balance with the natural reserve that straight men have to being touched by male strangers. If he was straight, either he'd never been frisked before or he was a good actor.

"Come on," I said. "Let's get inside."

"Thanks."

I unlocked the two front door locks, threw back the dead bolt, and pushed the door. It didn't move easily; when it had originally been fitted, the builders hadn't allowed for the weight of one-quarter-inch sheet of steel. Just inside was a small foyer with a grimy black-and-white tile floor. A dozen or so pieces of mail addressed to the various tenants were lying there, left over from Saturday, but I didn't bother. Sorting and delivering it would give the receptionist something to do with her day. Not just the morning, the day.

I relocked the door behind me and took Bonner up the stairs to my own office. My door had a double lock of its own. My mail had been slipped under the door, but otherwise the room was the same as I'd left it, two weeks before. A file cabinet, chairs, and a desk, all secondhand. The file cabinet was mostly empty except for a stack of paperbacks I read to pass the time between clients.

I motioned Bonner to one of the chairs. He unbuttoned his coat, looked around for a hanger, then shrugged and threw it over the top of the filing cabinet. When he sat down I saw a fine puff of dust rise off the cushion. Damn those cleaning people anyway.

I found a yellow legal pad and uncapped an Ace Check Cashing and Notary Service pen. At one time Ace had maintained an office upstairs, but when his second rent check bounced, the landlord changed the locks and put his things on the street. They were gone in half an hour, of course. Ace worked out of his house now, and his line had expanded to include crack and numbers.

"You said 'we,' Mr. Bonner."

"Uncle Chan's."

"The fast-food chain?"

"Franchise," he corrected. "And the fastest-growing one in the country. We've opened three stores in New Jersey in the last thirty days, with ten more planned for this year."

"I'm not licensed in New Jersey. And I don't know the territory."

"No, no. This is local. The work is for our franchisee for south-central Pennsylvania. Chadwick, Bruce Chadwick. He lives in Lancaster. We've had problems with the new restaurant. And threats."

"Go on."

"In the last week we've had almost daily vandalism. Some serious stuff, as far as cost is concerned. Between direct and indirect costs we're out more than fifteen thousand dollars already. We've had warnings not to open the restaurant."

"Have the police been notified?"

"Just on the initial problem, with the windows. Not as far as the rest. We wanted to have someone advise us before we do anything. If that's what you recommend, we'll do it, I guess. But you can discuss that when you see our franchisee."

"Not so fast. Just who are you?"

"Chief administrative assistant to the head of the Middle Atlantic Division, Corporate." He made it sound like he was chairman of the Joint Chiefs of Staff, but I let it pass. He was entitled; he was half my age and probably made twice as much as I did.

"What kind of threats?"

"Phone calls and letters. They tell us not to open, but we can't figure out a reason."

"This sounds more like a security job. I do investigations."

"We've already got some rent-a-cops on the job. If you have any suggestions to improve security, we'll listen. But mainly we want you to get out and put a stop to it at the source."

"How did you get to me?"

"We think you're uniquely qualified. If I've got my

facts straight, you have management experience in fast food.''

''If you count the five months as assistant manager of a Taco Bell, yeah. But I never intended it as a career; I was just doing it till I could get organized as a private investigator.''

''We know that. Still, you're oriented. That counts for something.''

''How did you locate me so quickly?''

''My boss is Bob Mosier; he's head of operations for the whole Middle Atlantic. He's in Lancaster now, helping Chadwick get the first restaurant open. He told me on Friday to locate someone. I made some calls and got your name. Found out you were in Cancun till Sunday; from there it was a matter of waiting. I got here at five-thirty. I didn't think there was much chance you'd show at the office any earlier than that.''

''It can't be twenty degrees out there.''

''I've got a job to do. My boss doesn't like to hear excuses.''

''You couldn't have any idea I'd come by this early. Or even that I'd be in today at all.''

''I was guessing. If you didn't come by here, I would have gone to your house. Sooner or later I would have run into you. Like I said, I have a job to do.''

I found myself liking him a little more. ''Well, your luck was good. I had the kind of vacation that makes you want to get back to work and forget it ever happened. Tell me about this franchisee of yours.''

''Bruce Chadwick. He's been in food service since college. He's around fifty. Very successful; his last position before this was business manager for a corporation that operated a dozen Holiday Inns. We're lucky to have him.''

''Any threats since Friday?''

''Not as of six last evening. I've been out of touch with my office since then. But the last I heard, they were getting worse. The last one could even be taken as a threat against him and his family.''

''How do things stand right now with your man in Lancaster?''

"I told him you'd be out to see him Monday morning."

"You take a lot for granted."

"We've heard you're very good."

"Then you know I don't have to scramble around for every piece of business I can find." I'd made a nice fee off my last case, and even after the overdue bills were taken care of, my checking account was in five figures. It wouldn't be there long—I needed to give some of it to Uncle Sam, and my Honda was going to celebrate her tenth birthday soon, but for the moment I was free not to have to take everything that walked in the door.

"We know that, Mr. Garrett. We'll pay five hundred a day, plus expenses. I have authority to give you a thousand-dollar retainer right now. And if the case resolves in less than two days, keep the change."

"I still haven't said I'll take it."

"But you're interested."

"I'm interested in lots of things. But not all at the same time. Besides, this sounds like something for the police, or a security company if you want this kept private."

"My instructions are to hire you."

I didn't feel like walking into a union mess or trying to break up some kind of protection racket. Or much of anything that required a lot of energy, just then. Last week had been the twenty-second anniversary of the day my platoon was ambushed, and each year it got worse, not better. I wasn't sure I was up for a project like this. Of maybe I was plain scared of it. "The city of Lancaster has a fine police force; your man doesn't need me."

He wasn't easily discouraged. "I'll make you a deal. Do you have any appointments today?"

"No."

"Go to Lancaster; talk to Chadwick and Mosier. If you still think there's nothing you can do, tell them so, call the police, come right back here, and keep the thousand. Half a day's work." He put a check on my desk.

"I don't take sucker money."

"I'm serious. Look, my job is just to get somebody there. Whatever happens from there, it's off my desk. It's not my money."

I fingered the check in my hand, trying to decide exactly how much trouble it represented. He saw me still hesitating.

"Look. Check your answering machine. If there's nothing more important than this, you take the case. If there is, I froze my ass for nothing."

I rewound the answering machine and set it to play. A lot of messages had accumulated during the last two weeks. A couple were from prospective clients; more were from existing clients calling about their cases. One was complaining about her bill. The building superintendent at my apartment had called; all carpeting was being replaced; please call and set a day for installation. The next call was from my lawyer; the state supreme court had refused to reconsider its decision disbarring me. There was nothing he could do—he was sorry. A final bill would be forthcoming. Two calls from the body shop; they were ready to fix the old dents in my Civic whenever I could get it down there. A phone solicitation for magazine subscriptions. And then one from a voice I didn't recognize.

"Mr. Garrett, sorry to have to bother you with news of this sort, but it's unavoidable, I suppose. This is Michael Fletcher at the operations center of First Pennsylvania Bank. We've just received a—I don't know exactly what to call it—well, something from the U.S. Attorney's office in Philadelphia, a court order freezing the twenty-thousand-dollar deposit you made several weeks ago. Something about RICO, that the government thinks the money could be from organized crime, or something like that. I've checked with our legal department and they assure me we have to honor this. Please understand that the money is still there—it's just that we're not allowed to honor any checks against it until this matter is resolved. And by the way, I checked for you. There was a check to a Mark Louchs, Esquire, which we had to dishonor in the amount of one thousand dollars. I'm very sorry to have to give you this news. Feel free to call in and speak to our customer service representatives about this."

They were sorry? Not half as sorry as I was. The

check to Louchs was only a part of the problem. I must have spent two or even three thousand of that money already, between the airfare and the hotel and meals. The hell of it was, I'd earned that money. Earned it the hard way, in hard work and sweat and danger. And now it was gone again, because some GS-12 hit a button on a computer. Two minutes ago, figuring that five of it had to go for taxes, I'd been eleven or twelve grand ahead. Now I was three or four in the hole. Or maybe eight or nine—for all I knew, the government would want me to pay taxes on it. I wished I'd been a tax lawyer. Or a ditch digger. Anything other than a private eye with money problems.

Bonner had heard every word, of course, but his expression didn't change. He just sat there, his hands crossed in his lap, waiting patiently for me to answer. He was good—good enough not to gloat when he knew that he'd won. Why didn't I take the damn messages in private? But it wouldn't have made any difference. It was time to sell to the highest bidder, and he was the only customer in sight.

Finally he broke the silence. "Mr. Garrett?"

"Huh?"

"Are you okay? You seem to be a thousand miles away."

"No, it's nothing you'd understand."

He squinted at me. "Well, are you up for it? This *is* what you do, isn't it?"

I looked at him, ignoring the edge in his voice. It came down to that. You did it not because it was a bright idea, or because you were bursting with enthusiasm for it. You did it—well, because that was what you did.

"Yeah. Tell your man I'll be out there this morning."

As soon as I said it I was regretting it, but of course then it was too late.

2

Monday, 8:00 A.M.

When I got back to my apartment I realized that I hadn't had breakfast. The coffeepot was too dirty to use, so I made some instant in the microwave. There wasn't any bacon or eggs, but I found a TV dinner and threw that in the microwave, too. It turned out to be lasagna, and I misread the directions somehow. When it was done it was boiling on the outside and still frozen in the middle. It went into the trash. I loaded the Honda's trunk with a few clothes, my cameras, binoculars, and some other equipment, put my .357 in its holster under the driver's seat, and headed west on Lancaster Avenue.

The traffic was starting to run heavy, but most of it was going the other way, toward Philadelphia. I broke out of the stop-and-go after I cleared Paoli and increased my speed. By the time I reached Malvern the sun was fully up, and I could afford to go a little faster. I didn't want to keep Chadwick waiting. That thousand dollar check might turn out to have a twin brother.

I rolled down Gap Hill into Lancaster County. As often happens in bitter cold, the air was perfectly clear. I could see across miles and snow-covered farmland, heavily dotted with houses, barns, small factories, and patches of woods. Gap itself is the intersection of two state highways, one of which leads to Wilmington, and truck traffic was heavy. I drove on for about half an hour as traffic and building density gradually increased.

Just east of the Lancaster city limit I stopped at a convenience store with gas pumps and a phone. Chadwick was in the book—124 President Buchanan Drive.

The kid at the counter didn't know the area—they never do—so I bought a city map and a cup of coffee.

I crested another hill and passed through the tourist strip. Dutch Wonderland. Amish Farm and Homestead. Dutchtown East Outlet Center. A wax museum on my right advertised lifelike depictions of the Amish. As I drove by, a buggy was going slowly up the hill in the opposite direction. I wondered if somewhere the Amish had a museum to show their kids what the rest of us—the English, they called us—lived like. An exhibit with all sorts of things they found incomprehensible: trash compactors, wall-to-wall carpeting, lottery tickets, golf clubs, credit cards, and pets living *inside* the house. The more I thought about it, I thought they probably wouldn't bother. It was already too easy for the Amish kids to learn about the English; and anyway, the Amish weren't big on irony.

Chadwick's street turned out to be easy to find, once I had a map. The neighborhood, School Lane Hills, was elegant. No other word fit. It was built back in the twenties, when people still built residences with class. The streets were lined with full-grown elms and maples that met overhead. Even without any leaves, the trees were impressive. The houses were set well back from the road, and mostly above the road level, as if to secure a height advantage over the rabble if the revolution ever came. The houses themselves were a mix of Italianate, Gothic, Tudor, and Federal, each carefully set apart from its neighbors. Every house had an inner defense perimeter of old plantings and hedges, most of them buttressed by windscreens of burlap and sticks.

Chadwick's house was a rambling Tudor style, two and a half stories tall, and covered in dormant ivy. The windows were arranged to keep a wary eye on both adjoining houses. It was the kind of place that new money buys when it's trying to look like old money. I approached on a long curving drive lined with boxwoods, and parked just short of the front door.

A heavyset Amish woman opened the door and regarded me without smiling. "I'm Dave Garrett, I believe that Mr. Chadwick is expecting me." There was a pause while she seemed on the edge of saying something but didn't. She moved back, half disappearing into the shadows of the interior. I stepped inside and she shut the door firmly behind me.

Inside it was dim, and there was a faint musty smell. While she was hanging my coat, I had a moment to look around the living room. However long the Chadwicks had lived here, they were still moving in. Inlaid cherry bookcases lined two walls, but they were empty. The sofas were still covered with their plastic shipping packaging. The Oriental rug underneath was evidently here on approval—the dealer's tag was still attached. I tried to read the price, but it was upside down and there were too many zeros.

She led me down a bare hallway, which seemed to go straight forever, and then took a hard right. I passed by doors on both sides, but all of them were shut. The corridor ended in an open doorway; she stopped in front and motioned me to go on.

I entered a suite of connected rooms. At one time they must have been a set of bedrooms, or perhaps some rooms for an elderly relative; but now they were packed with Chadwick's business operation. The room I was standing in was mainly taken up by workstations for three women, their typewriters, calculators, and files. All three were typing at once. Off to my left I could see a much smaller room furnished with a small round conference table and four chairs. To the right was a larger room that two men in ties and shirtsleeves were using as their office. One of them I recognized as Bonner. Both were squinting at a computer screen and arguing earnestly about effective gross transaction cost. Behind them I saw a door, freshly painted, with a panic bar. Labor & Industry compliance, I guessed. No one in either room noticed I was there.

I felt the presence of someone behind me, close, and bigger than the maid, bigger than me. At the same moment all of the typewriters stopped and the two men in the other room looked up.

"Mr. Garrett. I'm glad you're here."

I turned. Bruce Chadwick was tall and slender, and his smile showed impossibly even, perfect teeth. He was wearing a white shirt with no tie. Except for some gray at the temples, his hair was black. It was recently cut, but I could see that it hadn't been combed that morning. He extended his hand and pumped mine once. He made an effort to keep smiling, but it never quite reached his eyes, which seemed to look past me.

"Pleased to meet you, Mr. Chadwick."

I followed him into the conference room. Beyond, I could see into his private office. I got a glimpse of a bare desk with a few papers on a credenza behind it. Off to the side of the desk was a computer. In the far corner was an umbrella stand filled with rolls of construction drawings. Except for his own chair, there was nothing else in the room.

He shut the door leading to the central office, and immediately the clatter of the typewriters resumed. We sat down at the conference room table, which had started life as a dining room table, with matching chairs. His office chair looked like it was from the same set, too. I wondered what the family did at Thanksgiving.

He leaned back in his chair and rubbed his eyes. His movements were slow, and I wondered how much he'd slept recently. But his voice was clear and even. "I'd like to thank you, first of all, for taking on this case so quickly. I'm told you just arrived back from a vacation last night."

"It was explained to me how important it was."

"That didn't keep a couple of the big agencies from turning me down."

"Did they say why?"

He opened his hands in a sad, helpless gesture. "Too busy; not enough notice, this is what the police are for, blah, blah. They don't want to give me credit for—"

The door flew open and banged against the stop so hard that it rattled. I looked up; a big block of a man took up the doorway. "God damn it, Bruce. I told you, I wanted to be in on this from the ground floor."

Chadwick didn't seem to notice the shouting. "Mr.

Garrett, I'd like you to meet the chief of development for Uncle Chan's. Bob Mosier.''

I stood up, but when I was finished he still had a good three inches on me, plus the better part of fifty pounds. I recognized him as the man who'd been talking with Bonner in the other room. His face was deeply tanned, with heavy frown lines and the beginnings of jowls. His hair was mostly gray, and cut as short as the hair of any civilian I could remember.

He didn't give me any more time to size him up. He gripped my hand hard once and broke contact, the kind of perfunctory shake boxers give before they come out swinging. He closed the door and took a chair between Chadwick and me. ''So here's the miracle worker, huh? So what's been going on behind my back?''

Chadwick closed his eyes. ''Nothing, Bob. Mr. Garrett and I were just getting acquainted.''

''Well, let's save the sociability for later. If—''

''I was asking Mr. Chadwick what the other agencies said.''

Bruce seemed grateful for the chance to gain some control of the conversation. ''They were sure it was a crank, or some kids, that there was nothing—''

Mosier broke in. ''One agency even said that they'd have trouble getting paid if it turned out to be just some kids.''

I addressed my question to Chadwick. ''And how did you reach me?''

''Sheer luck. At least, I hope it turns out to be lucky.'' He chuckled and I smiled back, knowing that he meant it the right way. ''I mentioned the problem to one of the financial people, Bonner. He seemed real interested. Real helpful guy. He made some calls, got back to me within an hour. Offered to put a top-notch man on the case right away. He said they'd run the bill through corporate. But I turned him down on the second part. So you send me your bill, okay?''

''I've received a one-thousand-dollar retainer already. If we get beyond two days I'll let you and them fight it out. Did you contact the police about any of the incidents after the first one?''

He fidgeted, as if he weren't sure which answer would please me. I made a mental note that I would have to question him very carefully. Clients who try to tell you what you want to hear can be trouble. ''Well, sort of.''

''Go on.''

''My bookkeeper's husband is a detective on the city force—Lancaster's, I mean. I talked to him about reporting it, in general terms. He said that if I wanted to make a formal report they'd give it lots of publicity, make sure everybody knew about it.''

''That's the way they work. They want to keep the heat on people. Even if it doesn't result in some arrests, it may scare them off.''

''Well, Uncle Chan's is new in town here, trying to build up a reputation. What a hell of a thing for the community to know about a business as an introduction. I figure that if someone is trying to hurt us, making a big deal out of it might be playing into their hands. So I decided to sit tight until we know more.'' He looked at me anxiously. ''Did I do the right thing?''

I shrugged. ''I'm an investigator, Mr. Chadwick, not a bullshit artist. I'm not going to kid you or reassure you just for the sake of doing it. There's no way to know, except with hindsight, whether you did the right thing. But since we've waited this long, let's keep waiting until something definitely comes along. Then we can decide what to do.''

It was Mosier's turn again. ''And I hope you don't ever start bullshitting us. I need to have the straight dope. I've got a company full of b.s. artists already.''

''Nobody's ever accused me of that.''

''Have you had any breakfast?'' Chadwick asked. ''I gather we caught up to you pretty early.''

''I've just had some coffee. I'll eat later.''

''No; come on. You're going to be working hard. I'll have Mary get breakfast ready for us all. I haven't eaten yet myself.''

Eating a meal with Mosier wasn't my idea of a good

time, but before I could think of anything to say he had placed his orders with Mary over the intercom. "Come on, men, let's start the day right." We followed him back to the kitchen. Somehow, Mary had not only cleared the table, but already set it for the three of us.

"Let me tell you, Dave, I'm really glad to see you. I feel like a nightmare is ending."

I was having trouble reading him, or maybe I was just naturally suspicious of people who are grateful in advance of the result. "I haven't done anything yet."

"Still, I feel better knowing someone's working on the problem."

As we talked I tried to get a sense of the man. He paused every time before he spoke, and his voice was carefully modulated. Either he had taken voice lessons, or he kept himself under iron control. His movements, though, were quick and jerky, and I wondered how well rested he was. At one point he tipped over a coffee cup, which fortunately turned out to be empty. Then he held onto the cup tightly for a moment and took a deep breath. I could see the tension in his jaw muscles. I was going to have to allow for displays of temper and even bad judgment calls because of his fatigue.

Mary poured coffee and juice, and the kitchen began to fill with the salty, greasy smell of frying bacon and eggs. I remembered how hungry I was.

"Just what are your qualifications?" Mosier wanted to know. It was a fair enough question, but not with the tone he used.

"Ten-plus years of private practice as a lawyer, two years as a licensed private investigator, five months as assistant manager of a fast-food operation. And three years in the Marines."

"Combat?"

"One and a half tours in Vietnam."

Mosier nodded, and something passed between us. I could have asked him where he'd served, but it didn't seem like the right time. He was the kind of man who wouldn't engage in any small talk with the hired help until they'd proved their usefulness.

Our food arrived. Chadwick gestured with his fork. "You know why no one ever made a fast-food Chinese franchise work before?"

"Too much competition?"

"Heck, no. There are a million places to buy burgers, but that doesn't stop McDonald's. Hell, nonfranchise competition is good for you; it gets people used to the idea of Chinese food. That's the trouble with Taco Bell. Their food is good, but the franchise only really works in the West and Southwest, where people already know about Mexican food. No, Dave, the key is limiting the menu."

"Limiting?"

"Let's face it. Sit-down eating is white collar; fast food is blue collar. Except for the students, who eat there strictly based on budget. Your average working-class person is intimidated by a menu with a hundred choices, whether it's Chinese or Mexican or American. You give him ten things to pick from and he's happy. It's a scope he's comfortable with. And with a limited menu you can keep down the cost of food. Which is really low for Chinese food anyway."

I mopped up my egg with a piece of bread. "At Taco Bell we had a lot of theft. When you're operating, I assume you'll keep a tight watch on that."

It was Mosier's turn. When he was talking about something he knew, he could sound surprisingly reasonable. "For money, yeah, sure. The stats show that eighty-five percent of your employees will admit that they'd steal from you if they had the chance. You know what that means?"

"Go on."

"I've been in fast food for twenty years. It means that fifteen percent of the people taking the test were lying."

"And what about food going out the back door?"

Mosier shrugged. "If we sold steaks, we'd keep an eye on it. But it's mostly vegetables. You can lose a lot of rice and not be out more than a couple of bucks.

Uncle Chan's runs without any inventory control at all."

"No kidding."

"It seemed funny to me, too, when I first started. But from the beginning that's what they wanted. They said that they'd made a study; as long as we could control the cash, managing the inventory would cost more than it would save."

Mary poured me another cup of coffee. "Interesting."

"It's not as odd as you might think," Chadwick said. "The packaging helps. Take a high-priced item, like shrimp. The shipping package we use is way too big to conceal under your clothing. It weighs close to forty pounds. The case stays in the freezer in a compartment that only the manager or the assistant manager has a key to. All you have on the food line is enough for the shift."

"Good thinking."

"Same thing with beef, even the chicken."

I looked at my watch. It was time to take some control of the situation. "Ready to get started?"

"Sooner the better."

I got out a small notepad. "You have a restaurant nearly ready to open. Where is it?"

"Only about a mile from here."

"Most of what's happened has involved damage at the site?"

"That's right, you—"

"We'll get into the details later. Right now, I'd like you to take me there so I can see for myself." The two of them exchanged a look. I sensed surprise, and wariness. Perhaps they wanted to get to know me better, or they had their own agenda of how they wanted this investigated. I didn't care. Uncle Chan's check was already in the bank, and I was going to do the job my way.

Chadwick spoke after a moment. "Certainly, Mr. Garrett, however you want to handle this. I've had the staff prepare a little more history of the franchise, kind of a briefing, but—"

"Thanks, but I think I'll just ask questions as we go, if that's okay."

"Fine," he nodded. "Could you give me a couple of minutes with Bob? Then we can all go over together."

"I think I'll use the john while I'm waiting."

He turned to Mosier, and the two of them began discussing something about the training of crew chiefs. Perhaps they felt it wasn't necessary to explain to a professional investigator how to find a bathroom. I retraced my steps to the living room and opened a likely-looking door. I was in luck.

When I came out, a woman was standing by the sofa, looking out the living room window. I saw her in profile, with the morning sun shining strongly in her face. Her hair was done in what women call the frazzle style: golden red curls going in every direction and down to her shoulders. She had a redhead's pale complexion, but her eyes were dark, almost black. She was wearing gray exercise clothes, but not for working out—a couple of gold bracelets protruded from the cuff of her sweatshirt, and she was wearing heels instead of tennis shoes.

There was nothing outside for her to see, as far as I could tell, except the curve of the driveway and the little bit of street that was visible from the house. I couldn't tell if she expected something to happen, or if she was just thinking about something and happened to be looking out the window.

I shut the bathroom door a little harder than necessary. She turned around so that the sunlight struck her from behind, putting her face in shadow.

"Hi. I'm Dave Garrett."

She extended her hand; the nails were perfectly groomed and painted. "Nice to meet you—can I call you Dave? I'm Anne Chadwick. You're the investigator." It wasn't a question.

"Pleased to meet you, Anne."

She was a good deal shorter than Chadwick—and younger, too. Or perhaps she'd had a face-lift; Lord knows they seemed to have the money for it.

"You must have just come in. Have you been here long? I know Bruce was expecting you."

"Just long enough to have breakfast and get some background."

"About the restaurant?"

"Yes, that's right."

She tried to form an expression of disapproval but wound up with a pout. "This trouble with the business, it's awful, isn't it? I mean, people smashing brand-new things like that. Such a waste."

"I'm sorry, but we have to go," I said. "But I'd like to talk to you when I get back. Will you be around?"

She seemed startled at the idea I would want to interview her. "I have some errands to run this morning. But it's my husband's business. I don't know anything about it."

"If I understand the situation, most of the upper-level employees are in and out of this house all the time."

"Oh, yes. Bob and Larry practically live here these days."

"Sometimes these things are inside jobs."

"What does that mean?"

"This could be the fault of someone who works for the company."

"I can't believe anyone here would want to see the business hurt. They all work so hard."

"I hope you're right. But it's my job to eliminate possibilities."

She looked around. "I apologize for the condition of the house."

"It's fine."

"It's so hard for Mary to keep up with so many people underfoot. And Bruce won't let me have her every day."

"Having a home office has its drawbacks, I'm sure."

"You're going to be staying with us, aren't you?"

"It really hasn't been discussed. But if it wouldn't be any trouble, it would make my job easier."

"Oh, it wouldn't be any trouble," Anne said. "We

have lots of extra space. And we have another house-guest anyway, my cousin Kate. Are you married?''

''Not anymore.''

''Well, I'll have Mary make up a room. Do you play bridge?''

''I never even figured out hearts. I always lost.''

A boy in his early twenties came through the front door, carrying a bag of deicing salt. ''Jeremy,'' Anne said, ''I'd like you to meet Mr. Garrett. He's going to be staying with us for a few days. He's helping with your father's business.''

He had his mother's hair, thick, and blond, with reddish highlights, hanging down to his collar. He was every bit as tall as his father, but not as broad, and his posture was bad. His hands were small and pale, but his grip was surprisingly strong.

''Jeremy Chadwick. Pleased to meet you, Mr. Garrett.''

''Same here.''

Chadwick came around the corner and saw the three of us. ''Did you get those walks all taken care of, Jeremy?''

''Yes, sir.'' His voice dropped when he addressed his father.

''You remembered to do all the way around this time?''

''Yes, I did.''

''This is a place of business; we have to make sure that people don't slip and fall. The—''

Before he could lecture Jeremy any further, Mosier came in, wearing his coat. ''Come on, guys, let's roll. No point in screwing around here any longer.''

I said my good-byes and we were on our way.

3

Monday, Noon

Five minutes later the restaurant was in sight. Chadwick was driving and I was in the back. "As you can see," he said over his shoulder, "it's a good location. It's a major arterial with a daily traffic count of thirty thousand plus. Sixty thousand people within a one-mile area. The demographics make them a little old for us, but the household income picture is good." His voice lapsed into a singsong; he must have given this pitch a hundred times to investors, representatives from the corporation, lenders, the chamber of commerce, and anyone else he needed to talk to. "Labor's a problem; Lancaster County has chronically low unemployment, five, even three percent at times. We have to pay five bucks an hour as a basic wage, five and a quarters for closers. But the location, it's super. There are five other fast-food locations within half a mile, and we're part of a shopping center with seventeen stores. The signage is out of this world. When we come around this bend you'll see what I mean."

The road curved slightly to the left and then straightened. I could see a good quarter of a mile; the road was broad, two lanes each way and a center turning lane, and both sides were lined with businesses—car dealers, bars, restaurants, small shopping centers, office buildings. But what caught my eye was dead ahead, a little to the left, at the crest of the hill in the distance, an enormous green-and-yellow UNCLE CHAN'S sign in the shape of a takeout box, with thirty-foot crossed chopsticks underneath as supports.

"And the visibility is just as good from the other side," Chadwick continued. "Best on the strip. We figure this to be an eight-hundred-thousand-grossing store the first year. And we're hoping it'll be a million-dollar store in two years.'' We made a left into the parking lot and were stopped by a uniformed security guard. Chadwick rolled down his window. The guard gave him three security cards and waved us through. ''It's because of the threats,'' he explained unnecessarily.

The site was swarming with workmen, Uncle Chan's employees, and equipment installers, all wearing identical tags clipped to their jackets. There were just as many panel trucks and vans from the workmen as there were personal cars from the employees.

''The place looks a long way from finished to me.''

We got out of the car. The restaurant sat on a small hill, and the wind was cold. Chadwick shook his head. ''We're a lot closer than it looks. All the mechanicals are in, and the food-service equipment. The driveway and parking lot are paved. We've even had the food lines open already, as a test. It's a matter of finishing work. As a matter of fact, we have our first open house today. It's not general public. We're giving away free lunches on an invitation-only basis. You know about open houses?''

''The place I worked at, we did the same thing when we opened. We were the first Taco Bell in our area, so there was no other way to train the crews. Who got invitations?''

''You need the names?''

''No, just in general.''

''Employees and their families, our attorneys, the engineers, the accountants, the bank people we've worked with, our insurance agent, some friends, and some people we'd like to have aboard as investors.''

''Running a full menu?''

''Too expensive. No shrimp or lobster items. No desserts, only one beef dish. But everything else.''

''How many people you expecting?''

''Maybe a hundred, hundred and twenty-five. The invitations say one to seven, but I don't expect a rush till a little after five.''

"Is it too late to call it off?"

"What are you talking about?"

"I'm talking basic security. One, the people closest to you are those with the biggest motive to harm you. Letting people run around the site complicates things. Two, you think you've had problems so far? An open house would be a perfect chance to embarrass the franchise. Not just with the general public, but with the people behind it."

"I hadn't thought of that," Chadwick admitted.

"And our security agency didn't say diddly," said Mosier. "Great advice they gave us." He looked around the parking lot anxiously. "Shit, Bruce, he's got a point."

Chadwick looked around, too, as if that would give him the answer. I could see his eyes looking past me, not quite taking me in, as he thought through the problem. After a moment he nodded slightly, just to himself. "If the invitations weren't out I'd call it off. But once we invite people, what are we going to do? We go ahead." He looked at me. "But it's a good thought, Dave. Keep them coming."

We went inside, and I could see that they were indeed almost ready. The floors were still dirty from construction, but all the tables and counters were in. The workmen were finishing people, not basic construction—painters and paperhangers, plus a couple of computer installers working on one of the registers. With three days of hard work it would be in shape for a general opening.

"Here's where we had the first problem," Chadwick said. He pointed to the four big windows, each one about ten by eight, along the west wall. They looked like they had chicken pox. "The glazier says it was some kind of gun. Bigger than a BB gun, unless they were real close."

I took a look at the nearest mark. Something had hit the glass on the outside and dug out a neat, circular depression that glinted greenly in the afternoon sun. I stepped back and counted at least a dozen in that pane alone. "I bet it was a twenty-two pellet gun. It has a decent punch, but it's silent. And if they had a good one, they wouldn't have to be at point-blank range.''

''We thought it was kids, at first,'' Mosier said. ''We told the police so that our insurance would cover it. They came out and took pictures. They said there wasn't anything else they could do.''

Chadwick started leading us back toward the parking lot. ''They had a real problem a couple of years ago with kids slashing tires around here. Some jerk slashed the tires on something like a hundred cars in a year. They finally caught him, but they had a hell of a time. Anyway, speaking of that, this here was the next problem.'' He gestured around the parking lot. ''Our workers started reporting flats, lots of them. We checked it out; there were a couple of thousand roofing nails scattered around the lot. We had to bring in a special vacuum on a truck to get rid of them.'' He pointed at a bright-green dumpster, partly hidden behind a screen of pressure-treated wooden picket fencing. ''That same day we found that the bottom of the dumpster was ruined.''

''Some son of a bitch poured acid into it,'' Mosier growled. ''Ate the bottom out. The trash hauler says it's our responsibility to replace it. You know how much those things cost?''

I didn't, and I didn't want to know, because I had the feeling that Mosier would start a speech on how the haulers were ripping them off. ''Did you call the police on those incidents?''

''We were ready to,'' said Chadwick. ''But then we got the call from the newspaper.''

Workmen were passing by us on both sides. ''Is there somewhere we can talk privately?''

''There's a small office in the back. It's not much—they want the manager to be out on the floor, in sight.''

It was barely big enough for the three of us, and we all had to stand. But at least it was reasonably secure once the door was shut. ''Go on about the papers.''

Chadwick leaned away from me. I could tell he didn't like being crowded. ''Actually Larry Bonner took the call; he's handling publicity. We have a package of ads set up to run to announce the grand opening. It's the standard thing the franchise always uses, standard art and layout. It starts five days before we open and runs for five days after. It's calculated to a particular opening date. The first ad is, 'Do you feel like Chinese? Can you wait five days?' There's a four-day ad, and so on. There's TV time tied in with it, too. Anyway, Larry gets a call from the Lancaster newspapers, confirming our instructions to start the ads right away. God bless the ad manager; he said he had driven by that morning and we sure didn't look ready to open in five days, so he decided to check."

"None of your people had called."

"The paper didn't have a record of who they talked to—just someone who said they were from Uncle Chan's. The only people who were familiar with the details of the ad campaign were Bonner and Bob and me."

"Narrows down the suspects," I said.

"Well, not really. Every Uncle Chan's uses the same general publicity campaign, and there are only two papers in town. It wouldn't have taken a rocket scientist to guess that the right call could pay off."

"What a fuckin' mess if the ads ran," Mosier said. "Can you feature a thousand people showing up at a closed restaurant? We'd have been laughed out of town. Anyway, that was the same day we got the first call."

"What day are we up to?"

"Thursday," he said. "I took it. Everybody else was busy, and the receptionist said the guy was insistent. He said that there were too many fast-food places already and that we wouldn't open if we knew what was good for us. Then he hung up."

"What kind of voice?"

"Well, he didn't sound like a nut. Man's voice, not real young. I didn't recognize it."

"He say anything else?"

"Nah. It was real short."

"What happened next?"

"That day, nothing. But then Friday morning the shit really hit the fan. Bruce's housekeeper gets a call.

The guy says, 'Reached out and touched anyone lately?' "

"You mean, someone was hurt?"

"No. The guy just had a sense of humor. It's from the phone company jingle."

"The phone lines?"

"They're underground, and where they come up they're cased in plastic. He'd poured acid on them; fused all three lines together."

"Three lines?"

"We're pretty dependent on phones," Chadwick explained. "We have a general number to call in, plus a dedicated fax line to take orders. That's the big thing these days; advertise to the offices that they can fax in an order at eleven-thirty and send one person to the drive-thru to pick it up. And there's another dedicated line for the computers. The sales information rung up on the registers here is uploaded and goes to my office by modem. I can watch the daily sales as they happen without being here."

"At least, you used to be able to."

"We were lucky. When we put in the lines our installer talked us into duplicating all the underground utilities. We were able to cross-connect to the spare lines in a couple of hours."

It was Mosier's turn. "We've lost our spares, and someday we'll have a pain in the ass fixing the damage."

"Anyway, when the phone thing happened, that's when we decided we needed help," Chadwick said. "We called a security agency. They put in a pass system, like you see, and twenty-four-hour security."

"When was that?"

"Saturday."

"Any problems since then?"

"Nope."

"Look, Garrett," Mosier said. "If you know your job, get out there and do it. Bruce and I have an opening to run."

Chadwick shot an annoyed glance at Mosier, but he didn't notice. I nodded and went outside.

Without a guard on the premises around the clock, the site would have been hopeless from a security point of view. It was on a major highway and adjoined a busy shopping center to the west. People and cars went by like ants on an anthill. To make things even worse, a patch of thick woods came right up to the parking lot on the east side. Keeping an eye on the place would be like trying to police Grand Central if it adjoined Central Park.

The damage to the dumpster and the phone lines was so similar that I assumed it was from the same person. When I saw the area I decided I was dealing with the same smart person. The dumpster and the point where the lines entered the building were shielded from view by a six-foot solid wood fence. It was the only point on the property where a person could be totally hidden. And using acid was smart, too. As long as you were careful in transporting it, acid made more sense than starting a fire or cutting or smashing. Nothing to attract attention while you were doing it, and all the time you needed was enough to open a bottle and pour it out. So, was the pellet gun on the window the work of a different person? That was definitely higher risk. But it was the first job he did, before anyone was alerted. Yes, I decided, if he'd used a pellet gun it was safe enough.

I watched the guard at the entrance for a while. As far as I could tell, he was doing a good job. Everyone who entered was logged in. When things were quiet he made a quick tour of the exterior. He mainly seemed to be looking to see if the people had security badges—he missed a painter lifting the phone book from the booth beside the entrance—but at least he was a warning.

People started arriving in business suits, and I realized that it was time for the test opening. Inside, especially behind the counter, the place was a madhouse. The cooking area of the place was laid out, as most fast-food restaurants are, in two lines facing each other. Orders moved down the line, were assembled and packaged, and reached an expediter at the end, who put them on a tray and delivered them to the customers. At least that was the plan. The crew on hand didn't look like they could execute a fire drill. Twenty-five people, most of them new employees, were jammed into an area designed for half that number. Twenty of them had no idea what to do and were all shouting questions simultaneously at the rest, who included Chadwick and Mosier. I watched Mosier explain stir-frying to a couple of high school boys with bad skin and earrings, and I was impressed. He was calm, patient, thorough, and helpful. He was one of those people, I decided, who was calm in a crisis and frazzled the rest of the time.

I drifted into the back and looked at the sinks. Everything seemed to be in order. I walked into the cooler; the shelves were neatly packed with boxes and plastic bags, everything dated and labeled. Some had USE FIRST in bold letters. I wondered when they had been delivered. Next, I checked the dry storage. It was mostly paper products, but I also saw some nonperishable food items, like canned goods and freeze-dried pouches.

I don't know what attracted my attention to the dried wonton soup mix; maybe it was the novelty of it, or the picture of the smiling Chinese woman on the cover of the carton. But when I looked more closely, I saw that two boxes were open. I didn't know how Chadwick liked to run things, but when I was with Taco Bell, we never allowed that. Inventory control was based on the assumption that every box except the one in use was one hundred percent full. If the number two crate turned out to be half empty, we could run out of something before we could get in a reorder. It seemed funny that bad habits could be creeping into the staff already.

I reached into the first box; it was about three-quarters full of clear plastic pouches. Each pouch contained uncooked wontons, parsley, and a yellowish powder. Chicken stock, I guessed. The same directions were on the box and also on the carton: "Dilute with three quarts boiling water, stir five minutes.'' No one was taking any chances on misunderstandings.

I was putting the pouch back when it slipped from my hand and fell to the floor. My fingers were slippery. I rubbed them together; there was some kind of clear liquid on them. I smelled them and picked up a hint of lemon. When I picked up the pouch I found a pinhole in one corner; more of the slippery liquid was leaking out. I put a bit on my little finger and tasted it. Oh, good Christ.

I headed for the lines, fast, elbowing my way through the press of people at the counter. A balding man in a business suit was our first customer. If I had to guess, I would have said that he was Uncle Chan's accountant. He was talking to the expediter and looking around. And on his tray was a steaming bowl of wonton soup.

I stepped in front of the expediter and did my best to smile. ''I'm sorry, sir, but we're having a little quality-control problem with our first batch of soup. Please give this young lady another order and we'll get you a replacement in a jiffy.'' I grabbed the bowl and turned away before he could react. It was steaming, but I stuck in my finger anyway. It tasted the same as the liquid from the pouch, bitter and metallic.

I dumped the bowl into the nearest sink and grabbed the kettle of wonton soup on my side of the line with both hands. Chadwick came up behind me. ''Garrett, what are you doing? We only have two vats up. We can't have any more ready for half an hour!'' I shook my head and poured it into the sink while he looked at me with his mouth open. As it bubbled down the drain I stuck my finger in it.

The soup was hot as hell, but it tasted fine.

''Nuts!'' I said. ''The bowl must have come from the other line!''

''What are you talking about? Have you lost your marbles?''

I pushed past him, around the corner to the other line, and grabbed the other kettle of soup. Mosier and half of the restaurant were watching, and he started forward to stop me. I heard him yelling something, but he was too late. I upended the second kettle into the sink. The first one hadn't drained completely yet, and the soup overflowed onto the counter, my pants, and the floor.

And everywhere it landed, there were suds.

Chadwick and Mosier just stood there, staring at the yellowish froth. They looked at me and then at each other. Then Mosier pointed to the two nearest kids and told them to clean up the floor. I walked to the back and Chadwick and Mosier followed me.

I showed them the pouch. "Take a look at this. Somebody got soap into this bag without making more than a pinhole. They must have used a syringe of some kind. I think it's a dishwashing soap, not that it matters."

Chadwick fingered the bag and passed it to Mosier. "How many bags?"

"At least two, the one I found and the one in the kettle. There wouldn't be much point in doing any more. Once all your customers started getting the shits, you would have found the problem."

Mosier looked at Chadwick. "You know how close we came to a major fuckup? Imagine what would have happened if we served a gallon of wonton soap."

Chadwick looked at the floor. "These guys mean business."

"They certainly do. They're into more than just damaging things—they don't care if they hurt people, too."

"We'll have to increase security here."

"Fine, but what about your house? Not only is it your office; people know you're the man in charge," I said.

He bit his lip. "I didn't think of that."

"I did," Mosier said. "When we got the letter I told you. You just don't remember." He turned to me. "On Friday afternoon we got a letter. Lancaster postmark, no return address. It was spelled out with words cut from somewhere, a book or something. It said, 'No more games—we're coming after you.' I told

Bruce that I figured this was heavy shit, after all that had happened."

Chadwick looked uncomfortable. "I try not to panic. I thought that they had to mean the restaurant, not me. I mean, who would want to hurt me? I'm just a businessman. I pay my taxes and go to church and try to keep my nose clean."

"If I were you I'd have your security agency plant someone among the workmen to see if he can pick anything up. And have them start patrolling your house with a marked car. It might scare off whoever it is."

Mosier looked impatient, but it was Chadwick who spoke first. "Don't you think we're getting a little carried away?"

"Does Uncle Chan's have any place of business in the county other than here and your house?"

"We've bought a site in Elizabethtown, but there's no construction yet. We're waiting for the thaw. We don't expect to break ground till March first and we won't be opening till Memorial Day."

"So if somebody wants to hurt Uncle Chan's, and if security here makes that tough, where are they going to go?"

The two of them exchanged a glance. "Okay," Mosier said. "We'll do it."

"I'd like to get back to the house. I want to check it out from a security standpoint."

"I'm in the middle of an opening. I really can't leave," Chadwick said. "Bob, could you run him back? I can handle things here for a few minutes."

Mosier and I headed back toward the house, driving quickly. "Tell me, did Uncle Chan's have any trouble before this? With outsiders?"

"There were some zoning problems, but nothing unusual. We needed a height variance for the sign and we got it."

"Anyone appear at the hearing to oppose it?"

"Some neighbors showed up, but no one spoke out against it."

I wondered if Uncle Chan's had stumbled into some

kind of Asian gang turf struggle without knowing it. "What about your competitors?"

"Lancaster has the usual Chinese sit-down restaurants, but the nearest one is a couple of miles from us. We've never heard anything negative from any of them."

"What about the other fast-food operations?"

"You have to understand how fast food works. At least out here. The other operations around here—Taco Bell, Pizza Hut, Wendy's—they're happy we're here. The more restaurants in a location, or along a stretch of road, the better everyone does. A family decides to go out to eat but they don't decide exactly where. They drive past a couple of places and then pick one. Only McDonald's can afford to set up all by themselves. They can afford to break the rules. Everybody else needs to cluster together."

"Could there be somebody who doesn't share that view?"

"Everybody gets along, better than you'd think. Hey, the guy who's the crew chief at a Burger King today could be our assistant manager next. And then go on to manage a Hardee's. You can't go around pissing people off. On the record I'm not supposed to know this, but I do: When one place runs short of something, like vegetables or hamburger or cheese or whatever, they borrow it or swap for it from somebody else. Nobody likes to brag about it; they're supposed to be organized enough not to run out of inventory, but it happens."

"Any union trouble?"

"Not at all. This isn't a union area."

I was silent for a while. We turned onto Chadwick's street and then into his driveway. "So what's the answer?" he asked.

I closed my eyes and rubbed the back of my neck; the muscles always hurt back there in cold weather. "Mr. Mosier, I don't have an answer. It's just that for right now I've run out of questions."

When I got out of the car, he snorted and drove away.

4

Monday, 3:00 P.M.

The layout of the grounds of the house was the first and only thing in the whole case that satisfied me, professionally. The house was well clear of its neighbors on either side, with large front and back yards. I saw floodlights mounted in the eaves at regular intervals. The bushes close to the house were well trimmed—not much cover for anyone sneaking around. The garage was big enough to keep all the cars—except mine—under lock.

I went inside. Mary showed me to a bedroom on the second floor and pointed out the nearest bathroom. I showered, changed out of my soup-soaked pants, and sat in my room, taking notes and trying to make sense out of the case. Security wasn't my strong point. I was more at home trying to eliminate suspects. The problem was that I could easily eliminate everyone I'd met.

After an hour and a half of puzzling over lists that were too short and diagrams with too many arrows pointing toward nothing, I decided to allow myself a twenty-minute break and wandered downstairs. My destination was the kitchen, but I took a wrong turn and wound up in a library. On the opposite wall was a fireplace, with a pleasant little fire going. A small sofa faced the fire.

I worked my way around the room, browsing the shelves for some evening reading. Every sort of book was there, in no particular order. The first five books on one shelf were *Understanding Modern Physics*, *Dianetics*, *The Story of O*, *Cost Accounting for the Small Businessman*, and *Contemporary Philosophical Problems*. Some of the books were in pristine condition, with the dust jackets still on. Others looked like they'd been retrieved from under the tread of a tank after a war.

I worked my way around to the front of the sofa, wondering what kind of people could collect a library like this, when I heard a low, steady rumbling that was loudest near a door between a pair of bookcases. I opened it and was startled by bright lights shining on glossy white walls and a white tile floor. It was a small gym, with mirrors across one wall, a sauna, and half a dozen pieces of exercise equipment. The only one in use was a stationary bicycle that faced away from me. The rider was a teenaged boy wearing a yellow leotard. For a second I thought it might be Jeremy, but the hair was shorter, and bright red. I looked again and realized the rider was a very slender woman. She was riding the bike hard, and her body glistened with sweat. A book was propped open on a stand attached to the handlebars, although I couldn't imagine how she could read like that.

I was sure she didn't know I was there. I coughed once, deliberately, but the bicycle drowned it out. I walked around in front of her. She was wearing glasses, and she really was reading. She looked to be somewhere between forty and fifty, with large green eyes and a pale complexion. Sweat was running freely down the sides of her face. When she reached to turn the page she realized I was there.

"Hi," I said. "Didn't mean to startle you."

She took off her glasses and let the bike come to a stop. "No, not at all. You must be the detective." She didn't sound the slightest bit out of breath.

"That's me. Dave Garrett. And you must be some kind of relative of Anne's."

"Good guess. I'm just a cousin, but the whole family has the same skin coloring."

I took that for an invitation to study her skin. Mistaking her for a teenaged boy was understandable: she was delicately built, with tiny wrists and ankles, and long slender legs. There was no swelling under the front of the leotard at all. The neckline plunged deeply, and it would have been daring on a woman with any chest; on her it was quite demure.

I offered to shake. Her hand was as slight as the rest of her, but her grip was so strong I looked down at it. "Kate McMahan. Pleased to meet you."

"You must be the houseguest Anne told me about."

"I've been traveling for a few days. This is my first chance to work out. It feels good."

"You bicycle much at home?"

"No, I mainly work out with weights. They've got a nice setup here. This is just my cool-down."

I looked over at the weight machine. It was set up for bench presses, and I could see dampness on the padded bench. I could also see that the machine was set for a 140 pounds. I wished I'd been there to see her do it. It had been a long time since I could press my own weight.

I looked at the book on the handlebars. "What are you reading?"

"Marcuse. *Negations*. Ever hear of it?"

"I read it in college."

"Me, too. I wanted to see how it read twenty-five years later."

My first thought was to tell her that she didn't look her age, but something told me not to. A woman with a sense of humor, or irony, who would wear an outfit that showed off a nonexistent chest was a little too complex for casual flirting. "So what do you think?"

She picked up a towel and rubbed her face and arms. When she spoke, she looked me directly in the eye, without blinking. Either her parents had never punished her for staring, or she'd been a stubborn child. "I still think he's a very deep thinker. But now I read him as an academic. In college I thought it was the blueprint for revolution."

"Free the enslaved masses and right the wrongs of the world. Or at least burn down the ROTC building."

"You're making fun of me."

"No, of me. And all of us. We thought we could change the whole course of human history, before we even graduated, without having to miss any classes."

"Or any of the good parties. We were pretty arrogant." She put her hands behind her head and stretched, then looked at me again. "But you have to forgive the young their arrogance."

"And why is that?"

"Because it's all they've got to keep them going."

"Some people envy them their youth." I didn't say, *especially women*, but I was thinking it.

"Well, I teach college, community college, that is. Or rather, I did until recently, and I'm around young people quite a bit. I wouldn't want to be young again."

"Oh?"

"When you're eighteen in America, what do you know? They don't know how to support themselves, they don't have any money, they don't know how to live yet. They haven't even learned how to fuck very well."

I became conscious of the heat coming off her body, and of her smell—healthy, clean, and salty. "Where did you go to school?" I asked.

"UC Santa Barbara. And you?"

"Johns Hopkins. You're a long way from home."

"Home is for kids." She shrugged. "For grown-ups, it's where you make it."

"Then, where are you from?"

"The whole family's from Washington, the Seattle area. Until recently I lived in Miami." She got off the bicycle, reset the weight machine at fifty pounds, and sat on the bench with her legs crossed.

"And now?"

"For the next few days this is home. I just got divorced. The kids are on their own, and so am I."

The third finger of her left hand showed a band of white skin where the ring had been. She saw me looking at it and pretended not to notice.

"How long you been here?"

"Just a couple of days. It's been fun. I haven't seen Anne in a good ten years, maybe fifteen."

"You said you used to teach at a community college?"

"Near Miami. English lit. But the budget crunch hit, and I didn't have tenure, so I'm on layoff."

"Till when?"

"Hopefully my department can fit me in when the new budget comes out in June. They like my work. And if it doesn't come through, I'll have to fall back on my other job skills."

"Oh?"

"I've been a secretary, a long-distance operator, a veterinarian's assistant, and sold real estate. And I spent two years in the Army."

"And raised some kids, too."

"The Army was before the kids. My husband was drafted and I decided it was the best way to stay near him. I was assigned to a security unit. An MP."

"How'd you like being a cop?"

"If you could stay clear of testifying in courts-martial it was okay. I could never make sense of the UCMJ. And once in a while you'd get a jerk who couldn't admit to himself that a skinny little woman had brought him in, so he'd decide that you had to be a dyke. That used to fry me. But then I got pregnant and took a discharge."

"It's been quite a life."

"It sounds more interesting than it lives, especially the part about the children."

"How well do you know Anne and Bruce?"

"I'd never met Bruce before, and as I said I haven't seen Anne in years."

"You know about the problems at the restaurant?"

"Of course. It's all they talk about."

"Bruce and Anne?"

"Bruce and everyone but Anne. He's a driven guy."

"And Anne?"

"She stays clear of business talk. The business is his baby."

"He seems pretty upset about the sabotage."

"He is. From what Anne tells me, he was running flat out with just the regular problems of getting a new business started. This has kicked him into orbit."

"Well, speaking of that, you'll have to excuse me. I need to do some work of my own."

"The game's afoot, Holmes?"

"The meter's running, at least. Have you seen Larry Bonner? I'd like to talk to him."

She laughed. I didn't think a chest that slight could give such a rich sound. "If it's one minute after five you're too late."

"I met him this morning. He didn't seem like a clock-watcher to me."

"He's not. He's in love."

"Well, good for him."

"You won't see him till tomorrow morning."

"And Bruce won't be back till after seven, I'm sure."

"And Anne's busy making dinner. So there's nothing you can do, as far as your job is concerned. You might as well go in the library, pull down a good book, and throw another log on the fire."

"You do that; I need to work."

"From what I hear, you've worked a full day already. We won't be having dinner till late. Take it easy."

I shrugged. "You take it easy. People should do what they're good at."

She gave me the same look I must have given her when she said that the young should be forgiven their arrogance. "How do you mean?"

"If someone has a gift for taking life easy and finding enjoyment in lots of things that most of us miss, they should do it. If they're good at working hard, they should do that. Not everybody was meant to stop and smell the roses."

"You've had this conversation with someone before."

"My ex-wife and several girlfriends."

She pursed her lips. "Maybe it's the people who work the hardest who should be the most conscientious about taking time off."

"I'll make you a deal. Get yourself a shower and I'll sit with you in the library and read over some papers Bruce prepared about the case. You can read Marcuse and feel sixties again."

"Only if you build up that fire. My blood is thin."

She joined me a few minutes later, wearing a light-blue sleeveless dress that probably worked a lot better in Florida in June than in Pennsylvania in February. I stoked up the fire for her, and she pulled a wing chair in close. She read a couple of pages of her book, but didn't keep the deal from there. We wound up talking until eight, when Chadwick called us to dinner.

We ate in the library, but Anne had spread a tablecloth and lit candles. I was seated between Anne and Kate, with Jeremy across from me.

Chadwick, at the head of the table, signaled for a toast. "To Dave Garrett, our very own Sherlock Holmes."

"Without whose help, our accountant would be five pounds closer to his ideal weight," Anne added.

"News travels fast," I said.

Jeremy leaned forward. "You're the first one to beat him to the punch, Mr. Garrett. How did you do it?"

Kate hadn't heard the story, and neither Anne nor Jeremy had any of the details. When I was finished, I found that Kate was smiling at me. I liked the way she smiled.

There was hardly time to talk to Anne; she was in nearly constant motion between her seat and the kitchen. She brought in the food and Jeremy cleared after each course. I used the time to get some more information from Chadwick.

"How did you get in with Uncle Chan's?"

"We'd been here when I was with the Holiday Inn franchise. The Holiday people wanted me to take a transfer to California. I was ready to go; this hasn't been a town of good memories for Anne or me. But she insisted we stay. They insisted I go. Just then, the Uncle Chan's people came along."

"It must have been a switch—hotels to fast food."

He tore his bread apart and buttered it. "The emphasis is different, but it's still a service industry. It wasn't as hard as you might think. The big thing I had to learn was portion control." He chewed on a piece of bread. "Actually, once you understand—you said before that you were in the service?"

"Marines."

"Then you know how it works. You don't need to think for yourself, ever. There's a plan already in place to take care of everything. When to eat, what to wear, what to do when things go wrong. Unless you're an officer you never need to think at all. Not that plenty of enlisted men aren't smarter than their officers—a hell of a lot of them are. But they don't need to be; the system assumes they're not."

He stabbed his salad and took a large mouthful; he was eating like he hadn't eaten all day, and perhaps he hadn't, at least not since our breakfast. "But anyway, Dave, the connection is this. Every job in fast food is set up so that an illiterate fourteen-year-old can do it. No, I'm not kidding. Not the management jobs, but everything else. Let me give you an example. Can you make fried rice, or even boil rice?"

He caught me with my mouth full. "No."

"Most Americans can't, at least not consistently. So here's what we do. You start with your fourteen-year-old illiterate. You give him a premeasured bag of rice and a container he fills to the top with water. We don't trust them to measure to a line, we just have them fill it up. He puts the water in a pot, turns on the burner, and hits a timer. The timer is preset for the amount of time it should take to boil the water. When it goes off, and if the water is boiling, he pours in the rice. He hits another timer. When that one is through the rice is done. He greases the griddle by pouring the entire contents of a little bottle of oil, and throws on the rice. Again, he hits the timer. He looks at a wall chart for the exact kind of fried rice he's making. If it's shrimp fried rice, it'll have little pictures of an egg, a shrimp, a bottle of soy sauce, and a green box for vegetables. Each of those items is premeasured; all he has to do is throw in a little box of each and stir. When the timer goes off our boy has made fried rice." He put down his silverware and leaned closer. His voice became low and urgent. "And not just fried rice. Great fried rice. And it'll taste the same in San Francisco and New York, every damned day."

From the corner of my eye I caught Kate smiling. I almost asked her whether she thought she had the requisite breadth of vision to make it big in the fast-food game, but decided not to. I had the feeling that if I asked, she'd say exactly what was on her mind.

Toward the end of the meal Anne settled down next to me. "Bruce said that you think there could be trouble here at the house, David."

"It's possible. If they want to get at the franchise badly enough, this is the other logical place."

She bit her fingernail. "But what would they do?"

"It depends how serious they are. If they come at all, it could be just threatening phone calls, or it could mean slashed tires, or rocks through windows. Maybe even a firebomb, if someone's desperate enough."

"Do you think it's that bad?"

"I don't know. There seems to be a pattern of escalation, and I don't like it. How do you get your food here at the house?"

"I do all the grocery shopping myself."

"All of it?"

"Well, Jeremy gets a few things now and then, and we have the meat delivered, of course."

"How is the meat order handled?"

"I call it in, and the next day or the same afternoon it's delivered. If no one's home, and if it's cold, they leave it at the back door."

Oh, Jesus, I thought. "Anne, until this is over, stop your meat order. Don't allow any food into the house that you haven't selected yourself. And don't leave your shopping cart unattended."

"All right," she said in a small voice.

That gave me another idea. "When are you going grocery shopping again?"

"Wednesday is my regular day."

"You always go to the same place?"

"The Giant over near the restaurant."

"The next time you go I'd like to go along. I'll stay

way in the background and see if anyone shows any unusual interest in your cart."

"I don't have to shop for a few days. We have enough."

"Why don't you go ahead and pick up a few things anyway. It just might flush them out. Will you be home all day tomorrow?"

"I have a couple of errands in the morning and then I have a late lunch with a friend."

"The errands—does anyone know you'll be running them?"

She thought for a moment. "Yes, the caterer is expecting me."

"Maybe I'll follow you tomorrow, too."

She giggled. "You're going to ride shotgun, like in the Westerns?"

"No, I'll be way back, out of sight. I won't be watching you so much as seeing whether anybody else is watching."

"If you think it's a good idea, all right then."

"Scared?"

"Not if you're behind me."

Later on, I'd have lots of time to think about that one.

5

Tuesday, 9:00 A.M.

I'm normally a poor sleeper, and a strange bed doesn't help, but when I opened my eyes the next morning it was nearly nine. I shaved and dressed as quickly as I could and hurried downstairs. Anne was in the kitchen, engrossed in a newspaper. She looked up and gave me a warm smile when she heard my footsteps. Whatever her limitations, at least she was pleasant. "Good morning, David."

She put down the newspaper, and I could see that she was wearing a bright-blue dress with a belt at the waist, and a string of pearls. "Thanks again for dinner last night. It was great. Now, what's your schedule for this morning?"

"I have to pick up some dry cleaning, and then pick out a cake."

"A cake?"

"We're having a party for the office staff to celebrate the grand opening. I decided a cake would be nice. It's going to be in the shape of a . . . what's the word? You know what I mean, like, you know, a Chinese church steeple?"

"A pagoda?"

She nodded. "Right, that's it. Anyway, I want to have a red velvet cake with white and red icing, looking like a pagoda. Or maybe carrot cake. I like carrot cake better, but red velvet seems more Chinese—the color, you know."

"Cake consultations aren't in my job description."

She missed the irony. "Well, that's why I'm going to Party Time; it's a bakery and catering. They always have such good ideas. They do all our parties."

"I'm ready whenever you are."

"Sure you don't want any breakfast?"

"My fault for sleeping in; I won't hold you up. I'll get something later."

She stood up. The dress was simple, but her body made the most of it. She was wearing high-heeled shoes that were a matching shade of blue. I wondered where you get bright-blue shoe polish. "All right, then, Dave, tell me the plan."

"Where's your car?"

"They're all in the garage."

"Which one is it?"

She furrowed her brow and fingered the pearls for a moment. "I like the Fiero; but with the dry cleaning, I guess I'll take the Benz. Anyway, with the snow, Bruce would be mad at me for taking out the Fiero. He says it isn't a good snow car."

"Just get in and drive away normally. Now, I'm not really tailing you—I'm going to stay far back enough so that I can pick up anyone who is."

She looked worried for a moment. "You don't think I'm in danger, do you?"

"Not really. I'm just being careful."

"All the things at the restaurant, it must be some kids whose parents don't pay them enough attention, they have time on their hands."

"Well, I hope that's all it turns out to be. But these kids have gone pretty far. Breaking a window is one thing. Trying to make a hundred people sick is something else."

"I don't like to think about things like that. There's too much trouble in the world as it is."

"Ignoring it doesn't make it go away."

"Well, dwelling on it doesn't, either. But let's go, okay?"

"Tell me your route."

"Do you know the roads around here?"

"I know the main roads, at least."

"I'll be going south to Columbia Pike. Then I'll make a right and go about a mile to the dry cleaner's. It's in the shopping center next to the restaurant, as a matter of fact. Then I keep going west on the same road all the way to Columbia."

My Honda was in the driveway, where I'd left it. I pulled around to the exit side of the drive and waited. One of the garage doors opened and a big gray Benz pulled out. She waved at me and headed south. We drove slowly. Aside from a city snowplow and a mail jeep there was nothing on the road. I stayed back about a block until we reached the Pike, where we hit a red light. She put on her right turn signal, then turned. I counted to thirty and pulled out behind her. The only eastbound traffic was a school bus; I wondered if it was running late on a snow delay or taking kids home early. Nothing was going west at all, except us.

We retraced the route to the restaurant. I would have preferred to keep some cars between us as camouflage, but there was nothing I could do about that. All I could do was watch my mirrors and verify that we had the road to ourselves. Traffic appeared from time to time in my mirror, but everything either passed us or turned off. I never saw the same car twice.

She went by the restaurant, put on her left signal, and pulled into the shopping center. It was built on three sides of a huge central parking lot, with a supermarket in the middle and smaller stores on both wings. The lot was full despite the lack of traffic on the road, and we had to pick our way around heavily bundled women trudging through the snow pushing shopping carts.

I parked one row away from her, and about twenty yards closer to the exit. She went into the dry cleaner's with a small bundle. I scanned the parking lot; no one seemed to be paying her any attention. After a minute or two she came out, empty-handed, and came over to my car.

"Dave, I know this isn't your job, but I need a little favor."

I looked around and tried to keep my voice even. "It probably isn't a good idea for you to be seen talking to me out here."

"Oh, come on. There's nobody watching, is there?"

"No, probably not."

"Well, listen. The draperies are ready. I need to get them hung for the party. Can you give me a hand?"

If anyone was watching, they would have spotted me already. Helping her out wasn't going to make anything worse. "Sure," I said, trying to sound cheerful about it.

The dry cleaner's was crowded with harassed-looking women brandishing little yellow receipts. It was hot, and permeated with the pleasant, clean smell of freshly ironed cotton.

Anne wasn't kidding about the drapes; they were in two bulky parcels, each one as big as a man and a third as heavy. I muscled them out to her car, one at a time, while she loaded some smaller bundles. When we were through the back of the Benz was filled.

She brushed the hair out of her eyes with the back of her hand. "Thanks, Dave. I couldn't have done it myself. Maybe I should have brought Jeremy along, but I wasn't thinking."

"No problem. And now the caterer's?"

She nodded. "You go ahead," I said. "I'll give you a little head start and then pull out behind. In this light traffic I don't want to stay too close."

"Okay. See you in Columbia."

I got in my car and watched her exit the lot. A white station wagon followed, but it turned right when she made her left onto Columbia Pike. Then a green Ford with two women made the same left. I turned the key. Nothing happened.

I tried again. In eighty thousand miles the Honda had never let me sit. But there was nothing, not even the click of the rotor. No lights. No horn. I looked at the dashboard clock; it had stopped five minutes ago.

I jumped out of the Honda and ran to the edge of the lot, just in time to see the Benz disappear over a rise a few hundred yards away. I walked back to the car and kicked the side viciously. I was going to look like an idiot. I wondered if Mosier was going to be sarcastic with me, or just mad. Chadwick would just give a disappointed look and say that these things happen—and then call the franchise to tell them not to pay a cent to such a moron.

I put on my jacket and considered the walk back to the house. Maybe things weren't so bad. If I could hitch a ride, get back, and borrow a car quickly enough, I might be able to catch up with her before she left the caterer's. I wasn't going to come out of this looking like Sam Spade, but it would salvage something.

As I zipped up my jacket I looked at the car. It was tired and old. The paint was going in a hurry, and the rear bumper was badly rusted. Whether I could afford to or not, I was going to have to spend some money on a new car. For the clients that never came to the office, my car was my only chance to impress them, and mine didn't do it. The sides were gouged from a thousand skirmishes with other cars in parking lots. And there was a particularly bad one right near the front edge of the hood.

I bent down and took a closer look. The mark was half an inch long, which hardly made it unique. But it was fresh—I could see shiny bare metal instead of rust. I pulled on the hood; a latch should have held it in place, but it swung up easily. I propped it open and looked around. The battery had been disconnected from one of the terminals.

It took me no more than five minutes to reconnect the battery and get back to Chadwick's. The first person I saw was Jeremy. He was in a tie and shirtsleeves, carrying a typewriter.

"Jeremy, stop what you're doing. I need your help right away."

The typewriter went onto the nearest chair. "What do you need?"

"Someone futzed with my car. I was following your mother and I lost her. Do you know where the caterer is that she uses?"

"Yeah. I have to run out there for stuff."

"Come on and show me, then. If we hurry we can still catch her."

"What's going on?"

"I don't know yet."

As I drove I watched the road with new eyes. It was a crime scene waiting to happen, or at least it might be. I thought of what Mosier had said yesterday about the opposition meaning business.

Past the shopping center the road was two lanes each way, and in most places there was a turning lane in the middle for left turns. For a good five miles beyond, it was heavily built up on both sides—shopping centers, bars, gas stations, furniture stores, restaurants, motels, and supermarkets. I hardly saw a vacant lot before we reached Mountville, five miles from the house. Traffic was light, but I was able to count police cars from three different jurisdictions. Only a maniac would have attempted anything on this road.

Jeremy was starting to fidget, and I decided it was better to keep him talking. "Does your mom work in your dad's business?"

His voice was naturally soft, and he had to raise it to be heard. "Not in a long time. When I was little she did. She's a whiz at math. She could do payroll in no time, almost in her head. But she hasn't done that since we moved from Cincinnati."

"What does she do all day?"

"Cooks for us, takes care of the house. Dad entertains for his work quite a bit. There's a lot to do."

"Does she go out every morning about this time?"

"Sometimes. And sometimes, in the late morning or early afternoon. She goes out every day, even Saturdays. Dad works all the time. She comes back at three, maybe four, and gets dinner ready. When I was in school she was always home to meet me."

After Mountville the road narrowed to two lanes and development thinned out to an occasional gas station. Traffic dwindled sharply. I had a bad feeling about this road. "Are you in school now?"

He laughed. "I went to Millersville State for a while, but Dad said I'd learn more being in the business with him, so I quit. I help him out around the office. Doing stuff that needs to be done. It's good to get to work with him. At least I get to see him more than I did before."

"Is he training you to take over someday?"

"I don't know. I'd like to think so, but so far I spend a lot of time running errands. He hasn't really shown me too much yet."

I felt sorry for him. "If you show him you can do a good job on the small stuff, someday he'll have confidence in you for important stuff."

"It'd be nice."

"A long time ago, that's how they trained lawyers. You didn't go to law school; when a fellow was your age, or younger, he'd sign up as a sort of apprentice with a law firm. He'd empty out waste cans and sweep the floors—but after a while, they'd start showing him how stuff was done, and then let him do little things. Then, more and more complicated stuff. Eventually the firm would certify he knew as much as they could teach him, and he would be eligible to take the bar exam and be a lawyer."

"I'm hoping he'll let me do more. It's just so slow."

We came out of a dip and there was the Benz, parked off the road on the paved shoulder, just short of an intersection with a secondary road. Neither one of us said anything. I hoped he wasn't looking at my face—it wouldn't have told him anything encouraging. I pulled over and parked right behind.

We were completely alone. Up ahead, the road gently climbed a hill and crested about five hundred yards away. In the middle distance on the right-hand side was a Taco Bell, closed at this hour of the morning; on the left was an abandoned gas station. I turned around to face the way she had come. There was nothing but farmland on both sides. The country road didn't cross the Pike; it led only to the north. There were no buildings on either side, just farmland frozen under ice and snow.

"Jeremy, you have a set of keys to the Benz?"

"I have keys to all the cars. Just in case they need me to run one somewhere." He detached a key from his holder and handed it over. It turned out I didn't need it. The driver's door was unlocked and her keys were in the ignition.

I went over the car as carefully as I could. But when you don't know what to look for, it's hard to know what you've missed. I walked around it slowly; the tires were all inflated and there was no skid marks leading up to the rear ones. All the locks and windows worked fine, no new scratches or dents, no damage to the headlights or taillights. The gas tank was nearly full. Inside there were no cuts in the upholstery, no stains, no loose buttons on the floor—no evidence of a struggle at all. The dry cleaning she'd picked up was lying across the backseat, exactly as I'd left it. I tried the car phone by dialing Information; it was working fine. The engine started on the first try.

Jeremy came around the passenger's side and climbed in. I didn't like him being in the middle of things, but under the circumstances I wasn't going to order him out.

The ashtray was half full of cigarette butts, all of them ringed with a pale pink lipstick. "Does your mom smoke?"

"Yeah, she does. She's always saying she's going to quit, but never does." No one said anything for a moment. "Mr. Garrett, I think you'd better tell me what's going on."

"Just a second, Jeremy." I opened the glove compartment. Nothing but the usual maps and warranty books. Then I reached under the seat and my hand closed on a piece of paper.

It was ordinary typewriter paper, with a message created by cutting words out of another source. From the look and feel of the paper, I guessed the words were from a magazine:

WE'VE GOT HER. NO POLICE. NO TRICKS.
RANSOM DEMAND TO FOLLOW.

It was as bad as I thought it could be. The very first time she'd been alone on this road her car had stopped—or been stopped. It's the simplest thing in the world, and it doesn't require any brains. All you need is a car that looks generally like the cars police use, plus a twenty-dollar rotating red light to slap onto the roof. If you're wearing a suit—or better yet, a uniform—even the most suspicious citizen will stop, and then you shove a gun in their face. After that, it's rape, sodomy, murder—or kidnapping. Dealer's choice.

I handed him the note. He looked at the paper, blinked, and handed it back to me. When I took it, I saw that his hands were shaking.

"What do we do now, Mr. Garrett?"

"We go back and talk to your father. He's going to have to make some hard decisions."

"Like whether to go to the police?"

"Among others, yes."

"Would he get in trouble if he didn't?"

The question caught me by surprise. "You mean with the police? I don't think so."

"I don't think he'll want to tell them."

"What makes you say that?"

"Well, Dad's used to doing things his own way. I don't think he'd like being told what to do."

I got out and checked the trunk, but it was empty. I looked around once more, very slowly. The wind was picking up, and it cut right through my parka and leaked in around the wrist cuffs. Once, as a lawyer, I'd stood at a bad curve on a country road where my client's husband had been killed in a one-car accident. I'd stood there for two hours on a slushy November day, trying to—what? Meditate? Visualize what he had seen? Commune with the dead? I didn't know why I'd done it then and I didn't know why I was doing it now, either. But whatever had happened, happened *here*. Right where I was standing, in broad daylight. Figuring it out didn't involve inventing anything, or doing mathematical calculations. Any five-year-old who had been here could have solved the whole thing.

I looked around again but the landscape gave nothing back. Try as I might, it was just a place, nothing but gray skies, bare trees, and icy concrete.

"Jeremy, let's go back to the house. We'll lock the Benz up and leave it where it is. If the police get into this they may be able to find some clues. But there's nothing more we can do here."

6

Tuesday, 11:00 A.M.

Jeremy drove while I watched the road and thought. He was a good kid; he had enough sense not to pester me with questions I couldn't answer. Or maybe he already had me pegged as someone who didn't have many answers.

Kidnapping. In the couple of years I'd been a private investigator, since my disbarment, I'd handled a few. None of them had been like this, though. My experience was with the common kind—a child abducted by the losing spouse in a custody battle. The kidnapper was usually the husband, but not always. It was dangerous work—I'd been threatened several times, once with a gun—and emotionally draining, but as far as involving investigative skills, it was a joke. Most of the time the client would tell me who the kidnapper was in the initial phone call. A lot of the spouses didn't even try to hide—they were right at the address listed in the phone book when I showed up. The only creative intelligence required was when the spouse had skipped and I needed to run a trace; and even that was usually simple if the child was of school age. Other than that I was just hired muscle.

Not all of the cases I'd handled were quite that simple, but with a few variations you could cover the waterfront—grandparents snatching grandchildren, random child snatchings by strangers, and the occasional parent taking a teenaged child from a religious commune. I didn't like doing the last kind very much, getting into the middle of disputes like that. I didn't believe in God myself, but I respected people who did—even if their cosmology stemmed from too much acid in the sixties and too little red meat ever since.

A real kidnapping of an adult for ransom—not the smash-and-grab hostage taking by young punks with large guns and small brains—was a rare animal indeed. So rare that I'd never worked one, either as a lawyer or as a private investigator. It involved the kind of risks and effort associated with murder for less return than a well-organized stickup.

I took out the note and studied it, trying to get a sense of the people I was dealing with.

Jeremy looked over. "Does it tell you anything?"

"Yeah. First of all, it tells me they're smart. No handwriting, a garden-variety paper, not even an envelope—there's nothing to trace. But they've given away a couple of things."

"What?"

"Well, 'ransom demand to follow.' That's the kind of expression someone with some education would use. Someone with no education would say 'ransom demand coming,' or 'wait for ransom demand,' something like that. This sounds like someone who's worked in an office. And it says 'we've' got her. Not 'I've' got her. That figures in with how it was done. One man disconnects my battery, the other follows your mother and stops her."

He shook his head. "Mr. Garrett, you're the detective, but . . . couldn't one person have done both? If they were really organized and had it planned?"

I nodded, hoping he wasn't right. I would have rather dealt with a gang than with one man that good.

Chadwick and Mosier were both standing in the driveway when we pulled in. I took one look at their faces.

"They must have called here already," I said. No one responded for a minute. Mosier just watched me, the way a man with a shotgun might track a slow-flying bird. "Ten minutes ago," he said at last.

"They work fast."

"A hell of a lot faster than you do, Garrett, if you work at all."

"Somebody disconnected my battery." I was going to say more, but it wasn't coming out right, so I shut up.

Chadwick spoke. "Bob, you took the call. Tell Dave what happened."

"The office line rang and I answered. It was a man. He said they had Anne. We could find her car on the side of the road past Mountville."

"That's where it was."

"He said that they wanted forty thousand in cash. He'd call back at four with instructions. We're not supposed to call the police. He said if we play it straight Anne would be home safe and sound tomorrow."

"Forty thousand?"

"You heard me."

I looked at Jeremy; his face was pale and his chin was trembling. At first I thought he was going to lose control, but then I saw his jaws were clamped tightly together and that he was making an effort to breathe slowly and regularly.

"Jeremy," I said. "I want you to wait by the phone. If they call again, let me or your father know right away."

He was no fool; he knew I was shuffling him out of the way, but he took it well.

Mosier, Chadwick, and I went to Chadwick's office, where I told them what had happened.

"How the fuck could you let this happen?" Mosier wanted to know.

"I told you. We stopped at the shopping center and she asked me to help her load some draperies from the dry cleaner's. They were too heavy for her."

"So you just wandered off and left your car? You're lucky they took pity on you and didn't plant a fucking bomb!"

"She came up to me and asked. I was blown already."

"All the more reason not to leave your car."

I just nodded at him and looked straight ahead. I hate it when assholes are right.

"I'm not here to talk about blame," Chadwick said. "Just tell me, what are we going to do?"

"Go to the police."

Mosier shook his head. "I can't see it."

"What do you mean?" I asked.

"If we pay, we get her back, the whole thing's over with no publicity. It costs us what we gross in the first two days; big deal. If we go to the police they make a big deal out of this. People associate Uncle Chan's with heavy crime and danger, not a fun time away from home. The cops will be so eager to catch the crooks that they probably won't get Anne back, at least not right away. The whole thing drags on. We lose all the way around."

"Bob's right," Chadwick agreed. "Pay the forty and just get her back. If she's not free when they promise, then we can do something."

"But if you wait till after the ransom is paid, you have no point of contact with the kidnappers. There's no way to trace them down, at least not very easily."

Chadwick looked at me. "You mean that the police would arrest them when the money is paid? *Before* seeing that Anne is safe?"

"I don't know. I can't say how they'd handle it. Either they do that or they have to follow the pickup man."

"That sounds just as dangerous for Anne."

"No matter what you do, she's in danger."

He closed his eyes and rubbed his chin. "Then let's do as they say." He looked at Mosier. "You know that I'm good for it, Bob. But it's going to take a couple of days to raise it from my broker. I need a short-term loan from corporate."

"It won't be a problem."

"Would you take care of the financial arrangements with Bonner?"

"Sure. I'll get right on it."

The door swung shut behind Mosier. Chadwick and I both leaned back in our chairs.

"It's been a hell of a day, Bruce."

He looked at the top of his desk. "I don't know how much more of this I can take."

I took out my notebook. "I need to ask a few questions. And this isn't going to be pleasant. I might as well go right into it. How solid is your marriage?"

"Like a rock. What does that have to do with anything?"

"I have to consider whether her disappearance may be voluntary."

He shook his head vigorously. "Look, I know this woman. I love her absolutely. We've been married for almost twenty-five years. Five years into our marriage I had to go bankrupt. We built up everything all over again. She's been with me through eight different companies, ten or twelve houses. We had a child die on us. And we got through all of it. We had no problems. Everything was fine. Now don't you tell me that she'd walk out on me without a word of warning! That's plain nuts."

I shifted gears. "Who knew about the party the cake was for?"

"The invitations were out, so everyone we had invited—the office staff here, the main contractors, a few of the people at the bank, our operations staff for the restaurant—maybe twenty people."

"How long has the party been planned?"

"It was Bonner's idea originally; Anne liked it and she carried it through. The idea goes back to just before Christmas. We had a little party then and it went well. Having a party to celebrate the opening sounded like a good idea."

"Who knew about the cake itself?"

"Anne had mentioned it to me. I don't know who else knew."

"Did anyone know she was going to the bakery today?"

"You're the one who told me that the bakery was expecting her. I'm not even sure that I knew. She may have said something a few days ago about going, but I really don't remember."

"The car was found between Mountville and Columbia, on Columbia Pike. Is that the usual way to go?"

"There's another way, going up to Route Thirty, which is a limited-access road. It would be a little faster, maybe, but it's longer. And anyway, she had to get the dry cleaning."

"When she drove was she usually alone?"

"Sure. We all have things to do. She has no particular reason to take company along."

"Her age?"

"Forty-one."

"Any scars or identifying marks?"

"Why would you—" He stopped. When he spoke, his voice was soft. "Oh, I see. A small mark on her left breast. She had a benign tumor taken out years ago, not long after Jeremy was born. And a real old cut above the left knee, from a bicycling accident when she was a kid."

"Is anything missing as far as money, clothes, personal effects?"

"I took a quick look while I was waiting for you. I can't be sure, but nothing jumped out at me. As far as I know, all she took is the stuff she had on."

"Does she have any close friends she's been in touch with for a long time, for years? The kind of people she'd confide in?"

"Not really. But she's made a good friend here in town. Nancy Saunders. Lives just up the street. They see each other quite a bit, I think."

"I'd like to go see her, if you don't mind."

"How do you think it will help?"

"I have no idea, exactly. I don't know enough to have a theory yet. But there are no witnesses to the abduction and no physical evidence. You don't want me to bring in the police. Someone did this who had a pretty good idea of her routine, who probably knew her and was known to her. Talking to people who knew her, and learning about her, is about all we can do for the moment."

"Then go ahead, by all means. I have to trust you in this."

I stood up to leave. We could have talked for another hour, but I was anxious to get started.

"Look, Dave, I've had just about enough for one lifetime. Get Anne back for me."

"I'll do everything I can. I mean that."

His grip was firm, but his hand was sweaty.

7

Tuesday, 1:00 P.M.

We were in the unheated garage, and Mosier was glaring at me, which didn't make the conversation any more pleasant. Despite the cold he was in his shirtsleeves.

"Goddam it, Dave, why the hell do you want to go around looking for trouble? They call up and say, hey, no problem, just give us forty grand and she walks. What are you trying to do? Stay put and wait for them to call."

If the garage wasn't at twenty degrees I would have been flushed with anger. We were on our third go-around. Sometimes the educated are the hardest people to deal with. "All right, Mr. Mosier. We'll do—"

"If you're such a top investigator why couldn't you—"

"Excuse me, but—"

"Goddam, it's my money and I get—"

There were only two ways of dealing with people like him, and I didn't have the energy to shout him down. I hit the button to open the garage door and walked outside.

"Don't you walk away from me, Garrett!" I could hear his bellowing echo around the neighborhood. I walked over to my Honda and unlocked the door.

"Where the fuck do you think you're going?"

I got inside and started it up. It caught on the first try. White vapor poured out of the exhaust and enveloped the car. I rolled down my window. I didn't even bother to look first; I knew he would be there.

For the first time in ten minutes, he spoke in a normal tone. "What's going on here, Dave?"

"We're going to make a little deal right now, Mr. Mosier. It's very simple. I'm going to do the talking. You're going to shut up and listen. The first interruption, I put this thing into gear and drive back to Philadelphia."

He crossed his arms over his chest and waited.

"Mr. Mosier, I know how much you want to get Bruce's wife back. I want to get her back. But we do that by facing things as they are, not as we'd like them to be. Somebody went to a lot of trouble and took a lot of risk. In Pennsylvania, the fall is ten to twenty. Anyone who'd know the family well enough to select Anne as a victim knows that forty thousand is peanuts. So either something has gone really wrong with their plan—which I doubt—or the call didn't come from them at all. It's just someone pulling a quick con. So we go ahead and pay the ransom, if that's what you want, but let me keep looking. Because I don't think that we're anywhere near the end of this."

He'd finally calmed down enough to feel the cold. He rubbed his hands over his arms. "I sure hope you're wrong."

"So do I."

"Come on. Let's go back in the house."

We went into the kitchen. Mary poured coffee for both of us. He didn't speak until he'd almost finished; he wasn't a man who backed down easily, and he found it hard to find the right words now. "Do you think they're just playing with our heads?"

"I really don't know. All I can say is that the offer is fishy."

"Who else could know about Anne?"

"I don't know. Look, real kidnappers would want everything they could bleed us for, not a quick hit like this. So either some amateur got really lucky—which I don't believe—or this call isn't from real kidnappers. That means either the kidnapping isn't real, or there's a third party in the situation."

"What's your vote?"

"I vote for assuming it's real. That's the vote that keeps Anne alive. You have a different vote?"

"It can't hurt to keep checking around, I guess."

"My meter is running until I get back to Philadelphia. I charge the same for investigating or for drinking your coffee."

"You weren't kidding," he said slowly. "About not bullshitting, I mean."

"No. We've got three hours, right?"

"They said they'd call back with instructions then."

"No problem with the money?"

"The bank is working on it now. It'll be here by courier by the time we need it."

"Bruce mentioned that Anne had a good friend that lives around here. Nancy Saunders."

"I've met her once or twice. She only lives three doors up the street. It's a big stone sonofabitch with a turret."

I decided to try my luck dropping in unannounced. If she knew anything worth knowing, she'd try to put me off. She'd have to work harder at it if I was already on her doorstep.

The wind had died down, and it was starting to cloud over. Normally that meant warming, but I felt as cold as ever. A few snowflakes, big and puffy, started to fall.

The Saunders house was every bit as big as Chadwick's, but on a smaller lot. Instead of lawn, the Saunders's property had trees—at least a dozen maples, with ivy as a ground cover. In the summer it must have been pleasant; now it was gray and bare.

The house was a sort of Gothic revival by way of Italy. I trudged up the stone steps and rang the bell. The door opened a couple of inches and stopped.

"Yes?" It was a woman's voice, husky and pleasant.

"I'd like to speak to Nancy Saunders, please. My name is Garrett. David Garrett."

"I'm Nancy."

"This is about Anne Chadwick."

"What about her?"

"I'm from Sentinel Life Insurance. We're doing an investigation."

The door closed for a moment, and I heard the rattle of a chain. "Please, come in."

Nancy Saunders was the kind of seventy-year-old who was fighting age every inch of the way. She was tall and thin, with short gray hair. She was wearing a close-fitting black dress that went all the way to her ankles. A single string of pearls and a gold belt. She looked at me carefully, looking for something in my face. "You don't look like you work for an insurance company."

"I'm an investigator."

"But not for an insurance company."

"What makes you say that?"

She smiled. "Young man, by the time a woman reaches my age she's had a good deal of experience being lied to, and you're not as good a liar as you think you are. Anne would never go near an insurance policy. She said it was presumptuous. Trying to cheat death. Now if you'll tell me what you're really here about, perhaps we can see about a talk."

I was feeling like a jerk three times over. I decided to come clean. "I'm sorry. It's just that I'm trying hard to protect my client's privacy. I'm a private investigator, working for Uncle Chan's. And now Anne is involved." I told her about finding the car. I kept the ransom demand to myself, but I hinted that I thought she'd been abducted.

"Please come in. I'll do anything I can to help." She turned and headed down the hall. Her walk was poised and very elegant; when she led, she was used to being followed. Although the floor was tile, I heard no footsteps.

I followed her down a short hallway flanked with English hunting scenes into a sitting room. It was small, with a fireplace at one end, and the floor was mostly taken up with a huge red Oriental rug.

We sat across from each other on two facing love seats with a butler's table in between. She sat down slowly and relaxed only when her back found the support of the sofa. I wondered if she suffered from arthritis. From my vantage point I could see three tall case clocks, all showing different times.

"Thanks for seeing me. I won't take up much of your time. I'm told you know Anne very well."

"She visits often. We're both widows, each in our own way."

"Does she have any enemies?"

"Before I answer a question like that, young man, you ought to tell me why you want to know."

"You're aware of the trouble at the restaurant?"

"Yes, she mentioned it. But what does that have to do with Anne?"

"That, I'm not sure about. But if she was kidnapped it may be the same people who've been making trouble at the restaurant."

"Is she all right?"

"As far as we know, but we haven't had any confirmation."

"Ask me your question again, please."

"Does Anne have any enemies?"

"None, except for Bruce's job."

"I gather you don't care for her husband."

"Oh, he's a fine man. He loves her and he's devoted to her, in his own way. But he's a workaholic. He's not the kind of man who can fulfill all her needs."

"Do you know one who is?"

She smiled. "That's a rather large question. But no, I didn't have any particular candidate in mind."

"You don't seem to be taking the kidnapping of a good friend very seriously."

She looked down and fiddled with her ring finger for a moment. "I take it very seriously, Mr. Garrett. Don't patronize me by expecting me to emote around the room to prove my sincerity."

"I'm sorry."

"Do you know very much about her?"

"I've been trying. I only met her briefly. I was hoping you could help."

"I'll tell you what I can. Do you have a picture?"

"Not yet."

"Then at least let me give you one. It may help."

My eyes followed her as she moved across the room to a side door. When she didn't return after a couple of minutes, I got up and walked around the room. I hefted a crystal vase and held it to the light. It was the kind of thing my wife had loved; we must have received half a dozen as wedding presents. I wondered where they all were now. Probably with her—like everything else.

Nancy returned by another door, holding a snapshot. "This was taken last summer."

Anne was lying in a hammock in the shade, presumably in the rear yard of this house. A big white straw hat concealed part of her face, but a cascade of reddish blond curls spilled out all around the brim. She was smiling at the camera and her arms were behind her head, but something about the picture didn't add up.

"For somebody enjoying a summer day she doesn't look very relaxed."

"Anne isn't very relaxed. She's very full of energy, always in motion. This is as calm as she gets."

I put it in my pocket. "What made her that way?"

"She always was. We've talked a lot, over the years. I like to think I've been like an aunt to her, or even a mother. You know, you need parents at every age, not just when you're young. She told me that when she was a child, they called her 'high strung.' I suppose the term now is 'hyperactive.' She was always getting into things, always a discipline problem. But very bright; she told me that if she buckled down she could get straight A's. Let me tell you a story. One summer when she was twelve or thirteen she was bored; she found an old text on calculus and taught it to herself. She had a full four-year scholarship to Penn. Even as a freshman she was taking graduate-level math courses."

"You seem to know a good deal about it."

"We talked about it many times. Women of my generation, whatever our talents—or lack of them—never had the kind of chance she had. My father sent me to a finishing school and then placed me in an office job so I'd meet a suitable husband. I didn't—I met my first husband instead. But Anne was young enough that the world was open to her."

"But she quit to get married."

She stiffened. "That was about as much of a choice as the fox who decided to chew off his own paw to escape the trap."

"No one held a gun to her head."

"Oh, but they did. In a way. She slept with Bruce exactly once, and then found out she was pregnant. Abortion was still illegal. Adoption didn't appeal to her. Nowadays, I suppose she would have considered just having the child and raising it alone; but no one thought like that at the time. When she told him about it he begged her to marry him. He went to her parents, and even to his own parents, and all of them ganged up on her. So she agreed to marry him."

"Ain't love grand."

"So it seems. They were very unhappy at the start. I'm very fond of Anne, but I have to say that she can be very stubborn. In those early years they only stayed together because of the children, and because it was convenient. Don't get me wrong, Mr. Garrett. He was never abusive, or a drunkard, or a flagrant womanizer; there was nothing like that. They just weren't a good fit."

"I can see that you don't think it's a kidnapping."

"Then you haven't been listening very carefully. They had a difficult marriage, certainly at the start, at least. But they've had it for twenty-five years. And what was it that Hamlet said to his mother? Something like, at your age, love is tempered by discretion. My own first marriage was very unhappy. I'd get up every morning and think about whether to leave him that day. Eventually I met the man who became my second husband and the decision was suddenly easy. But until then . . . It's very *wearing* to live that way, rethinking your life every day. Many, many people just decide to make the best of it, especially when there are children. She was very devoted to Amy."

"The child that died?"

"Yes. There's quite a story with that, too, but nothing

that has anything to do with Anne's disappearance. Amy ran afoul of a motorcycle gang. Horrible thing. They never actually found the body, just her clothes, torn and burned. But to return to what I was saying, it wasn't a close marriage, but it worked, and it's worked for many years. She's proud of his success. He's a good provider. It's more than many people have."

"Did she have affairs?"

"Do you think it's important to go into that?"

"Unless you're certain she voluntarily disappeared, it could be a matter of life and death."

"I see. Well, I suspect so, and I'm fairly sure he did, too. But it's always been very discreet. Nothing public at all."

"Is she seeing anyone now?"

"I don't believe so."

"Could she have decided to disappear in retaliation for one of his affairs? Make him sweat it out, teach him a lesson?"

"No. He's been very busy with the Uncle Chan's project for a number of months. Whatever else he is, he's a damned hard worker. He doesn't play till the work is done. Besides, the affairs he's had in the past have hardly been worthy of the name; a little fling now and then with a secretary in a roadside motel. Nothing of any consequence."

"Were there ever any relationships—by either one of them—that weren't so tidy? Any with jealousy, possessiveness?"

"Just one, years ago, right after she moved here. He was one of the first people she met, besides me. It was at a tennis tournament, playing mixed doubles. He fell very much in love with her. At first she was flattered, but she gradually realized that he wanted more than she wanted to give. He asked her to leave Bruce and marry him, and then he persisted after she refused. So she broke if off. It all happened within a few months."

"Any chance they've renewed their relationship?"

"No. She didn't care for him that deeply to run the

risk. If you don't have marriage in mind, Mr. Garrett, Lancaster has any number of other attractive men."

"Could he have kidnapped her, trying to win her back?"

She laughed. "Ted was a bit headstrong, but violence isn't his forte. He was far too gentle and considerate a man to even think such a thing. If he'd been ruthless, he would have confronted Bruce and asked him to let her go. But he never even considered that, I'm sure."

"When's the last time Anne and Ted had any contact?"

"They see each other once or twice a year at parties. Ted travels in some of the same circles she does. But there's been nothing between them for years."

"When were you supposed to see Anne next?"

"A late lunch, at four, in Lancaster. We both love the English custom of tea. It breaks up the day so nicely. The difficulty is that American restaurants are so often closed, so we used to eat lunch as late as we could, to make the best of it."

"Did she have other errands planned for the day, after lunch?"

"None that I know of. And we had nothing planned for after lunch. We have lunch once a week, generally. Sometimes we go shopping afterwards, sometimes not, depending on the weather and our schedules."

"I'd like any thoughts you might have on what's going on."

She rested her chin on the point of one finger for a moment. "If I had to guess, I'd say she's been abducted, but I don't think it has anything to do with her. It has to do with Bruce."

"Go on."

"Anne is a housewife. She has no business, no information, no assets of her own. Anne is being used to get to Bruce."

"Who do you think is using her?"

"I don't know. Someone who wants Bruce to do something, or not do something, with the franchise. I can't believe anyone would take her in hopes of getting a money ransom. Lots of people in Lancaster have money, more money than Bruce. What's unique about him is the franchise."

"Why should anyone care so much about a fast-food restaurant opening on time?"

"I don't know," she said slowly. "I've been trying to think of just that as we sit here. But Bruce and I are hardly close; I don't know anything about the business. Certainly Anne never mentioned it."

"No offense, but I'm having trouble understanding exactly what you're trying to say."

She gave me a rueful smile. "Well, God love you, so am I. All I'm trying to do is make logical sense of a situation without having all the facts. I just have this feeling that the key is Bruce, not Anne."

I glanced at my watch and saw that it was twenty till four. "Thanks very much for your time. If you hear from her or learn anything else, please call me. If can be reached through the Chadwicks' number."

"Certainly, Mr. Garrett. If there's anything I can do, please let me know." She showed me to the door. "You will get her back safely, won't you?"

"If it can be done, I'll do it."

I was promising a lot of people something I had no way of delivering. But what the hell; I was going to be blamed if it didn't work anyway.

8

Tuesday, 4:00 P.M.

"Where the hell have you been?" was Mosier's greeting when I came into the kitchen. The room was long, with a series of skylights interspersed by dark wooden beams. Half of it was the kitchen proper; the rest was the large breakfast nook where Mosier and I were confronting each other. Jeremy sat in one of the chairs, trying his best to keep clear of Mosier's bad temper. The floor was reddish quarry tile. With snow starting to accumulate on the skylights, it was a dark and somber place.

"You know where. At Saunders's."

"You cut things pretty damn close, Garrett." Not knowing if he meant the phone call or the case in general, I said nothing. Whether the kidnapping was related to their problems with the franchise or was something personal wasn't up for discussion right now. And who knew, perhaps the ransom would bring her back and I'd never have to deal with it.

"Find anything out?" He was looking out the window.

"Not really. Just some background."

"I told you it was a waste of time. I need you here, where the action is. Not flitting around the goddam landscape."

"It's getting too cold for flitting." I was getting very tired of him. "What's the phone setup?"

He pointed a finger at his chest. "It's me they want to deal with. I do the talking, and nobody else."

"Fine. I just want to listen in."

"There's a wall phone near the stove, and the one here on the counter. Same line."

I went to the wall phone and unscrewed the mouthpiece. The microphone dropped into my hand, and I put it on the sink. I barely had time to replace the phone before it started to ring. I did my best to lift my receiver at the same moment as Mosier.

"Yes, is it you?" he asked.

"It's me," a muffled man's voice responded. I could hear street noises in the background, like he was calling from a phone booth. "Do you have the money?"

"Right here next to me."

"Put it in a briefcase and bring it to the square at four-thirty. You'll see a brick with a dab of yellow paint. Put the briefcase right on top and keep walking. Don't look back or the deal's off. And no cops."

Mosier started to say something, but the line was already dead. He looked at me, a little dazed.

"Was that the same man as before?"

"Yeah. At least, I think so. It sounded like he had something over the phone."

"Did the background noises sound the same?"

"Who knows? Who cares? The important thing is to get her back and stop dillydallying around."

"No problem, Mr. Mosier. Give me the briefcase and let me get going."

"You? I'm doing this myself."

"I don't think that's a good idea."

"All you've done is given us bad ideas."

"It's crazy to be paying me and not using me. I'm a licensed private detective. I have a permit to carry a weapon. I'm not emotionally involved. Let me do this."

"You don't even know where to go."

"The intersection of King and Queen. I spend a couple of weeks every summer with a friend here. I know the city just fine."

"You didn't think this was ever going to happen, did you?" There was a sneer in his voice. "You thought it was all a joke." He sounded pleased with himself. I wasn't surprised.

"For what difference it makes, I wasn't sure what

would happen. But there's a job to do, and pretty soon. We can't afford to be late."

"I'm coming along, at least."

"I need someone here in case they call."

"Then you stay here and I'll go alone."

"You're the only one they've talked to. What would they do if a new voice came on the line?"

"How are you going to play it?"

"Straight. I'm going to give them the case and not try to follow."

He snorted. "And you're the expert? Any idiot could do that."

"You couldn't." I picked up the briefcase and headed for the door. He was so stunned that I was in my car before he could start bellowing.

The snow was starting to stick, and the Honda wasn't worth much on slick surfaces. Fortunately, the main roads were heavily traveled. Even though traffic moved slowly I was in the center of town with ten minutes to spare.

Even on a lousy gray day, Lancaster is a handsome town. Most of the buildings are two or three stories, built between 1850 and 1920, and nearly everything is brick. Except for the very poorest neighborhoods, nearly every house is well maintained. The streets are lined with old shade trees—sycamores, oaks, and maples—and many of the sidewalks are still brick. That day, the trees were bare and the sidewalks glazed with ice, but at least the city was beautiful the rest of the year, which is more than most places can say.

I pulled into a parking garage on Duke Street and cut through Watt & Shand's department store, the main local retailer in the city. It was nearly deserted. A few hopeful signs advertised sales, but only a straight-up giveaway would bring out shoppers in that kind of weather.

I emerged from the front of the store and looked at the square across the street. The wind was picking up and blowing the snow in loose, swirling patterns. The square itself was dominated by a large Civil War monument with four cement soldiers standing watch at the corners; traffic flowed around it on three sides. The northwest corner, across the street from me, was a brick plaza for pedestrian use only. In the summertime it was crowded with concerts and charity events; at the moment there was no one in sight.

I crossed the street and entered the plaza itself. Unless someone was hiding behind one of the planters, I was alone. The snow was falling faster; if a blizzard was in the forecast, the offices would be letting people go for the afternoon soon. I paced slowly around the square, sometimes looking down at the brick, sometimes looking up at the windows of the buildings around me. I couldn't catch anyone watching, not that I expected to. But after a bit I spotted a swatch of yellow paint, hardly bigger than a golf ball, near the corner of the Fulton Bank building, on the Queen Street side. I rubbed it with my shoe to make sure—it was paint, and fresh, too. Probably from a spray can.

I put the briefcase down on the brick and stepped around the corner of the building. It was exactly 4:30. I couldn't see the briefcase, but in case the pickup man came up Queen, he would have to walk right past me. The wind was getting stronger, and I had to keep moving. No one was on Queen Street. I saw the blue-and-white awning of TMB, a clothing store, half a block to my right. Once, on a long lunch between pretrial conferences, I'd gone in on impulse and bought a suit. It was twenty percent less than I'd been used to paying at Boyd's, and it had worn well—at five years old, it was my second-best suit. I wondered when I'd be able to afford a new one.

At 4:37 I looked around the corner. The briefcase was still there. I pulled my head back. My vacation with Lisa came to mind; the sun, the heat, the blue sea. It was hard to realize that right now people were there, where we had been, only a few hours away by plane, while I was shivering alone in this snowstorm.

I looked again at 4:40. The case was gone. At the far end of the square I could see the back of a man, walking swiftly away, the case in one hand. He was wearing jeans, boots, a lumberman's jacket, and a ski mask. I didn't even try to follow. He hadn't just been lucky in figuring out which way to approach the case, and at what moment—he'd been tipped off by someone watching the square. Probably from one of the surrounding buildings, or from a car. Before I could cover half the distance to him, he'd be in a car and on his way.

I counted to thirty, slowly, and followed. When I turned the corner, as I expected, there was no one in sight. I checked the block anyway, on the off chance that he'd decided just to lay low in a storefront instead of taking a car, but it did me no good. I went back to Watt & Shand's and found a public phone.

"Mr. Mosier, this is Garrett. The pickup went fine."

"Where is she?"

"They never said they'd release her at the pickup point."

"Then what the fuck are you doing for me? I could let Chadwick's goddam kid give away forty grand on the sidewalk for me."

"My job was to deliver the money according to instructions so that Anne would be safe. For what it's worth, I told you not to pay it in the first place."

"How much the fuck longer are you going to argue with me?"

There was no answer to that question that wouldn't make things worse, so I said nothing.

"Get your sorry ass back here. I've got to get back to work." He hung up.

I was in no hurry to spend the waning hours of the afternoon with Mosier. I called my office and handled as much business as I could. By the time I finished, the store was closing. Traffic was barely crawling. The forecasters were predicting four to six inches, and visibility was poor. It was nearly a quarter to six before I turned onto Chadwick's street.

The lights were on at the Saunders house as I drove by, and I found myself turning into her driveway. Even without knowing about the ransom demand, she'd thought that Bruce and the franchise were connected to the kidnapping. Maybe, given a little more time to think, she could give me a lead in that direction. It could have been handled by telephone, of course. Mainly I was putting off the inevitable confrontation with Mosier.

The snow was already an inch deep on the steps, so I held onto the railing and took them slowly. I knocked and the door swung open at my touch.

"Hello? Anybody home?" Silence. "This is Dave Garrett."

I stepped inside. I didn't like it. When I'd been there at two, Nancy had a chain on the door. I checked; it was still intact, hanging loose. No forced entry, at least from this door. But why unlocked? "Hello?" I yelled. "Mrs. Saunders, your front door is open."

I decided to walk as far as the sitting room; if no one was there I was going to leave. Perhaps she was upstairs, having a bout of ever-so-genteel sex with the proper sort of person.

I didn't have to go further than the sitting room. Nancy Saunders was there, on the same sofa where we'd talked. She was wearing the same black dress. Except that now the back of her head was crushed.

I didn't move at all. First, I listened. I held my breath and strained my ears, turning my head for the slightest sound of footsteps or closing doors. As far as I could tell, Nancy and I were alone. Then I looked around the room, very slowly. The table had been cleared since I'd left. Except for that, and Nancy herself, everything was the same. I approached her, keeping my hands to my sides. She was slumped over, her right hand on the armrest and her left hand in her lap. She'd been hit from behind; if the first blow hadn't killed her, at least it knocked her out. Her hair was thickly matted in blood. Her dress glistened, and I assumed it was soaked, too, as was the back of the sofa. The rug was clean. I saw no streaks or smears of blood anywhere. Whoever had killed her had done it quickly, and hadn't disturbed the body at all afterwards.

I retraced my steps out of the room and picked up the hall telephone.

"Mr. Mosier, this is Dave Garrett. I'm—"

"You're missing the goddam boat is what you're doing! Where the—"

"Shut up and listen! I don't have time for your crap right now. I'm at Nancy Saunders's house. She's been murdered."

"Oh, my God."

"I waited around town after the pickup. I decided to stop by and ask her a few more questions. I just got here and found her, not more than five minutes ago." I found myself withholding the details; was I suspecting him? I startled myself with the thought. Mosier was a turkey, not a killer.

"Does this have anything to do with Anne?"

"I don't know. If the two are connected, then she's in serious danger."

"Look, can't you get back here and talk about this?"

"No. I don't dare leave this house. If someone sees me going out and then the body is found, I'm the prime suspect."

"What are you going to do?"

"Call the police myself."

"Huh?"

"Even if I got out of the house without being seen, there's no telling who she told that we'd met this afternoon. Plus I have fingerprints and maybe hair samples in at least two rooms. I've got to come clean. Besides, I could lose my license for not reporting a felony. Don't worry. I'll try to keep all of you out of it."

I hung up before he could argue with me.

9

Tuesday, 10:00 P.M.

I was in the squad room of the Detectives Division of the Lancaster Bureau of Police. I wasn't alone, but I was getting used to having company. In the last four hours, except for a trip to the station's bathroom, I hadn't been out of the sight of at least two officers for an instant.

The squad room of most detective units is a pretty bleak place, and this one was par for the course. It was, literally, one big room, about thirty feet on each side. It didn't seem big though, probably because the ceiling was only about seven feet. Fluorescent fixtures hung down at intervals; the taller men had to keep ducking their heads. The floor was green and white linoleum tiles—or at least they were white when they were put down, God knows how many years ago. A half a dozen battered metal desks were strewn around, all of them covered with files and overflowing ash-trays. Why did so many cops smoke? Three detectives were in the room, and all three of them were smoking. Two of them were at their desks. One was really working. The second, the one nearer me, was pretending to type. Actually, he was acting as a witness to the interrogation. The third and most senior detective was sitting on a desk right in front of me. His legs swung back and forth, but they were the only relaxed things about him. His grip on the edge of the desk was so tight that the tendons in his wrists were bulging. His eyes couldn't have narrowed any further without disappearing completely.

"We're going to do it all again, Garrett. But this time let me do the talking. You're a disbarred lawyer. Now you're making a living as a PI in Philadelphia. A few weeks ago you come into twenty thousand dollars—"

"I told you, it was a fee."

"Then who was the client?"

"You know I can't tell you that."

"The bank records show it was a cash deposit. What kind of client pays a bill like that in cash?"

"I filed a disclosure with the Treasury Department."

"That doesn't answer my question. You spend two weeks in Mexico. The day after you come back, you come to Lancaster, in the dead of winter. You missed the start of the tourist season by about three months."

"I told you, I'm here on a case."

"And you won't tell me who for. So just be quiet. You're seen by a neighbor when you go into the victim's house around one. Despite the fact that it's snowing, you arrive on foot. Why ditch the car?" He paused for effect, knowing I wouldn't answer. I couldn't tell him I walked because my client lived only three doors away.

"Anyway, she lives alone. You're in the house with her for Lord knows how long. You kill her. I don't know why yet, but I figure you're working for the kind of people that pay their bills in cash, so anything is possible. At some point you leave and come back with your car. Or maybe an accomplice drops it off for you and you never left the house at all."

"It's a tough racket. I can't afford accomplices."

"Come on, Garrett. It's only a question of time till we find the murder weapon. Or till the state police crime lab puts together enough forensic evidence. Why don't you come clean now? It'll be easier on you."

"Can I talk now?"

"Go ahead." The detective at the desk nearest me gave up any pretense of typing.

I'd been cooperative, even polite, for nearly five hours, and all I'd accomplished was giving the police the impression that I was on the verge of confessing. It was time to take off the gloves. "This is an idiotic conversation. I'm not an idiot, neither are you. So stop insulting my intelligence. You don't have jack shit and you know it. According to you, I plan this crime so carefully that I arrive on foot. You and I both know that a pedestrian in bad weather is a hell of a lot more conspicuous than just a car. But no matter. I then go up to the front door, in broad daylight, and announce myself to my intended victim. I go in, commit the murder, and hang around in the house with a body for hours. I'm not really doing anything; nothing in the house is disturbed or missing. Just passing time. Then I arrange for my accomplice to drive my car over and park it in the front driveway, right in front of God and everybody. Having performed his function of negating whatever advantage was gained by not parking my car there in the first place, he leaves. With my thanks for a job well done. Actually, he does a hell of a job, since he drives my car without leaving any prints or hairs. But when you don't exist in the first place, that's easy enough. Then I cap off the perfect crime by calling the police myself and waiting for you to arrive.''

The room was very quiet. His face was red, and I thought for a moment that he was going to hit me. Suspects had been worked over for a lot less. But I was mad, too, and I didn't care anymore. ''You think you're pretty damned smart, don't you?''

''No. But I'm pretty damned innocent.''

''We're not through with you.''

''You are for tonight. I've told you everything I know, three times. Somewhere out there is a murderer. Get out of my face and go find him. The show's over, detective.'' I raised my voice slightly so that everyone would hear. ''I demand that you let me see my attorney, immediately.''

''Make your call if you want.'' He was raising his voice, too; we were both playing to the audience.

''You'd better let me walk right now.''

''You're not going anywhere. We're in the middle of a very serious criminal investigation.''

My temper finally got the better of me. ''Investigation? Investigation! Then investigate! Take fingerprints! Call your stoolies! Sweat some dealers! Whatever it is you guys do. What are you doing here?''

I looked around the room. "I don't see any criminals here. I see three cops trying to finish out their shift without having to go out in the cold, and one suspect whose civil rights are being trampled. I don't see any investigation anywhere."

"We've all got our jobs to do."

"Your job is to uphold the Constitution of the United States of America and of the Commonwealth of Pennsylvania. And it looks like you may need my help."

"What do you mean by that?"

"We'll settle that at the suppression hearing, or on a habeas. Right now I'm tired. And I want to know if you intend to charge me or not. And you're going to make your decision without any more violations of my privilege not to incriminate himself."

"Your rights haven't been violated." He sounded sure of himself, but I saw a flicker in his eye. *I'm certain I didn't do anything wrong. But just maybe I overlooked something. Is there some damned new case somewhere I don't know about? What will the DA say? He wants to be a judge.* I'd seen that flicker a hundred times before. The police knew what to do, what procedures should be followed, and usually knew the drill better than the defense lawyers—but they didn't know why they were doing it, why the courts had drawn the lines where they did. And that gave the lawyers the edge.

"We'll see about that later." I had nothing to work with, but I wasn't going to tell him that. Uncertainty was the only weapon I had.

"We're preparing to charge you with criminal homicide."

"Don't kid me. You aren't going to charge me; you don't have a thing. You've talked to the DA and he's told you to sit tight. What did you tell the DA? That I was in the vicinity of a homicide. So were the next-door neighbors, he said. And they probably had more reason to kill her, being neighbors. Got your motive figured out, by the way?"

"You're a material witness."

"So are lots of people, including whoever had to identify the body. I don't see him here. Why pick on me? And don't tell me you're afraid I'm going to take off."

"It's occurred to us."

I sensed I'd pushed him as far as I could; it was time to try sweet reason. I modulated my voice and leaned closer. "Look, I'm a licensed professional. I only live sixty miles from here. I'm working on a case right here in town. And if it makes you feel better, I'll check in twice a day with you. Three times."

He said nothing. "Let me guess." I said. "The DA didn't give you authority to hold me on a material witness warrant, either, did he?"

"Get your coat and go. And we expect to hear from you."

"I won't leave the county without checking."

"See to it."

Outside the wind was picking up, blowing stinging crystals of ice into my eyes. The cold sliced right through my jacket and I found myself shivering after hours of overheated rooms. It was great to be outside, and free. I closed my eyes and breathed deeply until my head was clear.

I took two different cabs going home, and had the second one let me off several blocks from Chadwick's, just in case.

The neighborhood streets were poorly lit, and there was no moon. Despite the cold I took my time walking back. For the first time in six hours I had a chance to think about Anne Chadwick, and about all the people who were counting on me. I wondered where she was, if she was alive at all. Mainly I wondered how I was going to find her.

The sky was clearing, and I could see the familiar constellations. The sky behind them was completely black, and without any frame of reference the stars seemed close enough to touch. The illusion was compelling, but my hands stayed in my pockets.

10

Wednesday, 7:00 A.M.

When I got downstairs the next morning, Bonner was sipping coffee in the kitchen with a sheaf of computer printouts spread out in front of him. When he saw me he cleared me a spot. I poured some coffee and sat down.

"How you doing?" he asked.

"As well as can be expected under the circumstances."

"The last I heard, the money had been dropped off but there was no word about when she'd be released."

"That's as much as I know."

"You think she'll be free soon?"

"How well do you know her?"

He looked around the room. "Jammed in here like this, you can't help but get to know people."

"Did she have any good friends?"

"I wouldn't know anything about that."

"Does the name Nancy Saunders ring a bell?"

"Sounds like you don't think this is the end of it."

"I'm not sure it is. In case it isn't, can you answer my question?"

"I didn't know her, no."

"Any activities where she'd meet people?"

"She took math courses sometimes at a local college. But I don't remember her mentioning meeting anyone."

"Did you talk much?"

"Not about ourselves. She would look at the numbers a little from time to time, and ask a question or two. But I wouldn't let her go over just anything. None of her business."

"Or Chadwick's."

"No. At least, not the day-to-day. His job is to hustle chow mein. Period."

"How is it that Chadwick runs things out of his house instead of a real office?"

"Just another example of his mismanagement," he said casually. "Doesn't have the self-confidence to see that we need first-class facilities. Thinks that it's better to do everything on the cheap. And now it's coming home to roost. Important people come to see how the operation is coming and they see—well, what you saw. It's half-assed."

"Where were you yesterday afternoon?"

He started to answer, then stopped. "Does it stay between us?"

"Depends what it is."

"With my girlfriend."

"Where?"

"Nowhere anybody would have seen us."

"Sure?"

"She came to my place around one and left at three or so. We didn't leave the apartment."

I pulled out a small notebook. "I'd better verify it, for what it's worth. Her name and phone?"

"She's married. She had to leave at three to be sure she got home before the kids got back from school."

"I still need to check it out."

"You come back with a good reason and I'll tell you. Not before."

I put the notebook away. Later on, we'd see if it was important or not. "What about after that?"

"I was back here between three and five. Then I went to my place, had some dinner, and spent the rest of the evening with her till nine."

"What about the kids and her husband?"

"He was working. The kids went to their friends' house."

I shifted gears slightly. "Chadwick and Mosier didn't miss you at the open house on Monday?"

"If they'd wanted me there I would have gone. But I know shit about food preparation. I've never even eaten in an Uncle Chan's. I'm a bean counter, period."

"Like your job much?" I asked.

"It's only my second job after my MBA. First I did two years with Chase. Now I'm here—two years with a smaller company in an expansion mode. After this I'll spend some time with a major company, either manufacturing or retailing."

"So do you like it?"

"I just answered you. I'm getting my ticket punched. Well, it was okay till Mosier came along. You know, you meet somebody like him, and it shakes your self-confidence. You think, boy, most people I meet like me—what am I doing wrong that makes him so difficult? What you have to realize is, he's been an asshole since he was ten. Or two; I don't know. He's always treated people this way. You're just the latest one to encounter it. Thinking about it that way helps your peace of mind."

"How about Chadwick?"

"He's a good boss to a point. He's too driven for my taste. He wants a day and a half's work every day. But that doesn't mean I'd kidnap his wife."

"Who do you think did?"

"I don't think anybody did. I think she just decided she'd had the shits of things."

"Anything in particular make you say that?"

"Not really. I think I work hard. But Chadwick—he's established. He's at the point where he can afford to let up a bit. He's crazy not to."

"Is that the way she thought?"

"I don't know. We never talked about anything personal."

"So if she took off, why the ransom?"

"I don't know that, either. That's why I keep my mouth shut around the others. My older sister just got a divorce in Philly. She took her husband for half of what he was worth, and she'd never worked since they got married. Anne could have hired a divorce lawyer and cleaned up big. I've seen his financial statement. He inherited some money from his parents, and he made good investments. He's worth close to a million. Some is tied up in IRAs and pensions, and some isn't real liquid, but this guy could afford to make a serious divorce settlement."

I decided to take a flier. "Speaking of divorce, I've heard a rumor that Anne had an affair a few years ago with a local man. Someone who plays tennis."

"News to me, if it's true. What was his name?"

"All I have is a first name. Ted."

He thought about it and then shrugged. "I've met a couple hundred local people through the Chadwicks. Bruce has sold a lot of little pieces of the operation—a couple of points here, a couple there—he barely has a controlling interest. Every one of them wears blazers and rep ties and they're named Buffy or Ted or Barry. Can you describe this guy?"

"Not at all. I'm guessing that he's between forty and fifty-five."

"Not much help. Sure you don't have a last name? If he's an investor I could pin him down in a minute."

"I wouldn't know about that. Sorry."

"If you come up with it, let me know."

From the corner of my eye I saw Mosier come into the kitchen. "Larry! Where the hell have you been, goddam it?"

"I took half a personal day, Mr. Mosier."

"A *fucking vacation* right when we're ready to open? What the hell is the matter with you? What about the figures on the thirty-second spots? And the uniform count? And the handbills for the high schools?"

"It will all be ready."

"That's what you say. I'm the one that's responsible. When I hire somebody I expect a day's work out of them!"

Bonner refused to be irritated. I got the feeling this scene was repeated often. "I work sixty to seventy hours a week, Mr. Mosier. Monday I had to leave for Philly at three-thirty in the morning. I told the staff in advance I'd be taking the day. I was here at six this morning. Everything is current."

"Well, it better be. And I'm not kidding."

By way of response Bonner drained his cup and went off. A door shut, louder than it needed to.

"Any new developments, Mr. Mosier?"

"Aren't you supposed to be telling instead of asking?"

"I've been out of touch."

"You've been out of touch ever since you left Philadelphia, if you ask me."

"I've been sweated by half the detectives of the Lancaster police force for keeping the franchise out of this."

"You expect a medal? You're being paid."

"I'm going to ask you one more time. Any news?"

"No."

"Then I recommend we bring in the police."

"You're nuts! Either that, or they got to you. First you want me to pat you on the head, or give you a bonus maybe, because you kept me out of this. Now you want me to tell the world."

"I kept the franchise out of a murder investigation. Because you're the client it has to be your decision. But that forty grand wasn't a real ransom, and you know it."

"Let's talk to Bruce about this, too. After all, it's his wife."

We found Chadwick in his office with construction drawings unrolled across his desk. He looked glad to see me. It was a welcome change from the way everyone else looked at me.

"I went to bed before you got home," Chadwick said. "Jeremy told me they didn't charge you."

I wanted to ask him how he'd been able to turn in and sleep so peacefully under the circumstances, but I held my tongue. He was paying the bills, and the customer was always right. "I don't think they will, at least not now. They don't really think I did it, but they think I know more than I'm telling."

"What will they do now?"

"It'll take a couple of days for the state police crime lab to process the forensic evidence—hairs, fibers, blood, fingerprints, things like that. And then a day or two to digest it all. Then they'll want to question me again."

He had a strange, fixed smile, and he seemed to be looking past me. "We should have her back by then, right? She should be back anytime. I'll tell you, Dave, I'm still really keyed up, and I won't rest easy till she's back, but I feel like a nightmare is ending."

"Bruce, I don't think it's that simple. There's no reason for optimism that I can see. I recommend we go to the police."

He leaned back in his chair and the smile faded. "Why the change?"

"I never said that we shouldn't. All I said was, we should wait till we had more information. Now we do. We paid a ransom nearly eighteen hours ago, and there's been no word since."

"Maybe that will be later this morning. That's what I'm counting on. Should we be rushing?"

"Once they have the money, they'd want to put as much distance between us and them as they can. I would have expected to hear something within two or three hours of the pickup."

"Well, having paid a ransom, I hope now that you're finally convinced this is a real kidnapping, at least."

"I'm convinced that whatever it is, the law should be involved."

"What about the Saunders murder?"

"Once we start talking to the police there's no way to keep them out of that, too. Saunders knew your wife; they're bound to make the connection. I'd recommend we come clean about my working for you."

"That's my decision to make," Mosier said. "We've got a two-million-dollar property opening in a couple of days. The corporation isn't going to subsidize somebody spilling their guts at this stage of the game."

Chadwick looked at Mosier and his voice dropped. "I respect your judgment, Bob, but what about Larry and Karen? Aren't they bound to make a connection to us, one way or another?"

"Nah, I don't think so."

"What are you talking about?" I asked Chadwick.

"Well, we didn't want to tell you, and it doesn't do much for Uncle Chan's image as a family place, but for months Larry has been seeing a married woman. Her name's Karen, and she's Nancy's daughter."

"He seems to be taking the murder of his girlfriend's mother pretty well. We talked for twenty minutes this morning and he never mentioned it. As a matter of fact he said he didn't know her."

"Well, he's a pretty cool customer," Chadwick said. He looked at Mosier. "But let's get back to the business at hand. I think we should do as Dave advises with the police. At least as far as telling them about Anne. Maybe we can keep the Nancy thing out of it, somehow."

Mosier surprised me. "I'll go along," he said mildly, "*if* we can keep them away from connecting us publicly with the Saunders thing. Let's at least try."

Chadwick nodded and reached for the wall phone, but it rang before he touched it. "The intercom line," he explained. He listened for a moment, then looked up at us. "No, don't open it. Bring it right back here."

He hung up. He tried to sound calm and didn't entirely succeed. "That was Rosie, the word processor. She said there was a knock at the front door; when she answered no one was there. But an envelope was on the step."

I sighed heavily. I had a very bad feeling about the envelope. A stout woman in her early fifties came in, holding it like she was afraid if was infectious. After she handed it to Chadwick, she was gone so fast I never saw her back.

Chadwick handed it to me, just as gingerly. "Should we open it?"

"There's no way of knowing if this means anything unless we do," I pointed out.

"What about fingerprints?"

"If this is from the kidnappers, they'd be nuts to be so sloppy. Anyway, I'll be careful."

I held it by a corner. It was a standard white business envelope, with a folded sheet of paper inside. No markings on the outside. I asked Chadwick for a clean knife and carefully sliced open the edge. I tapped the envelope on the table and the paper slid out.

Using the point of the knife, I spread the paper out flat. The sheet was a blank piece of typewriter paper with words cut from a newspaper pasted neatly across the middle:

> TWO HUNDRED THOUSAND AS FINAL PAYMENT TONIGHT. INSTRUCTIONS WILL FOLLOW. NO TRICKS.

We looked at each other. Not even Mosier could think of anything to say. Not even Mosier.

11

Wednesday, 10:00 A.M.

The first order of business was checking to see if anyone in the house had seen or heard anything, which was a waste of time. No one knew anything. And it didn't even help much in excluding the people in the house as suspects. Except for Mosier and Chadwick, no one had much of an alibi. The word processor operator herself had been on the telephone with the restaurant until just before she found the note, but the two secretaries had both been in separate rooms on errands long enough so that either one could have dropped the envelope outside and rung the doorbell. Kate had left the house at nine to go shopping and no one knew exactly where she was or when she'd be back. Jeremy did a little better; he'd been taking a shower after shoveling off the walks. Bonner was completely unaccounted for.

I put on my coat and went out the front door. It was gray and cold, with a gusty wind from out of the west. Jeremy had done a hell of a job on the walks; except for a slight dusting of blown snow, they were perfectly bare. I couldn't detect any footprints other than my own. The front walk ended about twenty feet away at the curved driveway. I couldn't see any fresh footprints there. Either the messenger had been careful to walk in and out in the tire tracks, or he'd come in and out of the house.

The house had a perimeter sidewalk that was equally clean. I started around, my eyes straining for even a single good print.

The layout of the house didn't make my job any easier. It was riddled with exterior doors, any one of which could have been used. Besides the main front door and the garage doors, there were side doors on each side and three separate rear doors.

I worked my way around the side and then into the backyard. I was walking directly into the wind so I pulled my coat collar tight against my face. The yard had a line of pine trees across the rear property line, but they were too far away to provide any shelter. The yard sloped upwards as it went away from the house at least as far as the line of trees. I couldn't tell if the slope continued beyond that. I looked down again and trudged down the rear walk until I nearly reached the far corner.

Looking back, I know I remember it incorrectly; it can't have happened the way I recall, with the hole appearing in the side of the house quite silently and the crack of the shot coming seconds later. But in my mind the instant between the impact of the bullet and its sound seems like forever.

I went down as fast as I could and found shelter behind the four-inch berm of snow. In Vietnam I'd seen 250-pound men hide behind trees with trunks two inches thick, and nobody thought it was funny at the time. I hit the ground hard and pressed myself as flat as I could, spreading out my arms and pressing my cheek on the snow. I even remembered the old infantry trick of turning my feet outwards to keep my heels from sticking up.

Waiting was forever. My universe consisted of some dirty snow a few inches from my nose and the harsh, ragged sound of my own breathing. My pants were wet; whether the moisture was incoming or outgoing I didn't know or care.

I counted to 1,060 and tried to hold my breath so I could listen. I couldn't do it; the adrenaline had me too pumped up. I waited another sixty seconds, gulped down as much air as I could, and tried again. Aside from the distant traffic sounds off somewhere to my right, all I could hear was a low steady sound, somewhere between a moan and a whistle, coming from the wind in the power cables overhead.

For all I could tell, the sniper was working his way in closer for the kill. As dangerous as it would be, it was time to move. Keeping my face against the snow, I slowly turned my head in the direction of the backyard. I nerved myself to lift my head. This was the most dangerous moment; if the sniper was watching, and if he saw the movement, he'd know I was still alive. It all depended on how close he was and whether he had a scope.

A quarter inch at a time I raised my head until I could see over the snow. I looked straight ahead at first, then panned to the left and right without moving my head. It didn't seem like a suburban backyard anymore; it was an ambush site, and that's how I saw it. Where was he hiding? The massive birdbath on my left could provide cover for a man if he crouched down, only thirty yards away. No, the approaches to it were too open; and anyway, if he was using a rifle he could afford to stand off ten times that distance. In the center of the yard was a white gazebo, but it was completely open and I couldn't see where he could find a rest for his rifle. And, like the birdbath, there was no covered line of approach or retreat.

I studied the tree line in the rear. If he was there, he could run in either direction on the far side of the trees without being seen from the house. He could crawl from one tree to the next and be invisible from ten yards away on either side. And he had the advantage of height. The interwoven branches provided ample cover. Yes, that was where I would be.

Was he still there? Three possibilities. One, he was trying to scare me and had taken off after the shot. Two, he was out to kill me, thought he had succeeded, and had cleared out. Three, he was waiting to see if he needed to make a following shot to finish me off. There was nothing to be gained by waiting. Either he was still there or he wasn't. Without turning my head, I tried to think of the location of the nearest door. I thought hard. I'd stopped near a door before the shot was fired. I couldn't remember exactly where it was, but I knew I'd planned to go back in through it. I probably wouldn't have walked past it. If I'd stopped short, it would be on my left.

Okay, let's assume it's five to ten feet to my left. How do I get there?

I thought about the door, and how far away it was. A half a dozen steps, but it wasn't that simple. I rehearsed my move; up on my hands and knees, then into a crouch, spin around to the left while coming up, and sprint for the door. I tried to inch my right hand outward a few inches to give me a better purchase. A pain shot through my shoulder so intense that for a moment I thought I'd been shot. I'd landed wrong, really wrong. However I got up, it wasn't going to be on my right arm.

I took a deep breath and started to move. And the instant I did, somehow I knew that I was still in danger. I felt eyes and a long gun-blue muzzle pointing at me. I felt a finger gently squeezing a trigger. As I started my spin I knew I'd never make it. I threw myself down again, just as a bullet passed through where I'd been standing. This time I heard the crack at the same time the hole appeared in the wall. I was down on my hands and knees but I didn't stop for an instant. My only hope was to keep moving, to get to that door, and pray that the sniper had a bolt-action rifle and not a semiautomatic. I leaped right from my knees into a low running crouch, as fast as any sprinter. My left foot slipped on a bit of ice but I didn't go down. The door was only ten feet away. I ran as fast as I could, terribly conscious that I had to move in a predictable direction at a steady speed. No matter how fast I moved I was still a duck in a shooting gallery. All the sniper had to do was lead me properly.

Five feet. I looked at the door and panicked. It was the back door to Bonner and Mosier's office. What if it was locked from the inside? I saw the curved thumb latch above the lock. Almost there. I extended my left hand to hit the latch and tried to stop. My hand brushed it, but at the same moment my feet went out from under me. I landed on my right shoulder just in front of the door. At the same moment I heard another shot and saw the stucco above my head explode into a shower of white and gray dust.

I pulled myself up to my knees and reached for the latch. It happened in slow motion. I remember everything about that moment—the glint of sunlight on the latch, the color of my glove, the tiny bits of plaster that sprinkled gently down. I even remember how the shot echoed off the pine trees. I saw my hand reach up, drifting slightly above the latch, and then move gently until it pressed down. The latch resisted, just for an instant, and then, blessedly, moved downwards. I wrenched the door toward me. I didn't bother to get up; I flung myself inside and landed on the tile floor in a belly flop. The door swung shut behind me and clicked.

Mosier was on his knees, on the far side of his desk. "What the fuck is going on?"

I opened my mouth but nothing came out at first. I gulped and tried again. "Sniper out back! Rifle! Where is everybody?"

"The first round came right through the wall in the next room. Everybody hit the floor. Then we heard two more. They didn't come through!"

"Everybody okay?"

"I think so."

"Tell everybody to stay down till I come back." I got to my feet and ran through the house and out to the front, where my car was parked. I jerked open the glove compartment and grabbed my .357. Holding it in across my chest, I dashed around to the corner of the house. I stood at the corner, listening and trying to catch my breath. I took the gun in both hands and dropped to my knees. With my elbows extended and the hammer back, I swung around the corner. I took a quick look and pulled back. Nothing. Just the sheer white-and-brown bulk of the house to the right, and a six-foot grapestake fence to the left. Dead ahead was a side yard that broadened into the backyard.

I had no illusions about what would happen if I showed myself in the backyard. If he was putting slugs through the wall the sniper had a high-powered rifle.

I had no chance in the open; my only hope was to catch him at close quarters, by surprise.

I looked at the fence again; it didn't go all the way to the street in front. As a matter of fact, it started about even with the front of the house. I put the gun in the air and darted across the narrow side yard to the fence and swung around the far side, onto the neighbor's property. Chadwick's side of the fence was simply lawn, with no cover, but the other side was a tangle of bushes and shrubbery. Even without any blooms it provided plenty of cover. Even better, there were no trees in the rear. I moved through the bushes as silently as I could, hoping that the snow would muffle my steps. I wasn't as cautious as I should have been. Now that I had the means to defend myself fear was giving way to anger.

I reached the end of the fence. The line of spruce began on the other side of the fence, to my right. Everything I could see was peaceful. I saw no footprints in the snow; the sniper must have approached from the other side.

I crouched down and leaned out until half my head was around the fence. The line of spruce was end-on to me in a bluish green zigzag. The branches had been left to grow close to the ground, and it was impossible to see down the row more than twenty feet. From somewhere a car horn beeped several times; it was an impossibly irrelevant, ordinary sound. The *whap-whap* of the blades of the med-evac choppers would have been more in keeping.

I stood and moved out with the gun locked in front of me. I moved out slowly, keeping my right side against the line of spruce. The branches swished as I moved, and I waited for them to stop before I took another step. About twenty yards down, I saw footprints in the snow. They led to a spot just ahead in the trees. I looked more closely; there were two sets, one leading in and the other way. I moved ahead and crouched down. The spot was easy to identify. The sniper had packed down the snow with his body, and even broken a few of the lower branches. There was no sign of a rifle rest, but at that range he probably had figured he didn't need one. I looked over the site as carefully as I could without disturbing anything, but there was nothing else I could see. The real work of going over the crime scene would have to wait.

I moved down the line of trees a little farther, but both sets of footprints swerved to the right behind some rosebushes and disappeared behind the adjoining house. I put my thumb in front of the hammer and let it down with the other hand; I didn't trust myself to get the hammer safely down any other way. Then I stuck the gun in my belt and shoved my hands in my packets. They weren't cold; I just didn't want anyone to see them shaking.

I opened the front door. Chadwick, Mosier, and Jeremy were there to greet me; there was no sign of Kate, Bonner, or the secretaries. Chadwick came forward in a rush. "God, Dave, I'm glad to see you're all right." When he grasped my hand and my right shoulder, he saw me wince. "Dave, have you been hurt?"

"I just landed hard. I'll be fine. Everybody in here okay?"

"Sure thing."

Mosier had recovered from events quickly. "What the hell is going on around here?"

I leaned back against the wall for support and glared at him. "What the fuck do you think is going on?"

"Don't you talk to me that way!"

"Or I'll be in more trouble? More than being shot at?"

"Now, now," Chadwick said. "Dave has done a very brave thing. We're all a little overwrought today. Let's keep our heads."

Moiser looked down and mumbled something I didn't catch. For a man like him, it was the equivalent of a down-on-the-knees apology. I nodded at him and closed my eyes. "Has anyone seen Bonner?"

"He left just after you went back to talk to Dad," Jeremy volunteered. "I haven't seen him since."

"Have you called the police? I don't hear any sirens."

Chadwick looked down. "Bob and I have given this some more thought while you were back outside. He's convinced me there should be no publicity."

"I hope that if I'd been splattered across your back wall that you wouldn't have just put me out with the trash."

"Oh no, no. Come on now, Dave. If there was anyone injured, that would be another matter. But if there's any way this can be kept confidential . . ."

I pushed my way through the crowd, not trusting myself to give an answer that wouldn't get me fired on the spot. "Let me think about that."

I went to my room and slammed the door. I lay down on the bed and stared at the ceiling, trying to pull myself together. These people were nuts, they had lost all sense of proportion. In the past two days we'd had a kidnapping, a murder, and a near-miss murder attempt—and all they could think about was their restaurant opening. So what if the publicity scared people off, when lives were at stake? I turned it over in my mind, trying to see Chadwick's point of view. After a while I stopped shaking. The adrenaline drained out of me and left me hollow. What would he say? That the publicity was certain to hurt, but might not help Anne anyway, so why take the chance? And my cards were weak. There was no unarguable advantage in going to the police; all I could offer was the hope it might help. Not good enough, he would say, and Mosier would back him up. And the customer is always right.

Stripping off my clothes, I was pleasantly surprised to find that I hadn't peed in my pants after all. I stepped into the shower and let the water run a long time. It washed off a lot of things; sweat and dirt and snow. By the time I finished, I was better. And I even had the beginnings of a plan.

12

Wednesday, Noon

The first thing was finding Chadwick, which was easy. As usual, he was in his office working. Fortunately Mosier wasn't in. I told Bruce I wanted his authorization to speak to his attorneys. He agreed and gave me the name of the firm and their address. I dictated an authorization to one of the secretaries, and he agreed to get it signed and put in my room as soon as it was typed. Time for part two.

Bonner was sitting behind his desk with his hands folded in front of him. His computer was on but he wasn't looking at it. He wasn't looking at anything at all, at least not anything I could see. I sat down on the edge of his desk.

I took a breath and did my best to be impersonal and businesslike. I was handling an investigation, period. The fact that I was the latest victim shouldn't change things. At least that's the theory. "I want to know where you've been this morning."

He looked up at me. "Taking a walk alone."

"You know what happened here."

"Bruce told me." I expected him to add some expression of concern about me, but I was wrong.

"You took a walk in the middle of February for an hour?"

"Yep."

"Can anyone vouch for that?"

"Not even Karen. I went for a walk to clear my head about her bullshit, as a matter of fact. We had a big go-around this morning. When I went to my office after I talked to you, she called. She's upset—she says her whole world is coming apart; her marriage is on the rocks, her mom's been killed, a whole ton of stuff."

"Do you own a rifle?"

"No."

"Know how to shoot?"

"I was on my prep school's rifle team."

I shook my head; he saw the movement and smiled unpleasantly. "You didn't think I'd volunteer something like that, did you? It's because I'm not guilty of anything more than not taking the world's oldest advice."

"What's that?"

" 'Don't play poker with a man named Doc, don't eat at a restaurant named Mom's, and don't sleep with a woman with more problems than you.' "

I felt my blood pressure rising. My first thought was to hit him, hard. I had an image of catching him with a short uppercut, right on the underside of his chin, and knocking him backwards clean out of his chair. I got as far as clenching my fist and shifting my weight before I got control of myself. Once I laid a hand on him, I wouldn't get any cooperation unless I beat it out of him. It was better to keep him talking. "Buddy, I've just been shot at with a rifle that would have blown my spine clean out of my back and I don't think very much is very funny right now. And you're the prime suspect."

He met my eyes. "And what's my motive for attempted murder?"

"There's two that come to mind. You could be in with the kidnappers. And if that's not enough, maybe you're putting on a front—just maybe you care about Karen Saunders and you think I killed her mother."

"Smart people don't think like that."

"What do you mean?"

"As far as Karen. That would be a stupid way to get revenge. Assuming I gave a shit in the first place."

"You must be telling her something different than you tell me or she wouldn't be involved with you."

He spread his hands. "Hey, I'm nice to the woman.

Good pussy's hard to find. But it is what it is. Nothing more."

"Let's go back to the first motive."

"Okay. I was here in the house the whole time you were gone with Anne. Bob and I were in conference. I couldn't have done anything, not even made a phone call." He leaned closer and his voice took on a more serious, earnest quality. "And besides, look at this from my point of view. If something happens to Anne, even if I'm completely cleared, it's not exactly a gold star for my career. I want to move up, man. This country is run by people from finance, not sales or manufacturing, and I want to get my piece of it. I'm not spending my life counting noodles. I don't want my next interview to start, 'Oh, so you're the guy whose boss's wife was kidnapped from under your nose, huh?' "

"You're all heart."

"I watch out for myself and I don't go out of my way to fuck with anybody." He looked at me, his hands folded. "Anything else I can do for you?"

Our conversation reminded me of my talk with the police, only this time I was on the short end. It was time to quit hunting until I had more ammunition. I got off his desk and walked out.

The rest of the interviews were a blur. I needed to make the rounds before anyone had time to check with anyone else and build up alibis. When the shots were fired Jeremy was in the photocopy room, putting more toner in the machine. He showed me the flecks of black on his hands. He wanted to learn everything about what was going on; I had to send him away. Mosier was with Chadwick. Kate was in the shower, but Mosier and Chadwick said that she'd came in from shopping just before it happened, and was working out in the gym at the time. They'd seen her car drive in and heard the creak of the pulleys in the weight machine. The secretaries had nothing to add about the shooting; all they knew was that they'd heard a noise and then two more noises. I made up some implausible story about vandals and thanked them for their time. I drove out to the security people at the restaurant and asked if they'd seen anything unusual; the answer was no, and I didn't feel like taking them into my confidence. I made sure everything was quiet and went back to the house.

Kate was in the library, on the sofa. She stood up when I came in and put her hands over both of mine. "David, are you all right?"

"Yes. Well, the client can't stand me, I'm a sort of suspect in a murder, and I've just been shot at. So I guess not."

Her green eyes moved over my face without blinking. "You look like hell."

"I'm tired of this case. And tired of trying to handle things alone. I feel like I'm going backwards."

"I'm worried about you."

"That makes two of us. Where have you been since I talked to you last?"

She smiled. "I took a cab to the newspaper office and tracked down the reporter covering the murder."

"What did you do that for?"

"I thought you would be too busy. And Anne is family, after all."

I thought of the old military maxim that the most dangerous thing in the world is a second lieutenant with a map. "Do you realize that your poking around could lead the papers to make a connection to the Chadwicks?"

"Of course I did, so I lied and told him I was a distant relative of *Nancy's*."

"Good job. So what did you find out?"

"He tried to pump me for family information, but I dodged it by saying I was new in town and didn't know her well. But he told me that the police have identified the murder weapon. She was hit once on the side of the head with a big crystal vase." She saw my face. "What's the matter?"

"I handled the vase when I was there. I picked it up and admired it while she was out of the room, getting a picture of Anne. And I didn't have gloves on."

"I don't know that much about fingerprinting. How bad is this?"

"There's no way to tell. Glass is a good place for prints, but mine could be smeared, and who knows how the murderer picked it up. If he gripped it the same way I did there may not be anything from either of us."

"Where do you go from here?"

"I was just looking for you. You've been a cop, at least in the military. I'd like you to assist me."

"There must be detective agencies down here."

"I don't want to have a stranger watching my back. I've got enough of that already. I haven't exactly known you for a hundred years, but I know you're in the clear and I need some help."

"I don't think I can do you any good. That trip to the newspapers shot my entire stock of ideas."

"Look, I'm in a crazy house that makes the Black Hole of Calcutta look like a nice place to spend the weekend. I've met half a dozen people since I got here, and the only one I trust besides you is the cop who thinks I might have something to do with the murder. If I'm not careful somebody's going to set me up for a fall—kidnapping or murder or both. I need a second pair of eyes."

"Is it that bad?"

"Yeah. As far as anyone knows I was the last person to see Nancy before the murder. If my prints show up on the vase they'll have enough to make an arrest. And as far as the kidnapping goes—well, the same thing. There's no one to verify my story about the battery. I'm as good a candidate as anybody—and better than some. If this thing goes south there's going to be trouble."

"What do you want me to do?"

"Help me out. We need to start with a small mountain of records and old newspapers, and we don't have much time. I'll put you on my payroll."

"I couldn't take money for helping family."

"Then you'll help?"

"When do I start?"

"You know that this could be dangerous."

"No kidding."

"Okay. You start right now."

We drove to the Lancaster Newspapers Building on West King Street and went to the library. Then I found a pay phone and a fistful of quarters and had a long conversation with the Corporations Bureau. With two of us the job went quickly. A little more than two hours later we were back at the house.

"I want to confront Bonner myself," I told her.

"Suits me fine. I can't stand him."

I went into his office and shut the door. "Larry, we need to talk."

He turned away from his computer but didn't say anything.

"I figured it out."

"You've been listening to old musicals again?"

"No. I've been at the courthouse and the newspaper library."

"Solved the kidnapping?"

"No, but I've solved one mystery. Who my client is."

"Uncle Chan's, corporate."

"I mean who's behind Uncle Chan's."

"Like every other business, there are stockholders, bondholders, investors. That's not my end of things. And it isn't yours, either."

The sharpness in his voice told me I'd hit a nerve. I smiled a little, just enough to let him see it.

"Let's talk about the franchise a minute."

"What's this got to do with your job?"

"What are the geographical limits of Chadwick's franchise?"

"What did he tell you?"

"Suppose you tell me and I'll tell you if you're right."

"What kind of crap is this?"

"Or we can walk over to his office right now and I can lay out everything I suspect for him. I might be able to tell him things he's never thought of."

"Lancaster and York counties."

"That's about six hundred thousand people between the two, right?"

"Give or take."

"And that supports how many restaurants eventually?"

"That's marketing. I don't know."

"You're lying."

"I think they're going for twenty-two."

"You're lying again."

"The forecast is six."

"How long to do all six?"

"Five years, maybe six or seven."

"Tell me how the land deal works. And if you don't give me one hundred percent I go across the hall and blow the whole thing."

He didn't answer right away. As I watched him sit there, he changed. His jaw firmed up and his feet took a firm stance on the floor, on his toes, like a boxer. He leaned a little toward me and tucked in his chin. The yuppie melted away and left something behind, something that had been underneath. Something harder.

He looked at me with narrow eyes. "What's your play?"

"You're paying me for a job. Don't make it harder by feeding me bullshit. I worked in fast food long enough to know the score."

"What do you think the score is?"

"Uncle Chan's isn't being run in what a lawyer would call a commercially reasonable way. You run without inventory control; that's crazy, no matter how cheap the product is. If nothing else, you need inventory control to keep track of theft and to know when to reorder. Otherwise someday you'll have a trainload of fried noodles show up on your doorstep when you don't need them. And how are you going to know your cost of goods so you can figure out pricing? Now, why would you *not* want to do that? The only possible answer is that Uncle Chan's doesn't care if it makes money selling Chinese food or not. It only cares that it has a big cash flow. And the less documentation on the cash flow, the better. Is Mosier in on it?"

"No."

"And I know Chadwick isn't."

He didn't answer.

"I checked the records. I know, I think, how the land deal works. Uncle Chan's has already bought six sites in Lancaster County. I assume there are the same number in York County?"

Again, no response.

"I have a classmate from law school who practices there. I can have the records run in an hour or two. Does that help your memory?"

"Okay. Four."

"The corporation's already bought more sites than it will ever need. Dumb for a profit-making business. Smart if you're looking to dump money." He made no response, so I went on. "The franchisee has to buy a site from the corporation. It's illegal—it's an antitrust violation—but that's the deal, isn't it?"

"It's all in the records. You can look it up."

"Oh, I just think I'll go ask Bruce."

"The answer is yes. The franchisee has to buy from corporate."

"You create some weird paper transaction between the corporation and your franchisee with sales and leasebacks and second mortgages until the IRS doesn't know whether to shit or go blind. The franchisee keeps his mouth shut, because he gets a good deal. And when it's all done you guys have control of an operation with a cash flow of six million a year, that deals exclusively in cash. You can launder money like crazy."

"Since you know so much, I guess there's nothing for me to say."

"And that's where men like you come in. Organized crime doesn't need muscle anymore; it needs CPAs. And you're one of the new breed."

"So, I've been listening. What's your point?"

"Does the money behind Uncle Chan's figure into anything that's happened?"

He shook his head. "Absolutely not. There's no way

this is inside. If we thought it was, we never would have brought you in."

"I bailed your people out of a mess last month. I thought that you trusted me, after that."

He shook his head slowly. "Trust? You're outside. You could do jobs for a hundred years and we wouldn't trust you. And let me tell you something more. This doesn't get mentioned again, ever. You know what you have to. More than you have to. Knowing too much can be bad for your health."

"And since we're in the spirit of clearing the air, what about Karen Saunders?"

"What about her?"

"I've been thinking. Lancaster is a small town, but it's not that small."

"What are you talking about?"

I enjoyed watching him squirm. "I don't buy that you knew Karen without knowing Nancy."

"A married woman isn't likely to parade her boyfriend around. Especially to her own mother."

"I don't mean after you started sleeping together. I mean, how you originally met. You didn't know either one of them. But you knew Anne. I bet there was some time Anne needed another man for some party or something, and you were it."

"You're guessing."

"Sure I am. But I can check that with Bruce. Or Bob." I paused. "Or Karen."

"Leave her out of this!"

"You're awfully protective of someone who's just a piece of ass to you."

"She treats me okay. I respect that, and I owe her to keep her name out of things."

"So give."

"So in the fall Anne and Bruce drag me to a little dinner party at Nancy's house. Six, seven couples. Karen's husband was called out of town at the last minute and they asked me to substitute."

"Was that the first time you'd met Karen or Nancy?"

"Karen, yes. Nancy had come to the house a couple of times. So what?"

"So you lied to me about knowing the murder victim."

"Yeah."

"You don't put a hell of a lot of effort into clearing yourself, Bonner."

"I don't need to."

"You're tough."

"I'm not stupid. We brought you in. If I killed our own investigator to settle a private grudge, it's the same as killing myself."

"You care about this girl a lot, don't you?"

He considered the question. "She's been good to me. She talks about leaving her husband and going off with me when I'm transferred."

"Sounds pretty serious to me."

"That's her agenda, not mine. You know what the Afghans say? If we could teach sheep to cook, we wouldn't need women at all."

"You always this sentimental?"

"You want an answer?"

"No. Just one more thing. Could Anne have picked up on the money laundry?"

"No way. I spend a hell of a lot of effort keeping Chadwick and Mosier in the dark, and believe me, they are. They see figures every day, they have MBAs, and she's just a fucking housewife."

"You sound pretty confident."

"I hear you. All right, let's assume she made a lucky guess. Where does that take you?"

It was my turn to stop and think before answering. "Nowhere, really."

"Right," he smiled. "Fucking nowhere."

13

Wednesday, 4:00 P.M.

I found Kate in her room. She had her glasses on and was reading the briefing paper Bruce had given me on Uncle Chan's. "Kate, it's time we talked to Mary."

"She won't be in until Friday, as far as I know; she doesn't work every day."

"I know; I just found out from Jeremy. But he told me where she lives."

We put on our coats and got into my car. "I hope you know your way around here," she said. "The best I can do is find the downtown and get back again."

"If his directions are good, no problem. A friend of mine has a cabin in the eastern part of the county near where she lives. She's not far from Intercourse."

"You've got to be kidding."

"No. That's the name of the place. You ought to see the tourists in the summer. The main street is jammed with buses and cars and Amish buggies."

"Is that where Mary lives?"

"On a farm just beyond, if I've got my directions straight."

"I've never known anyone who lived on a farm. I grew up in a suburb."

"Until I started coming out here in the summer, I'd never been on a farm, either, and I certainly didn't know anything about the Amish. I've picked up a lot, though, over the years."

"I was looking at how Mary dresses, all black, no buttons, clunky black shoes. And she told me they don't have electricity. Doesn't sound like much fun to me."

I took the exit for the Old Philadelphia Pike and

headed east. "That's not the way they see it. They don't consider what they believe as a religion of denial. Actually, it's not as odd as you might think. The basic idea is, if you get too worldly, too wrapped up in material things, you lose touch with the really important things. It's the same thing Thoreau said, except he meant nature and they mean God. They don't think there's anything sinful about electric lights, or cars, they just think they're distractions."

"I can't begin to imagine living without electricity."

"Until a hundred years ago, we all got along fine without it. And they don't sit in the dark and freeze. They use lanterns and kerosene heaters and wood stoves."

"If they don't have electricity, they don't have telephones."

"For the farmers, yes. But if you have a business, you can have a phone for the business so long as it isn't in the house. And some Amish are a little more liberal and have a personal phone in a little shed somewhere. Hey, there are Amish businessmen with fax machines. They run them off generators. It's real hard on the machines 'cause the current fluctuates so much, but it can be done."

"Amish are in business? I thought they all farmed."

We passed a pair of buggies, and I slowed down to give Kate a good look. "At one time, most of them did. Some of them were always in farm-support jobs, like machinery repair and carpentry and things like that. It used to be that there was enough farmland so that every son who wanted to farm could do it. But not anymore. To support themselves they get into all kinds of things—residential construction, plumbing, lawn furniture, storage sheds, just about any light industry you can think of."

Past Bird in Hand, the country opened up. Except for the road and an occasional farmhouse, there was nothing but the gently rolling hills, covered with snow. We passed by a frozen pond where a dozen Amish children were skating, their clothes black against the white. A couple of sleighs were nearby. The horses were covered with blankets and tied to trees. Even from a distance we could see their breath fogging the air.

"What do they think of all the tourists coming out to gawk at them?"

"The same thing your family would think if you were the last Irish Catholics and people came to see you. Some of them are bothered a lot, I'm sure. Some don't care. And some don't mind as long as you don't take their picture. They believe that photography offends the commandment about graven images."

"Do they ever do anything to keep their pictures from being taken?"

"I've seen some of the men yell at tourists, but they wouldn't dream of getting physical. Their religion is very pacifistic. They teach their children about cooperation and group effort, not about competition. And for that matter, even though the kids only get six years of school, they don't have forty hours of television a week or any of that Nintendo garbage. If I'd ever had children I would have thrown out the TV the day the baby came home from the hospital."

"No kids?"

"My wife and I tried for years. Nada. Then we got divorced, and I haven't remarried."

"Does it bother you?"

"Once in a while my guard will be down, and I'll see one of those cute commercials where the little boy, maybe seven or eight, is wearing a baseball cap sideways and looks up at his daddy while they're eating cornflakes or something, and I can get to feeling pretty sorry for myself. Fortunately the solution is easy."

"What's that?"

"Spending an hour with a real seven-year-old."

I'd delivered that line a dozen times, but this time the reaction was different. She put her hand on my arm. "It bothers you, doesn't it?"

I was too startled to answer for a moment. Then I just told the truth. "Yeah. Of course."

She squeezed my upper arm gently and put her hand

back in her lap. ''Take a look,'' I said. ''We're coming into Intercourse.''

At first glance it was a sleepy country village, strung out along both sides of the road. But as we drove slowly through town, we could see that the houses were antique shops and that nearly every structure advertised something—Amish quilts, pizza, tourist information, ''collectibles,'' jellies, leather goods, gift items, mass-produced duck decoys, movies about the Amish—a thousand things, none of which had anything to do with the people who lived there.

''Jesus Christ,'' was all she could say.

''This is the slow time. Come back anytime between Easter and Thanksgiving and this place is wall-to-wall people.''

A young Amish couple was standing on the sidewalk by a horse and buggy tied to a rail. ''The Amish women must be tough.''

''Oh, it's not such a hard life. You marry at seventeen or eighteen, start having children right away, raise ten or twelve kids without a microwave or a washing machine or even central heat, and help your husband run the farm. In your spare time, in the summer, you run a roadside stand selling jellies and jams and breads and pies that you've baked. In the winter, when you're not farming, you can relax and quilt.''

''Speaking of farms, are we close? It's starting to get dark.''

''He said it was the third farm on the right after Intercourse, a white house with a white barn.''

''They all look like that.''

''Yeah, but he said this one had a big roadside stand out front. There it is.''

''All I see is a big wooden box.''

''That's it; they just have it boarded up for the winter.''

I stopped the car in a snow-covered square with a two-story house, a large wooden barn to my right, and a small barn to the rear of the main house. Smoke was coming out of the house chimney, but no one was in sight.

"Why do they have two barns?" Kate asked.

"The small one is for horses and to store the buggies. The big one is for everything else, and for drying tobacco. Looks like he's keeping some dairy cows."

She pointed to the small barn, and I saw that half of it was being used as a house. "David, you said they didn't have electricity."

"They don't, at least they're not supposed to."

"That light in the little house back there. That has to be electric. It's too bright to be a candle."

"That's a place for the older folks. There's a word for it, but I can't think of it right now. The Amish don't believe in old people's homes—they take care of their own. It could be that one of the kids who didn't join the church lives there. Or maybe it's a lantern. Some of them are pretty bright." I looked overhead. "I don't see any power lines. Or phone lines. But listen a minute, there's something else we have to get straight."

"Yeah?"

"Remember they don't have radio or TV, and they may not take a paper. As far as I know, Mary only knows that Anne is missing. She doesn't know about the ransom or about Nancy or my being shot at. I've gone to a lot of trouble already to keep this quiet. Don't blab anything."

"Got it."

We stumbled through the snow to the front door and knocked. A skinny, serious-looking girl with large brown eyes opened the door.

"We're here to see Mary Fisher."

She looked from one of us to the other without saying a word, then shut the door and vanished. We waited so long I started to think she'd just decided to forget about us. Then the door opened again and we were facing a tall, gaunt man with dark hair and a beard with no mustache. He was wearing a pale-blue shirt with black pants and suspenders.

"My names is Dave Garrett. I work for Mr. Chadwick. I'd like to speak to Mrs. Fisher, please."

"Who are you?"

"I'm an investigator, for Mr. Chadwick. The reason—" He turned and left me talking to thin air. Once again the door shut in our faces.

"Real country hospitality, huh?" Kate whispered.

"They don't teach charm school. Polite listening isn't part of the repertoire."

After another long pause the door opened again. The man looked at us sternly and waved us inside.

It was a low-ceilinged room, sparsely furnished, with a highly polished linoleum floor. The house smelled of kerosene and oil soap, and faintly I detected the smell of bread baking. He sat at an old table and looked at us. Although there were extra chairs, he didn't invite us to sit down.

"Would you be Mr. Fisher?"

"That I would."

"Your wife works for the same person I do. You heard that Mrs. Chadwick is missing?"

"I've heard tell of it."

"My job is to find her, and we think your wife might be able to help."

"Are you the law?"

"No, sir. I'm a private investigator. I work just for Mr. Chadwick."

"What's Mary supposed to know?"

"We don't know. We'd just like to talk to her for a minute. It won't take long."

He left the room. A few minutes later Mary came in, standing very stiff and wringing her hands together. Her eyes were focused on the floor. "My husband said you were here."

"Mary, we'd like to ask you a few questions."

"My husband doesn't like being in English business."

"We're sorry to have to bother you, but you know how important this is. How long have you worked for the family?"

"Three years this Christmas."

"Did you know Mrs. Chadwick well?"

"She paid me good wages and she was always fair."

"I don't expect you to tell tales, just help us out if

you can. Okay?'' She didn't move, so I went on. ''Did you answer the phone?''

''If no one else was about I would.''

''In the last few months do you remember any threatening phone calls—not about the business, to her directly?''

''No.''

''Were there any . . . odd calls, like when you hear someone breathing but they won't talk, or someone using bad language?''

She shook her head.

''Did she seem any different to you the last few weeks?''

''Different?''

''Her moods. Was she more nervous or scared or happy or angry or anything different than normal?''

''No. Not that I seen.''

''Any visitors to the house besides the business people?''

''No.''

''After she disappeared, Mr. Chadwick asked you to check her room to see if anything was missing. Was there?''

''I looked good. Just the clothes she had on was all. She didn't even take a heavy coat with her. I set it out but she let it lie.''

I turned to Kate. ''Can you think of anything else to ask?''

''Who do you know best in the house, besides Mrs. Chadwick?''

''Jeremy, I'd say.''

''Has he acted at all unusual recently?''

''He's a worried boy. But no different lately.''

''How do you mean, worried?''

''His parents, they're never satisfied, always pushing at him.''

''What about anybody else in the house, like Mr. Mosier or Mr. Bonner?''

''I hardly see them, they're working so hard.''

''Did Mrs. Saunders call much?''

''Once't I can think of.''

"Was that unusual?"

She shrugged.

It was Kate's turn to look frustrated. "Thanks very much, Mary. We'll see you Friday morning. Good night."

Mary nodded and walked out, leaving us alone.

We didn't talk until we were back in the car. "So what do you think?" Kate asked.

"I was thinking that there was a difference in the way we asked questions. I was looking for a kidnapper, and you're looking for facts to show Anne ran off."

"Don't you think we should consider it?"

"It was at the top of my list, right up to the moment we got a two-hundred-thousand-dollar ransom demand and I got shot at. How do you fit those things in?"

"Maybe she ran off on her own at first, and now she's being held," Kate ventured.

"By who? If she ran off by herself, who else would even know?"

"There has to be somebody else, either way. Even if she was just running off, she had to have an accomplice to disconnect your battery. Maybe he's holding her now."

"Why?"

"I don't know."

"We've done everything they've asked. Can you think of why they would change their behavior?"

"Well, no."

"And if Anne's as smart as Nancy said, I have trouble seeing her getting herself into a situation she couldn't control. She'd have to very badly misjudge people to be in that kind of a mess."

"We all make mistakes," she said.

"You're right about that. I shouldn't be making assumptions that everyone else's plans are running smoothly."

"So who's shooting at you?"

"Well, I started out assuming that it's connected to the kidnapping, but that could be wrong, you know. Maybe whoever killed Saunders wants to pin it on me, and it's a lot easier to pin a murder on a corpse than a live person."

"How does killing you prove you killed her?"

"It doesn't. But if I'm dead it would be easy to plant some evidence somewhere linking me to Saunders. Just as an example, suppose Nancy's killer gets me. Then he dummies up a note linking me to the killing and plants it. Or suppose he took something from her house; now he arranges for the object to be found in my effects. Or he mails it to my office, or my home. Get the idea?"

"How do we know, I mean really know, the Saunders murder and the kidnapping are connected?" she asked.

"What makes you think they're not?"

"I asked you first. Anyway, when you assume there's a connection, you're forgetting the timing. If you'd announced you were going over to interview a witness and the witness is dead when you arrive, you've got a connection to whatever crime you were investigating. But she was killed after she talked to you. How would the killer know that the cat wasn't already out of the bag?"

"By asking her what she'd told me, after I'd left?"

She shook her head. "Too unreliable."

"What if she was killed to punish her for talking to me? An example to the others. If there are others."

"Nope. Killing her just draws attention. I'm not convinced there's a connection."

"So then who killed her?"

"Could have been anybody. Except me, that is."

"Not funny," I said. "But don't you think her killing is connected to the kidnapping?"

"Only if there *is* a real kidnapping. If Anne ran off, there's nothing for Nancy's murder to be connected to."

"I only believe in coincidences as a last resort."

"I thought you said you thought there really was a kidnapping, at least now. Why do you think that?"

"Mainly because of what I just said, that blaming things on coincidence is lazy. You're halfway to missing connections between things because you stop looking hard enough. But to answer your question about right now, this minute, I don't know what to think. We don't have enough facts, and we're kidding ourselves if we think we do."

"What's it going to take?" she asked.

"I don't know. Something will turn up. I just hope it isn't Anne's body."

I'd broken our tacit agreement not to talk about the worst. We were both quiet for a while after that.

"So what do you think of Mary?" I asked after a while.

"I've never dealt at all with the Amish. They're different."

"She didn't fall all over herself to tell us anything, but I don't think she was holding back, either."

"Do you think she'd lie to cover for Anne?"

"Good question," I said. "You've got things pulling both ways. Family life is very important to the Amish, and they just don't divorce or separate. Of course, Anne's not Amish, and they wouldn't hold her to their standards."

"No. So what's next?"

"Tomorrow morning we can go and see the family attorneys and see if they know anything. And at some point we have to think about going to the police, but not right now. There isn't anything more I can think of to do tonight, except go home and have some dinner. Did you have any plans? Besides the case, I mean?"

"No. I've been traveling for most of the last two weeks, and this is my last stop. I've seen what I wanted to see and I'm basically waiting for the plane."

"When's that?"

"Friday morning, out of Philadelphia."

"Where else have you been?"

"A couple of days with friends in New York, then I tried to learn to ski in the Poconos. I saw the sights in Washington, and now I'm here."

Conversation drifted further from the case. I heard about her children—one was a first-year medical student, the other was a sophomore at the University of Florida with no declared major but a great tan. I talked about my own days in college, and told a couple of stories I thought I'd forgotten. By the time we reached the house I was in as fine a mood as circumstances would allow. And all it took to ruin it was the sight of a Cadillac in the driveway. It was a vintage seventies gas hog, decorated with more chrome than was decent. Without being told, I knew it had to belong to Mosier.

"I think we have company for dinner."

14

Wednesday, 7:00 P.M.

It wasn't my idea to have dinner with anyone but Kate, but when we got inside Jeremy was waiting for us with his father's invitation. And yes, Mr. Mosier would be joining us, too.

I washed my face and shaved quickly, then Kate and I went down to the kitchen. She had changed into a pair of jeans and a dark-blue clinging turtleneck. Chadwick and Mosier were already waiting at the table, with a half-empty carafe of red wine between them.

Bruce looked up when we came in, but not right away.

"Dave, Kate," he nodded. "Find anything out from Mary?"

"Not really," I answered.

"What did you figure to learn from her anyway?" Mosier wanted to know.

I sat down and poured myself a glass of wine. "You don't know until you ask. There's all kinds of things she *might* have known—unusual calls or visitors, breaks in routine, mail that Anne seemed upset about. There could have been things that were missing, or something in Anne's effects she'd never seen before. But I struck out."

"Again."

I locked eyes with him. "Yeah. Again." We glared at each other across the table.

Chadwick broke the confrontation. "Dave, you've done everything you can for one day. What's the plan for tomorrow?"

"First, we wait till morning. Something might happen yet tonight. But if there's nothing new by breakfast, it's time to reconsider bringing in the police."

Mosier drained his glass and refilled it. "Can't you make up your mind?"

I was thankful I hadn't been drinking. Even stone sober I was on the edge of losing my temper. "Certainly. When I have enough information, it's easy. Sometimes the best thing to do is let the situation mature. Besides, if you decide to go to the police in the morning, they'll have a full day to work on it. Not much is going to get done if you call tonight, anyway."

"Makes sense to me, at least to review our options," Bruce said. "Okay, we'll sleep on it." He toyed with the stem of his glass. "Dave, what do you think it means, that we haven't heard from them?"

"It's not good."

"What are you saying?"

"Well, maybe you paid off a con man and we were never dealing with kidnappers. That would explain it. Or maybe these were the real kidnappers, and the forty was just a test."

"You didn't mention that one before," Mosier broke in. His voice had the triumphant tone of a chess opponent who sees mate in five.

"Because it's pure guessing. And even if it's true, it doesn't change anything. If Anne's not back in the morning we should go to the police, regardless of whatever little private theories we have. This isn't a science experiment—trying to see whose guess is right. Let's just get her back and worry about the rest later."

Bruce drained his own glass and looked at it. "Yeah." I glanced at Kate, who'd been looking at Bruce. She and I were thinking the same thing, that Mosier was a jerk, but at least his heart was in the right place. But where was Chadwick's? Did he know himself?

Jeremy had prepared baked chicken, with linguini in an herb-butter sauce on the side. And, of course, there was more wine with dinner. Several kinds, as a matter of fact. Mosier and Chadwick had evidently been doing some drinking of their own before dinner, but only Mosier was showing any significant effects. The only evidence that Bruce had been drinking was that he became steadily more quiet as the meal went on.

I had a one-man fan club in Jeremy. He made me repeat every detail of my episode in the backyard.

"If you don't mind me asking, were you scared, Mr. Garrett?"

"Sure I was."

"Were you in Vietnam?"

"That's right."

"Was it like what happened today?"

I had to give it some thought. How do you discuss close quarters fighting with modern weapons to people who weren't there—let alone someone like Jeremy, who looked like he'd never fired a gun? "In some ways, the feeling of being in danger, yes. But in a war you're not alone very often, the way I was today. You may feel alone, like during a bombardment, because you can't see anyone else, but you know that your friends are all around you. That helps you get through it."

"Did you ever do anything like today?"

I stopped and thought. I remembered another day of fear, one near the DMZ more than twenty years ago. It seemed a long way away—that day had been hot and noisy and green, and dusty from the med-evac helicopters that were passing close overhead every few minutes.

"Yeah, there was something like this once."

"Would you mind talking about it?"

A lot of vets did mind. I respected their decision, but I couldn't see the point of keeping silent. Compared to living through it, and reliving the memories that were there anyway, talking a little didn't change anything. Besides, if I stayed quiet too long, Mosier would think of something new to needle me about.

I looked at the fork in my hand. "Our squad had to cross an open piece of ground about fifty meters across, and we were taking sniper and light mortar fire from our left. The lieutenant planned for us to cross on our bellies, but before we could start, the gunny—that's the gunnery sergeant—took him aside. I was right next to them, holding the M-60 and waiting for orders. The lieutenant said, 'Sergeant, I hope you're not questioning my orders.' They spoke very quietly. Even right next to him I had trouble catching all the words. 'No, sir,' he said. 'But the mortar fire's light. I think they're firing blind, or they're low on ammo. And I don't hear any MG fire. If we take our time we're just giving the snipers a better target. I suggest we space out the men and do it in a rush. Sir.' And that's what we did. It was pretty scary, standing up and walking out there. The stand of bushes we were in looked pretty safe by comparison."

"Was everybody okay?"

"We all made it. Except for the lieutenant; halfway across he stepped on a mine so big he never knew what hit him." I stopped for a minute, trying to remember he face, but nothing came to me, just an impression of youth. Was he blond or was I remembering it wrong? It saddened me. He died getting me and the other men across, and I couldn't even remember his face. "He was a good Marine. For all I know, I'm alive because he was willing to listen to good advice."

Mosier surprised me yet again. He raised his glass. "Absent friends."

"Absent friends."

I decided to get the subject away from war. "Jeremy, the food is delicious. Did your mother teach you how to cook?"

"No, she always said it was easier to do it herself. But some of the housekeepers we've had taught me a lot. Except Mary—the Dutch cooking isn't for me."

"How'd you get into cooking?"

He smiled a middle-aged smile, the kind you give when you're thinking of long-ago things. "I thought Mom would like me being able to help."

There was an awkward silence; even Mosier sensed the evening was turning sour. The conversation drifted back to Anne. Then Jeremy got up and started collecting plates.

By the time Jeremy finished clearing off, we had exhausted every possible comment and speculation about Anne. I decided to try changing the subject again.

"Bruce, just how long have you lived here?"

"Oh, four years, going on five."

"Did you have a fire or something?"

"No, why?"

"Well, it's a nice place, but it looks like you still haven't moved really moved in."

He shook his head. "Every other house, she loved to decorate. She has really great taste, better than most of the interior decorators. We always knew we'd be moving, that no house was forever. That never stopped her before. We've left a trail of really fixed-up places behind us. But this one, she doesn't care about. She'll do nothing for months. Then I'll bug her. She and I will go out for a whole day and she'll buy one lamp. And half the time she sends it back the next day. I let it go. Someday when she gets up a head of steam she'll get it done." He swallowed, realizing what he'd said. "I mean, I hope she does."

"But why this house?"

"It's the first house we've moved to since Amy died. She hasn't taken much interest in things since."

"Your daughter?"

He nodded. 'She was just seventeen."

"How long has it been?"

"Eight years this March."

"Nancy talked to me a little about it. I'm sorry."

He nodded; he was used to getting sympathy and shrugging it off. Then, after a short silence, he raised his wineglass. "Allow me to propose a toast of my own." We followed suit. "To solving our problems." We all drank, except for Kate, who took only a token sip. I was surprised; she didn't seem like the type who played with a drink. I realized she considered herself on duty. Then I saw her drumming her fingers under her napkin and realized she was upset. I had a feeling I knew what it was.

"Jeremy," Bruce said. "Get us some of that German brandy."

"Not us," I said. "We have to compare notes and get ready for tomorrow." I said our good-nights, and Kate and I went to my room.

I sat on the bed and watched Kate pace back and forth, her arms across her chest.

"What have you got against Bruce?" I asked.

"He's do damn *encapsulated.* His wife is in danger and he spends the evening hosting dinner parties to relieve his boredom."

I agreed with her, but I wanted to draw her out. "Some people would call it grace under pressure. You want him sobbing onto your forearm?"

"No, but—it's when you're a family you make a commitment to care. You watch out for each other. You all count on each other. That's the way my mother raised us. Everything that's happened, with Anne, with Amy, he talks about it like it happened to somebody else."

"Maybe he just isn't letting it show."

She sat down in a chair and uncrossed her arms, but she was still scowling. "My instincts tell me there's nothing to show."

"Maybe you're right. But anyway, I did want to talk business. What do you know about Amy's death?"

"Not much more than you heard tonight. When it happened we were out of the country, in Canada on a summer vacation. I've never discussed it directly with either Anne or Bruce. They both took it very hard, I can tell you that much. But it's become one of those taboo subjects in the family."

"Did you know Amy yourself?"

"Not really. I hadn't seen her since she was a small child. I don't think she was more than eight the last time I saw her. All I can remember is that she was really attached to her mother."

"What do you think after an evening with them?"

"Let's start with the one who wasn't here."

"Who?" I asked.

"Anne."

"I'm listening."

"I don't know what to think. The time I've been in the house, I didn't get any sense of anything wrong. And according to Bruce their marriage is Thanksgiving on Walton's Mountain. If he's telling us the truth this has got to be a kidnapping. If he's kidding us, or himself, then maybe she left on her own."

"Nancy did say she had affairs."

She made a face at me. "One, years ago, that meant something. I listened to everything you told me and I didn't hear anything that would wreck a marriage. And even if there was something spicy, why all this production? Why not just get a divorce? Bruce isn't the kind of man who would beat her if she tried to leave, and Anne knew it."

"No, he's not."

She put her chin down on one hand and tapped her cheek with her forefinger. "Jeremy, I can't figure, either. He wants to be accepted by his parents. To say the least, he's eager to please. He can't have directly participated in the abduction; he was home. And besides, a child involved in a conspiracy against his own mother? Spouses, sure, but not kids. It's unnatural."

"So is kidnapping for ransom. Now what about Mosier?"

"He's guilty. Of being an asshole. What kind of criminal would go out of his way to antagonize the investigator?"

"Maybe he's an asshole *and* a criminal. It's been known to happen."

She shrugged. "You've got me there."

"And he's the one who works so hard at keeping the police out. He fights me every step of the way on that."

"Yeah, but he could have good business reasons for that."

"I doubt they're *that* good. Let's go worst case: The police are called in, there are a couple of stories on TV, and a couple of days of headlines. Then a baboon in Bangladesh gives birth to a human baby and it's old news. If you ask me, the publicity helps the name recognition. After all, it's about an Uncle Chan's employee, not about the food they're serving.''

''What about the story about the soap in the rice?''

''The police could be persuaded to keep that little angle quiet. The big news would be the kidnapping.''

She frowned. ''Maybe. Might brave of you to risk Uncle Chan's money like that. And the fact that your logic holds up doesn't implicate Mosier in itself.''

''Since you're so eager to leave him out of it, let's move on. I'm waiting to hear what you think of Bruce, beyond disliking him.''

''I'm suspicious of him.''

''We've been over that,'' I said.

''No, not just that I don't like him. He's keeping a lid on some information.''

''Like what?''

''I wish I knew. Something about Anne. He knows more than he's telling.''

''You don't think that he's behind the kidnapping?'' I asked.

''He couldn't have participated himself, but he could be in charge.''

''Come on, Kate.''

''I'm just thinking out loud, is all. You know, your theory of how they got Anne to stop, pretending they were police?''

''Yes.''

''I've been thinking about it. It's too cute. It's one think to pull that stunt on I-70 in the middle of Kansas at two in the morning. But here, someone could have driven by. Someone who would have remembered seeing an unmarked car pull over an attractive woman in a Benz. It's just enough out of the ordinary to stick in someone's mind.''

''The odds were against there being any witnesses. There wasn't much traffic.''

''People staging six-figure abductions don't leave things to chance. They want situations they can control.''

"To the extent they can, sure," I admitted. "But there are some risks there's no way around. And anyway, what's that got to do with Chadwick?"

"If she didn't stop for a fake police car, why did she stop? There was nothing wrong with her car and there's no reason to stop at that spot. Somebody got her to stop. And we're sure there was no one hiding in her backseat, right?"

"I put in the dry cleaning myself. There was no one there when I opened the door. After we were through there wasn't room for a good-size cat."

"That's my point," she said. "No one was in the car and no one used any force to get her to stop, at least as far as we can tell."

"Right. So what if she pulled over voluntarily, but not because of a fake police light?"

"Who would she do that for?"

"If Saunders told you the truth, she wasn't there, and she didn't know Anne would be out there. Anne didn't have any other close friends. She was a woman driving alone. I don't see her falling for the stranded motorist ploy. Jeremy was at home. That leaves her husband."

"Oh, Jesus," I said. "Are you serious?"

"He knew where she was going. He could either have gone out and waited by the side of the road, or come up on her from a side street. And gotten home in time to get the ransom call."

"I sure as hell hope you're not right."

"So do I. Because if I am, she's dead."

After that, there wasn't anything more to say. For the moment we reached the end of the road.

15

Wednesday, 10:00 P.M.

I looked at my watch. "We've reached the end of our ability to think straight for one day. We need to get some rest and start fresh in the morning. And my shoulder is killing me."

"I'll rub your back for you. I used to do that for my husband; I was pretty good at it."

"That sounds good. Thanks." She went out the bedroom door and shut it behind her. I started getting out of my clothes; when I pulled my T-Shirt over my head, pain shot from the shoulder blade up into my neck. I rolled my head around, trying to relieve the tension. I got the rest of my clothes off except for my boxer shorts and lay down on the bed. She returned with a small clear bottle in her hand and shut the door behind her. She put it on the table beside the bed; it was baby oil. "It's not ideal," she said. "But it'll have to do." I rested my face on my hands and closed my eyes.

"What are you thinking?" she asked.

"How different you are from anyone else I've known."

"How so?" Her fingers moved over the back of my neck, feeling for the knots in the muscles.

"You're very . . . direct."

She put both hands on the back of my neck, the thumbs barely touching. She pressed down with her thumbs, increasing the pressure with her thumbs, putting her full upper-body weight into it. I felt a crack. She must have heard it, too; she eased off and worked the spot gently in a circular motion.

"Yeah, that's been said about me, not usually so politely."

"What are *you* thinking?" I asked.

"About this crazy house and this crazy family. That I'm a part of, however distantly."

"There's a lot of self-deception going on around here."

"Oh, that's the best kind," she said. "It saves the trouble of someone else having to fool you."

She moved down my neck half an inch and pressed down hard, again. There was another crack, even louder than the first.

"That felt good."

"Your muscles are really knotted."

"It's been a hell of a day."

She pressed down, not too hard, on several points on my shoulder blade, and I winced. She found a spot that didn't hurt and pressed down with all her weight. "How does that feel?"

"That spot's fine; just be careful if you go any higher."

She pulled off her top and tossed it onto a chair. "Don't get the wrong idea," she said. "But this is going to be warm work." For five minutes neither of us said anything while she massaged the shoulder. She worked the spots that didn't hurt, stretching them out, then slowly she moved into where it ached. Several times she stopped to put on more baby oil. Then, when the rest of the shoulder was mobilized, she gently went after the center of the pain, just below the base of my neck.

"That doesn't hurt much at all now."

"Your arm isn't numb or anything?"

"No. It feels good."

"Your muscles are tough. This is hard work."

Her hands paused for a second but she didn't say anything. She cracked my spine at the base of my neck and started working her way down.

When she reached the middle of my back she stopped and stood up. Then she unzipped her jeans; they fell down to her ankles and she stepped out of them. I looked back over my shoulder at her. She was wearing a turquoise lace bra with a matching stretch-lace bikini. Except for a slight curve at the hips, her body was nothing but straight lines.

She looked at me. "What are you thinking now?"

"Nothing real important. A couple of different things."

She pulled off her shoes and socks and straddled me again. "Go ahead."

"Earthshaking thoughts. Like, how did your jeans just fall down like that? On most women they stay up even if they're not zipped."

She poured some baby oil into her palm and started rubbing my neck and shoulders. "Most women have hips a lot wider than their waist, and there's fat over the bones. I'm just bones. I thought you'd be thinking, why does she bother to wear a bra? And the answer is, I don't need to, but it came as part of the set with the panties. Before I had kids I was a perfectly respectable B cup. After my first pregnancy, when I was done nursing, I went to an A. After the second one, there was nothing left."

"Don't be so defensive. Think of all the women who try to diet down to your size and can't make it."

"It's a bad habit of mine. I dump on myself before anyone else gets the chance."

She put some more oil in her palm and spread it on my lower back. She shifted down towards my feet to give herself more room to work. Then she stopped. "I was just thinking about a vacation I took last year. Waking up early one morning and watching my husband sleep."

"Tell me about it."

"It was just dawn, and the window was open. I could smell the wind off the ocean and hear the gulls. He was lying on his side, facing me, with his arm under his head. He was so quiet and relaxed; he was never like that when he was awake. His hair was a mess and I could see a little bit of a beard stubble. He was snoring, just a little, and I could smell tequila on his breath."

"I just got back from Mexico, myself. I was with somebody. I woke up before dawn and watched her, too."

"Your girlfriend?"

"At the time she was. But we broke up while we were down there. She said I was crowding her, but I think she was just afraid to get more involved. We came back on separate planes."

"That's too bad."

"Thank you. So, what happened to your husband?"

Her hands were at the level of my hips, and her thumbs were working my tailbone. "I refused to accept the things about the world I can't change and just get on with life. My husband and I went round about it a hundred times. I'd say, it's not going to work between us. He'd say I was sabotaging it. I always asked him what he was talking about, but I knew. He'd say, you tell me you want your freedom, that you've never had a chance to play the field. He would say, fine, take a little vacation from our marriage if that's what it takes. Then you say you want to settle down and stay with me and the kids. That time is running out, that you want to get moving on your life. You want to stay in Miami and move back to Seattle and travel around the world with a backpack and go back to school and get your Ph.D. He said he could deal with any one damn thing I threw at him—he just couldn't deal with them all."

I turned over and looked at her. The same steady green eyes, but this time there was moisture in them.

"Are you still in love with him?"

"I'm still in guilt with him. I don't know that I've ever been in love."

"What makes you say that?"

"Because being in love means someone else's happiness is more important, or just as important, as your own. I never felt that way about him, and I'm not even sure I feel that way about my children."

She started rubbing my shoulders and making circular motions on my chest, but her mind was elsewhere. I watched the play of her muscles and tendons under her skin. She was right about it being warm work; her body was glistening with sweat, and a little rivulet ran from her chin down through her bra and down her stomach. I traced it gently with my finger.

Her hands gradually came to a stop and rested on my chest. "I think we've reached that point, David."

"Point?"

"Where I go or stay."

"I'd like you to stay."

She blinked once and wiped her eyes, but they stayed on my face while she unhooked her bra and lay down beside me. I put my arm around her and ran my hand through the back of her hair. Her body was so narrow, she was barely there.

Afterwards we slept, or at least I did. I had my usual dream. And woke up in a cold sweat. As usual.

Her eyes slowly opened, at first not focusing. Then there was a moment when I think she saw me but didn't quite recognize me. The moment passed and she held me so tightly I thought she'd break one of my ribs.

"How are you doing?" I asked.

She rolled on top of me and ran her hands over my shoulders. "My heart is glad, as my mother would say. Although she was never in a situation like this, I'm sure." She kissed me. "Are you ready to go again?"

"In a minute," I smiled. "Jesus, woman, give me a little time." I held her face in both my hands and slowly ran my fingers over her neck, shoulders, and back, as far as I could reach. "Has it been a while for you?"

"You're the first since my husband. I hope I was okay."

"No, you weren't." I paused for a second, feeling her backbone tense. "You were wonderful."

"You're only the third lover I've ever had, counting my husband."

"You say that with an edge."

"I'm forty-seven years old and I've only slept with three men. And one of them, just once."

"It's nothing to be ashamed of."

"How many times have you seen a play of Shakespeare's?"

"You ask the damndest questions."

"Just tell me."

"God, I don't know. Counting movies, all the plays, well, I guess fifty times, maybe more."

"How many friends have you had? Good friends."

"In my whole life? At least twenty."

"How many different countries have you visited?"

"Eight or ten. Where is this going?"

"I could ask you about foods and wines and books, or what kind of skills you have, but it all comes down to the same thing. You're either the kind of person that goes out and experiences the world or you're the kind that hides in the house and lets it all go by. For a long time I fooled myself that I wanted to stay inside, indoors, safe inside my marriage and my job and never step one foot outside of my routine. I've done a lot of thinking lately and I've decided that I was being what everybody else wanted, not what I wanted. And I kick myself when I think back on all the men who wanted me that I turned down. Not that I missed out on screwing them, that I missed out on learning things. Things I would know now if I hadn't been such a scaredy-cat."

"I wish I had your attitude, that everything in life was worth knowing."

"It's not all pretty, I know that. But I'm a teacher. I'm committed to the idea that knowledge is good."

"Not all of it. You can know things that tear you apart." I tried my best to keep my voice casual, but I clearly didn't succeed. She touched the side of my face. "What is it?"

"There are things that are hard to live with."

"I'm listening."

"Were you or your husband ever in country?"

"No. But most of the people we knew were, at one time or another."

"My second tour I was in I Corps, near Quang Tri. One day we were in jungle in a platoon-size patrol, two squads up and one back. I was in command of the reserve squad. Just before dark the first two squads walked up a road right into an X ambush. They never had a chance. We could hear a lot of firing, but after about two minutes, none of it was American weapons. Off to one side of the road was a secondary trail that went deep into the bush. The men wanted me to take it, try and get to our men. I said no, we'd wait for an artillery mission. The men got ugly; they said that Marines don't leave their dead, let alone their wounded. No one was shooting at us at all, there was plenty of time to look at that trail head. It was big and black and closed in by trees on both sides so that it looked like a square. And for all we knew it would have brought us out right on the flank of the VC, broken up the ambush."

"Or led your men into the middle of it, too."

"That's what I said. So we stayed put. The artillery came down twenty minutes later. By that time the firing was over and Charlie was gone. When we moved up the road three men were missing, prisoners. All the rest were dead. Some had been shot at close range when Charlie was cleaning up after they'd been overrun."

"Did the prisoners ever come back?"

"All three died in camps. One of them right near the end of the war."

She took my hand in both of hers and pressed it against her chest. "You did the right thing, you know. You all could have been killed."

"Or I could have saved some lives."

"Which way did the other trail lead?"

"We had orders to clear out before dark, and we never went back. I never found out. A week later I stepped on a booby trap and that was the end of the war for me."

"Don't you think you'd be better off knowing whether taking that path would have helped?"

"Now you're the one who doesn't get it. It's not the path, it's me. I knew everything I needed to know. I didn't sit tight because I knew one thing or another. I was scared, and I found a reason to play safe. I know it, and that's what I have to live with."

"Of course you were scared. You were in combat. That doesn't make what you decided wrong. You *don't know* if it was wrong. You just focus on the fear and blame yourself. For nothing more than being scared."

It was like I'd been slapped. Twice in one day, first

about children and now about the war, she'd cut right through. "I've never thought of it quite that way."

"You think about it a lot, though, don't you?"

"Are you an English teacher or a psychiatrist?"

"Don't you?"

I looked at the ceiling. "I've never been to a unit reunion. And I have dreams."

"How often?"

"At first it was nearly every night. Now it's maybe once every couple of months. Anything gets burnt out of you eventually."

"What's the dream?"

"Seeing that black hole, with the green jungle on both sides and meeting above it. There're noises, but the main thing is the hole. I keep staring at it even when I don't want to. It comes closer even though I don't move toward it. Then I wake up."

No one said anything for a long time after that, for which I was thankful. She knew when I was ready to pay attention to her again. She started kissing my nipples and then worked her way down my chest to my stomach. "Boy, they really gave you enlisted man's stitches."

"They had no way of knowing I was going to be a professional man. And they had their hands full; it was a pretty dirty wound. Most of the booby traps were like that."

Slowly she kissed her way down the scars on my belly. Not the regular skin, just the scars. There were a lot of them, and she took her time. It was sexual, of course, but there was something healing about it, too, something of recognition and acceptance. "No one's ever done that before."

She looked up at me. "Better late than never. The war's over. Welcome home, Marine."

"I think I'd be ready if you could give me a little help."

She looked up. "Honey, you can have all the help you want."

16

Thursday, 9:00 A.M.

"Do you have an appointment?" The receptionist said it just right; pleasant, even cordial, but just a hint that someone who just dropped in to see Mr. Weaver was pushing their luck.

"No. This is an emergency. Mr. Chadwick sent us."

She nodded and picked up the phone. "I'll check for you." Her expression was a lot more serious than a pretty blonde in her early twenties should have. Either she had a bad personal life or she took her job very seriously indeed. "Could you see if Mr. Weaver could see a couple of people without an appointment? They say it's an emergency, and that they were sent here by Mr. Chadwick."

I looked over at Kate and caught her smiling. We were both thinking the same thing. If this girl was doing what I thought she was doing—talking to Weaver without letting us know he was in—she was worth her salt.

"He'll be down in just a minute. Please have a seat."

We took her advice. I was wearing my business suit, partly for the occasion and partly to cover up the shoulder holster for my .357. I hardly ever carried it, but the events of yesterday morning had changed my mind, at least for the duration of this case.

The law firm of Fisher, Stoltzfus & Weaver had its offices in a converted row house next to a parking garage. We were only half a block from the courthouse, and about every third sign advertised a law office. The reception room was small, but when I glanced at the firm's brochure on the table I saw that there were only six attorneys. Kate was reading a copy of the brochure with interest. In what, exactly, I couldn't imagine. I spent my time looking around the room. I'd only been to a couple of law offices in Lancaster, and this was furnished very much like the others: stark, with Windsor chairs, small area rugs, and Amish quilts on the walls.

A tanned blonde woman in her early forties came out from the back and whispered to the receptionist. I leaned over to Kate. "Weaver's secretary?"

"You've got to be kidding. That's a good silk suit she's wearing."

"So?"

"If it cost less than six hundred bucks she got a great deal. The shoes are Papagallos—two hundred. And if that diamond is real I'd trade my car for it."

The woman walked over to us and I stood up. "Hello," she said. "I'm Marjorie Kligman, the office manager."

"Dave Garrett. And this is Kate McMahan." I didn't feel like volunteering anything more, at least not yet.

"I understand the Chadwicks sent you?"

"That's right."

"Are you an attorney, Mr. Garrett?" I was as thin-skinned as a man could be about that question, but she had a way of asking it that didn't rub any nerves raw.

"No, I'm not."

"I thought you were, that I just didn't recognize you." It would have been easy to explain myself, but I didn't. "No. Sorry."

She tried again. "You're working for the Chadwicks?"

"He sent us here."

"But are you working for him?"

"I have his authorization. Here you go." I hadn't been planning to show it to anyone besides Weaver, but it seemed like the only way to get past the dragon at the gate.

She unfolded the paper and glanced at it. I saw that

her eyes were blue and that she had freckles under her makeup. "This is signed only by Bruce."

I shifted my weight to my other foot before answering. Sometimes playing dumb can work. "Yes. That's true."

"Do you have something signed by Anne?"

"This is what I have now."

"Can I ask what this is about?"

"We have an authorization. Please feel free to call your client and verify it."

She shifted her attack. "As a matter of office policy, you understand we'll need to do that. I'm just asking so that we can help our mutual client."

"I've already told you, I'm not an attorney."

"Are you working for the government?"

"No."

"Are you a private investigator?"

"Yes."

"Licensed?"

I pulled out my wallet and showed her my card. She studied it a long time before she handed it back. I got a good look at the diamond Kate had mentioned; it looked big enough to shave by.

"And Ms. McMahan?"

I glanced at Kate; she was going to leave it to me. "She's assisting me."

"Is Mr. Chadwick your client?"

"I can't say."

She moved in for the kill. "Are you here to collect information against Mrs. Chadwick?"

"No, I'm not."

"Well, why can't she sign an authorization of her own?"

"I can't discuss that."

"Don't you know why she can't sign an authorization?"

"I can't discuss that, either."

"Some of our representations of the Chadwicks are joint matters. Having only one authorization puts us in a difficult position."

"I can assure you, we're acting on behalf of both."

I looked at Kate, who was looking at the floor. I think that was the moment when I fell in love with her. We both knew that if she looked at me, her expression couldn't say anything except, why the hell did you tell her that?

"Well, that's some progress, Mr. Garrett." She moved a little closer and I could smell her perfume. "Now if you're on a joint representation why don't you have a joint authorization?"

"I can't discuss that."

"Has she refused?"

"No."

"Is she under some kind of disability?"

That was a tough one. I was tempted to say I didn't know, but that would have sounded like hell. "No."

"Has she had a chance to sign an authorization?"

"I—no."

"Is she in some danger?"

"I can't say."

"Are the police involved?"

"No. Not yet."

"Is there—" Mercifully, the door opened and a tall, slender man in shirtsleeves came in and offered his hand.

"Joe Weaver. You're Mr. Garrett?"

"Mr. Weaver," Marjorie Kligman said, "before you go into conference with these people I'd like to have a word with you." She touched him on the sleeve and led him to the back of the office.

"She's tough," Kate whispered.

"Another minute and I'd have confessed what I did with the neighbor's daughter in the bathhouse when we were six."

Whatever Ms. Kligman said to Weaver, it didn't take long. He came back, holding the authorization like it was a fish wrapping. "I suppose we ought to go somewhere and talk," he said vaguely.

"Fine. Lead the way."

He took us through a door to a conference room that was a smaller version of the reception room. I introduced Kate and we sat down across the table from him. He had wavy brown hair, parted in the middle in a vain attempt to hide the widow's peak that was climbing up his forehead. His face was pale and unlined, and I couldn't get a sense of how old he was. Whatever his age he was working too hard; there was dark bags under his eyes, and he had reading glasses sticking out of his shirt pocket. He looked the way I used to look at about four-thirty on Friday afternoons.

"I gather you want us to give you information about Mr. Chadwick's representations here."

"As you know, I'm a private investigator. We've been hired by the Chadwick family. There's a problem involving Anne. We're hoping that something in your records may give us a clue."

"I'm going to need a little more to go on than that."

"We can't say. And time is precious." I wasn't up for a second grilling this early in the morning.

"I can tell you that we represent the family."

"We already know that. That's why we're here."

He studied the authorization like it was going to solve the world's problems. "I'm going to have to check with him personally." Without making eye contact with us once, he found a phone book and placed a call.

"May I speak to Mr. Chadwick, please? Tell him it's Joe Weaver calling. Yes, I'll hold." A long pause. "Thank you," he said, and hung up.

"I'm sorry, but Mr. Chadwick's in the middle of a long-distance conference call. They expect it to take at least half an hour."

"Look, we're agents for Mr. Chadwick. I want you to respect what I'm about to tell you as an attorney-client confidence."

"Well, if you really are acting on his behalf, that would apply."

"This one is particularly sensitive. It has to stay within this room. Do we understand each other?"

"Yes."

"Anne Chadwick was kidnapped Tuesday morning. We paid a ransom demand the same day, but she hasn't been returned. We need to know if there's anything in her dealings with this firm that could be relevant."

"Like what?"

"I don't know until we ask."

"I see. I don't know—" He looked at me again. "Say, did you have a brother at Villanova Law?"

"I went there. Class of 'seventy-four."

"No kidding. I was 'seventy-six. I thought you looked familiar. You went out on your own in Philly, didn't you?"

"That's right."

"What happened? You get the shits of private practice, or what?"

"Remember a couple years back there was a story about a Philadelphia lawyer who took the bar exam for his wife and got disbarred?"

"Yeah. I wondered how he ever got in to take the test."

"That was before they started using photo ID. As a matter of fact, that's why they started doing it. But if your wife's name was something like Lynn, who's to know? Mine's was Terry."

"Jesus."

"You might as well hear it all. I hope you'll think I was just stupid and not a slime bucket. She'd tried to pass eight times. After she failed the last time she tried suicide. It was a complicated thing with competing with her dad—he was a big litigator at Morgan, Lewis—and test anxiety and fear of success and a lot of shit that cost us a lot of money to sort out. But to cut it short, I let her talk me into taking it for her."

"They were really hard on you."

"One more supreme court justice like you and it would have been just a two-year suspension. But the hell with it. Let's talk about Chadwick."

I'd broken the ice. "Let me tell you what I know off the top of my head," he said. "I don't know about letting you see the files. I mean, not without verbal confirmation."

"Fine. Just go with what you've got."

"The first thing we did for them was eight or ten years ago; it was a real estate settlement. I remember it because I did it myself. They'd just moved here from the Midwest, Ohio or someplace like that. About four years ago they sold that house and bought another one."

"Did you do that settlement?"

He shook his head. "Damned realtors steered him to a title company. It happens all the time. They're afraid a lawyer will queer the deal. So after the settlement is over the client wants to know how come no one told him that there's a sewer easement running right through his stand of mature oak trees?"

"Is that what happened?"

"No. I'm just on my soapbox. Sorry. No, as far as I know the settlement went fine. Bruce was in to see us about two years ago. He was changing jobs and had to negotiate his way out of a noncompetition clause with Holiday Inns. One of my partners handled that. Right after that he brought in the documents when he bought the Uncle Chan's franchise."

"Did you do that?"

"I met with Bruce. Our associate handled the documents, for all the difference it made."

"Oh?"

"He might as well have signed it without reading. The deal was absolutely nonnegotiable. Uncle Chan's wouldn't even correct the typos."

"He must have wanted it badly."

"It was a great deal. I'm no expert on franchises, but we've done a few from time to time. To get a major national franchise you normally have to show a net worth, without real estate, of at least a half a million, liquid. If you're talking about McDonald's, you may need to show a financial statement with something close to a million. Uncle Chan's didn't care as long as the franchise looked like he had what it took to operate the restaurants. And Bruce really impressed them."

"He's a hard worker."

"Does this stay between us?"

"Depends what it is."

"Well, he's a very valued client, but just between you and me, he's not real popular around here. That's why I had to have an associate handle the franchise review; the junior partner told me flat out he wouldn't do it. Bruce is extremely demanding. Not only does he want everything yesterday, he'll bug you every few hours till he gets it."

"I didn't get that sense of him."

"Oh, he's polite about it, but he can drive you nuts. It's Friday noon, and he'll call up about getting a redraft of some document done by five so he can look at it."

"So he can get it back to you for Monday?"

"Monday, hell. He means Saturday morning. He has no concept that people take off at the end of the day, or on weekends."

"I don't think he does."

"That's what I respect about him. He'll demand that I drop whatever else I'm doing to get papers ready. But if his runner picks them up at five, they're back in our mail slot the next morning with his corrections and suggestions. He doesn't do it just to bust our chops."

"What about other matters?"

"We formed a Sub S corporation for him to operate the franchise. Penn China, it's called. Anne wanted to use Tso What, but she couldn't talk him into it."

"Was she involved with the franchise?"

He shook his head. "No, that was her only contribution, thank God."

"Why do you say that?"

"You think Bruce is tough to work for; we used to head for the hills if she came in."

"Go on."

"She was never rude or anything, but she was smart as hell. And she had the only genuine photographic memory I've ever run into. The first time I met her was when they bought their first home here. She glanced at the settlement sheet—and I mean glanced—and said that the school taxes had been incorrectly prorated by four dollars and seventy-three cents. She said it must have been because our clerk excluded one day, since the taxes were that much per diem. I can still remember how I stared at her when I ran the figures and found she was right. I mean, I do a couple of settlements a week, and I need a couple of minutes with a calculator to prorate the taxes. And she did it in her head. Instantly."

"What other work did your office do?"

"For Bruce's corporation, Penn China, we handled the settlement when he bought the real estate for the restaurant. And we've been negotiating for financing for another location."

"What about wills?"

He swallowed and looked at the door. "That's a joint matter with Bruce and Anne. I can't discuss it."

Kate spoke up for the first time. "But there are wills; at least you can tell us that."

"Sure. Yes, there are."

"And without going in to any details," Kate asked, "Has Anne ever been in for anything on her own?"

He leaned back in his chair. "I really can't say."

"If you can tell us that there *are* wills, without showing them to us, can't you tell us if she saw anyone, even if you can't tell us what it is? I mean, isn't that about the same?"

He hesitated. "Oh, I suppose you're right. She had a consultation with Charlie Fisher. I'm sorry, but I can't discuss any details."

"When was that?" Kate asked. "I mean, just roughly."

"I shouldn't say. Hey, I'm sorry, but my hands are tied."

"We understand. David and I have to get to our next appointment anyway." She stood up and extended her hand. "Thanks so much for your time."

Weaver stood up, too. Clearly he was happy to be rid of an uncomfortable situation. I had a few more things I wanted to ask, but I held my tongue. Inside of three minutes we were back on the street, at my car. It was a little warmer today, but a light snow was falling.

"What the hell is going on?" I asked.

"We need to talk to Bruce right away. I think I'm on to something. Let me tell you on the way."

17

Thursday, 11:00 A.M.

Chadwick was in his office. He seemed to have aged in the last two hours, especially around the eyes. "Boy, am I glad to see you. We've just had another note delivered, not half an hour ago. We're supposed to pay the money tonight, at ten, at the Watt and Shand parking garage."

"I know the place. Four or five stories, right?"

Chadwick nodded.

"Where's the note?"

"Right here in my desk. I treated it just like you handled the other one. I didn't get any fingerprints on it."

He handed it over by a corner and I examined it closely. It was like the first, a pasteup on common blank white paper.

"How was this one delivered?"

"The same way as the first—the doorbell rang, and then it was there."

"Who found it this time?"

"Mosier was in here talking to me and we both heard the doorbell. I got Jeremy on the intercom and told him to answer it."

I handed the note back to him. "My advice about not paying it still stands."

"We can talk about that in a minute, Bruce," Kate said. "I need to ask you some questions first."

"Sure. I'll have them hold my calls."

We sat down and waited till he was ready. Kate tapped the edge of the law firm's brochure against the edge of the desk. I decided to let her do the talking while I concentrated on watching Bruce. "Bruce, we have some information you ought to think about. We're not sure anymore that your wife was really kidnapped."

The color left his face. "What are you saying? You think she's—been dead all along?"

"No. Well, first of all, let me tell you what we're thinking about. Four things, basically. One, when she left she was dressed to kill. Two, it was an errand she could have handled by phone in the first place. She knew David would be following her, and his car was sabotaged—"

He waved a hand in a dismissive gesture. "I was over this same ground with Dave yesterday. It was stupid then and it's stupid now."

She didn't say anything for a while, making sure that he was finished. "Bruce, I know you're under a lot of stress. It's not easy to deal with my questions or what they imply. But you wanted our help, and I'm trying to give it in the best way I know how. If we were sure Anne had gone off to get away from you, we wouldn't be sitting here. It's just one of the possibilities all of us have to consider." Chadwick didn't look impressed.

I tried another tack. "And anyway, we need to know as much about her as possible if it is a real kidnapping. Crimes like that don't strike from out of the blue. A lot of the time the victim is well known to the kidnapper."

He shook his head again. "Listen, Dave, you do good work. But think about it. Sure, she was dressed up. She was meeting her friend for lunch and they were going shopping. The fact that the errand might not have been necessary—who can say? Maybe she wanted to talk face-to-face about the cake. And you know, it makes sense to me to handle it that way. She didn't work. If it wasted half an hour driving out there, so what? The car doesn't point anywhere. Somebody wanted you not to see what they were going to do with Anne. I'm no investigator, but the business with your car points toward a kidnapping, not away from it."

Kate didn't back down. "She went to see the divorce specialist at your law firm."

"When?" He sat up and his mouth dropped slightly open.

"We don't know."

"Do you know it was for her? Maybe she was there on behalf of someone else. A couple of times a year she'll take some poor soul under her wing; helps them out of legal or financial trouble. She's done things like that before for people in our church. Couldn't that be it?"

"We don't know that, either."

"And if she wanted a divorce, why would she go to my own law firm? There's a ton of lawyers in this county. No, it doesn't wash. Who was it, by the way?"

"Charles Fisher." Kate held out the brochure and put her finger on his picture.

"Charlie handled a problem for Anne a couple of years ago. About Jeremy. No, it must have been about four years ago, 'cause he was a juvenile. Used his mother's credit card without permission. Are you sure that wasn't the consultation they had in mind?"

"We don't know, but there could have been more than one."

"We'd like you to call and tell them we want a reinterview with Weaver, and he should tell us everything he knows."

"If this is the kind of thing you're coming up with, the hell with it. You've talked to them, you know what kind of legal business I have, and that's that. She's not in my lawyer's office. Go find where she is and get her back."

Kate gave me a quick glance and I shook my head. Let it go. Chadwick was in a bullheaded mood, probably from talking to Mosier. This wasn't the time to go head-to-head with him. If we could come up with a better reason to go back, we could always ask for authorization again.

"Okay, then, let's say I'm all wet." Kate put away the brochure. "We still need to know who she talks to, what she's been doing recently. The odds are that she was talking to her kidnappers, or at least someone working with them, and didn't know it."

"What can I tell you?"

"Did she ever consult with a psychiatrist or psychologist?"

"When Amy died, yes. And once or twice over the years. She took it very hard. We both did. But the fellow she used to go to died a couple of years ago, and she hasn't been to anyone since."

"If she was under a lot of stress, would she have confided in her priest?"

"No. We see him twice a year, Easter and Christmas. And when they're raising money for the church." A vague look of resentment crossed his face, like a man who feels he didn't get value for his money. I wondered if his beef was with the priest or with God.

"Didn't she work with him as part of this church work she did?"

"No. It's a big church. There're layers and layers of volunteers and lay staff to get through before you actually get to the priest, even if you're a big donor."

She leaned forward in her chair, nearly hunched over, and put her hands together in her lap. "You've been married a long time. You've had your arguments over the years, like my husband and me, right?"

"Every couple does."

"Of course they do. Nothing to be ashamed of. And you always worked things out."

"We sure did."

"When was the last time you had a fight that you remember?"

"At least a month ago."

"And you resolved your problem?"

"Oh, sure. We always did."

She cocked her head to one side and shrugged a little, emphasizing how unimportant the question was. "Just tell me if you could; what was it about?"

"I can't see how that can have anything to do with her kidnapping."

Her tone was relaxed, mild, even a little humorous.

"I can't either, Bruce, at least until you tell us about it."

"Well, if you need to know, it was about Amy."

"Tell us about it."

He grimaced. "It's been a fixation with her. Amy, I mean."

"She can't get over her death?"

"In a way. It's worse, really." He took his time before he went on. "She still thinks Amy's alive."

"Is that what you were arguing about?"

"It was three weeks, maybe a month ago. It wasn't the kind of thing I needed dumped on me right before our major opening."

"They never found Amy's body," I said.

He acted like he hadn't heard me. "Amy was our favorite. We sheltered her. She was like her mother—she studied hard at school, always getting straight A's—she was only a junior in high school, but she was already getting letters from colleges, inviting her to apply. She was in the National Honor Society, the math club, the chess club. She had lots of activities and stayed after school. She didn't have time for a bad crowd. I don't think she even knew those kind of people existed."

"What happened?"

"There's a bar up near the turnpike. Passin' Thru, it's called. I sort of knew it was there—you can see it from 222—but I never paid any attention. It looks okay from the outside, but it's a rough place. From what the police told me it attracts the worst elements. It's near the turnpike and it has a bad reputation, so the truckers looking for a wild time go there. There's a campground nearby where bikers hang out in the summer. And the local bad element goes there, too. There's underaged drinking, and drugs, and girls. The state police are there all the time in the summer breaking up fights. I don't know how they keep their license."

"How did Amy wind up there?"

"She was with the wrong kind of boy. I'd met him, and he seemed all right. He was a year older than her, a senior. Anyway, he took her there. It was the Saturday night of Labor Day weekend. You can imagine what the place was like."

"What happened?"

"We never got to the bottom of it. The police tried. I hired a detective agency; they tried. I put pressure on everybody I could—I contribute a lot to the local Republican party, they owe me some favors. But no one really found out much. The boy she was with, he and some bikers got into a fight and he was beaten up. Served him right. But when he woke up Amy was gone."

"People don't just disappear out of a crowded bar."

"Don't tell me that. I spent a year saying that. They questioned everybody they could prove was there. Only a couple people would admit to seeing her at all; no one saw her leave. The police figure that whoever beat up her date figured that she was the prize, that they took her somewhere and then killed her when they were through." He swallowed. "They figure that her body will turn up somewhere one of these days."

"That's all they know?"

"I'm not bitter about the police. They did everything I asked, and they were very professional. But if there are no clues, no witnesses, there's a limit to how much anyone can do. They told me, someday there'll be a break. Someone who knows something will get mad at one of the people responsible. A hunter or a swimmer will find the body. Or somebody with information will get caught for something and want to trade for a lighter sentence. Something will happen. It just never has."

"Anne didn't want to let it be a closed book."

"Until they find her, it never will be, for either of us. It would be better if we could be absolutely sure, if you know what I mean. We could put it to rest. I take nerve pills, every night, ever since it happened, and I probably drink more than I should. But it's been worse on Anne. She's convinced Amy's still alive."

"What makes her say that?"

"Just a feeling, she says."

"What was it that happened a few weeks ago?"

"Well, over the years there have been people who've come and taken advantage of us. And I mean 'us.' I was the biggest sucker in the world for a long time, too. People who would offer information for money. The police had publicized the case, and the detective agency we'd hired had sent out lots of circulars, so it wasn't hard for people to find out we had money and were desperate to find out anything we could."

"What kind of people?"

"Exactly the kind that killed her. And that was the worst part; when I passed out money, for all I knew I was giving it to her murderer."

"What kind of information?"

"Anything they could sell for money. So they could buy drugs, or a bottle, or a way to the next town. She's been seen here. She'd been seen there. She'd lost her memory. She was being held by a white-slavery ring. She was running with bikers. She'd been killed and buried upstate. She'd been thrown into the Susquehanna. She died of hepatitis in Texas. She'd been living with a trucker and died in a crash on the interstate in Ohio. Take your pick. The only thing they had in common was nobody had any proof."

"Did one of those people come by a couple of weeks ago?"

"He had the most nerve of all. He said Amy was alive, and that he wanted ten thousand dollars to produce her. It was crazy. The most anyone had ever demanded before was a couple of hundred dollars, and this fellow offered nothing to back it up. Just this scruffy guy showing up at the door, and not smelling very good."

"But Anne wanted to pay."

"Yes, she did. She would have, too, if I'd let her. She was ready to write him a check on the spot, that's how desperate she was. But I sent him away. I told him if he showed up again I'd call the police."

"You know, this could be the key to this case, right now."

He looked at me hotly. "To you it's a case. To me it's my life."

I kept my voice low and steady. "That's what the argument was about."

"She was upset."

"I understand that. It's a pretty volatile situation. But what exactly did she say?"

"Things she didn't mean."

"Tell me anyway."

"That I'd run her daughter out of the house and now I was trying to keep her away when she was trying to come back."

"But it blew over, between you and your wife?"

"After a day, sure it did. Anne has a bit of a temper, but she doesn't stay mad long."

"Bruce," Kate asked, "why are you so sure that Amy is dead?"

Impatience crossed his face. "The police found her purse, with her money missing, and her clothes, in a ditch along the turnpike. Everything was badly burned, with gasoline, but they could tell that there were slashes in the clothing. There was some freshly turned earth in the woods nearby, and the police dug all around. They never found the body, though. Besides, if she was alive, even if she was being held against her will, she would have found a way to contact us years ago."

"I think you're right about one thing, Bruce," Kate said.

"That would be a change."

"I think you had a good instinct about the man who came here. But maybe for the wrong reason."

He looked at her and waited.

"I think Amy is dead. And I think he may know something about it."

"But if he knows she's dead, why say she's alive?"

"Because he *knows* no one can prove him wrong. He'll have some vague evidence, like a blurry photograph or something—who knows? But the point is, he wouldn't be making the play if he wasn't sure Amy hadn't ever been in touch since she disappeared. And there's only one way he can know that. He has to know she's dead. Either he was there when she was killed, or he talked to someone who was. Or at least he's seen the body."

He nodded as she spoke. "What did you two mean about he was the key to the case?"

"He's the key to Amy's case," Kate answered. "And I have to think that there's a connection to Anne."

"Why?"

"Suppose Anne disobeyed you and tracked this man down, that she met him behind your back. She tells him she can't get him the money but she stays in touch. He decides to hold her hostage the next time he sees her."

He nodded. "If he can't get money for my daughter, he'll get it for my wife."

"You said yourself he seemed like he could be dangerous."

"All right, then, what next?"

I answered for us. "There's no point in waiting around here. That gives the other side all the initiative. We should go to them. If you'll tell us where it is, we'll go to the bar where Amy was last seen. It's as good a place to start as any."

"Do you know where Denver is?"

"Up near the turnpike?" I asked.

"Yes. The place is on Adamstown Road, about half a mile east of Denver. It's all by itself; you can't miss it."

"This man who came to the door. Tell me about him."

He squinted, trying to remember. "He was in his twenties, no more than thirty. Dark hair and a scruffy beard. Medium build, I guess you'd say. Kind of rough looking, but not as bad as some of the others."

"Did he say how to get in touch with him?"

"He left a phone number. I threw it in the trash."

"Did he mention where he was staying?"

"He said he was staying that night at a truck stop. If he said which one I didn't catch it. But he said he'd be in town till he heard from me. I didn't like the sound of that; it sounded like a threat. That's why I got mad."

"There's something else we need to talk about," Kate said. I knew what she was going to ask and I let her go ahead. It was the kind of thing better asked by a family member anyway.

"I hope it's more related to Anne than Amy's story is."

"We don't know what's related and what's not, yet," she pointed out. "We have it on good authority that Anne had an affair with someone named Ted, someone she met playing tennis."

"Ted Grigg?"

"If he plays tennis, that could be him."

"When is this affair supposed to have happened?"

"Not long after you two first moved here."

Chadwick looked baffled. "I can't say that it didn't happen. I'm not in the habit of chaining her to the nearest radiator when I go out of the house. But if there was something going on between them, it's news to me."

"Tell us about Ted Grigg."

"He comes from a very wealthy family, old money people. He's not married, at least not the last that I heard. His parents have a big estate a few miles north of town, and he lives in the carriage house. All the money belongs to his folks. If I understand his situation right, he has nothing of his own. But he's an only child, so someday it should all be his. As far as him having an affair with Anne, I just don't believe it."

"Why?" she asked.

He threw up his hands. "If you met him . . . well, I just don't."

"Did she ever speak of him?"

"Sure. He's one of the people we know in town. Like a hundred others. Look, even if something happened ten years ago, what's that got to do with now?"

"We don't know. There are a lot of possibilities. We're just checking."

We said our good-byes and got into my car. I

checked my .357 and made sure all the chambers were loaded.

"Is this that dangerous?" she asked.

"I don't know. But it's more dangerous than walking in the backyard, and that almost got me killed."

I directed her through the light traffic and onto Route 222 headed north. "Just go straight for about fifteen miles till we come to the Denver exit, then go left. When you get to 272, head south and then go right on the Denver–Adamstown Road."

We drove for a while without talking. Then I looked over at her. "I don't know what to think."

"About what?"

"Your talk with Chadwick."

She was smiling a little. "Go on."

"That was total nonsense, about that trucker knowing Amy was dead."

"It made no sense at all."

"And he bought it completely. How did you know he would?"

"I didn't. But he was so obstructive about Anne, I started thinking. When smart people do dumb things, you have to look for a reason. Bruce is a very smart man. But he won't let his brain work to logical conclusions, so he winds up saying stupid things. And believing them, too. Amy may be dead. Anne may have been kidnapped. But there's two ways to look at it, and he won't look at the contrary. He didn't spot any flaws in my reasoning because he has so much invested in buying into it."

I put my hand on her leg, just above the knee. "You've got a good instinct. I'm glad you're along."

I removed my hand and we drove in silence for about ten minutes. I was thinking about how I would handle things at the bar when she drummed her fingers on the wheel.

"I'm sorry, David."

"Sorry? About what?"

"About last night."

"Last night was wonderful. There's nothing to be sorry about."

"Yes, there is."

"Don't tell me—you figured out that I faked my orgasms."

"This is serious, David."

I took note of the tone of her voice. "I have a feeling I'm not going to like this."

"No, I don't think you are."

"You don't want it to happen again?"

"I do, very much. But listening to Bruce back there, talk about him and Anne, things go through my mind and I can't stop them."

"What kind of things?"

"About my marriage and my husband and how I treated him."

"You were married a long time. It takes a long time to get over it. You said yourself, you were in guilt with him, not in love."

"Sounded pretty pithy, didn't it?"

"Are you still in love with him?"

"I don't know. But—I am still married to him."

She was right about my not liking the conversation. "You'd better go over this one real slow."

"I lied to you. Or, made you a part of a fantasy, really."

"Go on."

"Remember last night, I said that my husband told me I could take a vacation from our marriage, no questions asked?"

"You said that was one of the options you wanted."

"Well, this is it. We live together. It's just that he's given me these last two weeks . . . off."

"And at the end of the vacation you get back on the plane and go back to Miami?"

"That was the deal."

" 'Was'?"

"I could make a big speech about my emotional state and how well I relate to you and get all mushy, but I don't have that right after just one night, so let me keep it simple. For right now, let's just say that I like sleeping with strange men more than I thought I would."

"Done it with any others?"

"No."

"Good." I struggled with how to continue. "I wish I could keep on seeing you."

"My husband was right, you know. I want him at home for security and you for excitement and to live in Miami and Pennsylvania and to travel and not be tied down anywhere. I want everything and wind up with nothing."

"I'll tell you what I think he'd tell you. All I can deal with is what I can offer, and you have to make your own choices. I'm not going to be the one to take responsibility for helping to end a marriage, if it's working. But if you decide it's over, I'd like to see you again."

"Life is complicated."

"We make it that way," I said.

"You're right. I'm sorry about not being up-front with you."

"It's okay."

"No, it's not. Being a mess is not okay."

"You're not a mess."

"Thanks for saying that, even though it's a lie. Look, there hasn't been anybody else, not since I've been married. I'm not used to this kind of thing."

"I understand."

"I'm very . . . fragile right now."

I didn't say anything back. I just took her hand and held it till the sign for the Denver exit came up.

18

Thursday, 2:00 P.M.

"Chadwick said that Passin' Thru was easy to find," I complained.

"He must have come here a lot, after it happened."

"Poor bastard. What a hell of a place this is. Do you see any color around here except gray?"

"There's some red clay over there, near the dumpsters."

Adamstown Road was narrow and winding. On our left was a line of barren hills, dotted with an irregular mix of bare trees, small houses, and industrial buildings. To the right was a rolling plain, partly covered in snow. Except for a few rusting storage tanks, and some deep gashes half filled with trash, the landscape was empty.

We'd already been all the way into Denver once; we were on our way back toward the turnpike when I saw it. "Over there, on the left."

She slowed. "Where?"

"Just beyond the gas station."

"If you say so."

"It's below road level. I saw the roof and a sign."

Kate made the turn onto a dirt road barely wide enough for the Honda. Even though it was mostly covered with snow, we could hear gravel pinging off the bottom.

The road curved to the right and then dipped down so steeply that for a moment the hood seemed to be suspended in midair. The road leveled out, just as abruptly, and we bottomed out so hard that the glove compartment flew open, showering me with maps, food wrappers, and miscellaneous debris.

"Here we are," she said.

We were, indeed. Passin' Thru was a one-story cinderblock rectangle with a cheap, warped hollow-core door and what looked like plywood over the windows. It was hard to be sure because of the snow, but from the angles of the vehicles clustered around, it looked like the parking lot was unpaved. Jeeps, four-by-fours, and Camaros were strewn around the lot, not a one of them in decent condition. A number of the cars had out-of-state plates; Ohio, New Jersey, New York.

Kate was careful to lock all the doors as we got out. "Sure is busy for two in the afternoon."

"Most of these boys probably work shifts. Or quit at noon to get in more drinking time."

We passed by a rusting pickup truck with a rifle rack behind the seat and a bumper sticker that read PUSSY—BREAKFAST OF CHAMPIONS. Kate shook her head. "What do you want me to do?"

"You were a cop. You know the hard-and-fast rule for fighting in bars?"

She smiled thinly. "Hit hard and hit fast."

"Good. Just watch my back, and let's not separate."

I pulled on the front door; it resisted so firmly I thought it was locked, then gradually and noisily came open. Inside it was completely dark and thick with cigarette smoke. Off to my left I could hear a jukebox, and straight ahead and above me I saw the blue rectangle of a TV mounted high on the wall.

I moved a short distance into the room, just enough for Kate to come in behind me and shut the door. As my eyes adjusted to the dark I took in the layout: a rectangular bar straight ahead, a few ratty chrome chairs and tables to my right, and a couple of pool tables to the left. I'd thrown away better chairs than the bar offered its patrons; the red-plastic seats were ripped and dirty-gray stuffing bulged outwards, spilling onto the floor. No one was sitting in any of them. A few figures were on the stools at the bar with their backs to me.

I took my time unzipping my coat. I left my gloves

on and kept my hands in plain view. "Let's go over to the pool tables; that's where everybody is."

"Don't you want to talk to the bartender?"

"I don't see one. And he wouldn't tell us anything, anyway."

I couldn't tell if the floor was linoleum or wood. Whatever it was, I didn't touch much of it. Mostly I stepped on peanut shells, napkins, candy-bar wrappers, and God knows what else.

The pool area was better lighted, at least as far as the tables themselves. I saw a row of folding metal chairs along one wall, empty except for a couple of girls in jeans and leather jackets. Half a dozen young men, between eighteen and thirty, were gathered around the nearest table. Their clothes told the story; the bikers wore black T-shirts and heavy boots and the construction workers wore heavy flannel shirts and dirty jeans. The biggest one, and the only one with a beard, wore a T-shirt with a down vest. Most of them were holding pool sticks; one was hefting a ball in a way I didn't like. All of them were looking at me.

I turned to Kate. "I don't like the looks of this. There must be people who drop in from time to time, strangers. I don't think they get a reception like this."

"Maybe we were expected."

"Yeah."

I turned to the group and raised my voice. "I'm not here to hassle anybody. I just want to ask a few questions and I'm out of here."

"You a state pig, or local?" the bearded one asked.

"Neither one. My name's Garrett. I'm looking for somebody."

"He ain't here. Fuck off."

"You guys have no reason to get excited. I'm just looking for somebody."

"Half the cops in the state are, too," someone said from the rear. "Bunch of shit if you ask me."

"I'm a private cop. I don't want any trouble."

"Then get out. This is our place." There was a general rumble of agreement, and a couple of them started moving to cut me off from the door. I sidestepped in front of them and stood with my legs apart, knees slightly bent.

"I've got business with somebody who hangs here, or used to."

"What's his name?" said the man with the beard.

"I don't know. I just know what he looks like. Twenties, maybe thirty. Brown hair, short beard. He may drive a truck."

"Yeah, I know him. There's about a million of him." He made a quick gesture with his hand at the two nearest me, and they came toward me. They were younger than me, and faster, but I had three advantages: I was making the first move, I'd done two tours in Nam, and I had a backup I trusted.

The first one, a heavyset kid in a checked shirt, lowered his head and charged. I stepped into him, doubled my fists together, and nailed him on the side of the head so hard he went right to the floor and stayed there. The second one came on in a boxing stance with his head well back. I raised my own fists, let him get to arm's length, and floored him with a quick front kick to the groin.

A sharp blow caught me on my bad shoulder, knocking me back against a pool table. I looked around; the bearded one was raising his pool cue above his head for a second shot. I couldn't move quickly enough to avoid the blow, but I got close enough that it only glanced off my good shoulder. I gave him a hard elbow in the ribs and a short right to the stomach, neither of which had any effect. He reached toward his belt and I pinned his arm with my left.

"Whatever you've got there, don't try it," I said. He grunted and kept trying to get his hand free. In a straightforward wrestling match, his right against my left, he had the advantage.

As we struggled I felt another pair of hands grab me by my bad right shoulder. My arm went numb. They felt my .357 and began to go for it. I turned my head; it was another of the bikers. There was no way to deal with him without letting go of the leader. The most I could do was try to turn away and drop my shoulder to protect the gun; it made his job more difficult, but it was only a question of time. I couldn't see his face, but there were prison tattoos on his hands. His right inched inside my jacket and onto the pistol grip.

The biker leaned heavily against me and I began to fall backward; then I realized his grip had gone slack and he was limp. I took a step back, and he fell to the floor in a heap. Kate was standing behind him, the butt of a pool cue protruding from her fists.

My grip on the bearded one's arm had loosened when I stepped back, and now he had his hand on some kind of weapon—gun, knife, or razor, I didn't know. I stepped into him, hooked my leg around his knee, and pushed forward. He went down on his back with me on top. He landed hard, but he was still full of fight. I tried banging the back of his head on the floor with my right while trying to keep his weapon arm pinned with my left, but I couldn't exert enough force to control him. Then something hit me hard just behind my ear; one of the women had kicked me with her cowboy boots. I heard a thunk, saw the toes tilt, and then she fell limply on top of us. She landed mostly on my left side, which helped keep his weapon arm pinned.

Time wasn't on my side; I was hurt and starting to tire. It was time for a calculated risk. Letting go with my left, I pushed myself up a couple of inches and went for my gun. My hand found the grip and whipped it out before my own weight could pull me back down. I had barely enough clearance between him and me to draw it. It wound up pointed directly into his right eye, with the muzzle brushing his eyelashes. "Show's over, buddy."

He didn't give me any argument.

I shoved the limp body of the girl off me and slowly stood up. Kate stood behind me and to one side, the cue across her chest. She didn't look at me. He entire attention was focused on the other people in the room.

I took my time getting my breath. No one rushed me. I kept the gun leveled at the man on the floor.

"What's your name?" I asked when I felt like talking again.

"Barton. Jack Barton."

"I'm looking for someone. You ready to help now?"

He stared into the muzzle. "Whatever you say, mister."

"They guy I want hangs with a girl, about twenty-three, twenty-five. Her name is Amy Chadwick, but she may be using an alias. She's on the short side, thin, with reddish blond hair. She's from this area originally."

"What do you want with this guy?"

"I want to talk to him."

"You here to take him in?"

"Nope."

"You kidding about that?"

I kneeled down and put the muzzle against his cheek. "I told you once already. I'm not going to play twenty questions with you, asshole."

"Okay, okay, just let me up."

I backed off. "Come up slow and keep the hands high."

"Let's go over to the corner. I want to talk private."

We sat down at a table across from each other. Kate stood behind him with the pool cue. The girl she'd knocked out lay where she'd fallen. The others moved to the far end of the bar and left us alone.

"Let's have it, Jack."

"You sent by the Chadwicks?"

"Yeah."

"By the father or the mother?"

"What's that got to—"

"Oh, Jesus," Kate said.

I looked up at her. "What's the matter?"

She put her hands down so that the tip of the cue touched the floor. "If I'm right," she whispered, "We've solved half the case." She looked at Barton. When she spoke, her tone was sharp. "You're in deep shit, buddy, and you've got one chance to stay clear of a fall for extortion, theft by deception, and maybe even a federal rap. Ever hear of the Mann Act?"

He twisted his head around to stare at her. "Huh?"

"Transporting a female across state lines in furtherance of a crime. You brought her here from out of state, right?"

"Sure—but, hey, *she* brought *me*. You got this ass-backwards, honey. You can't—" Kate grabbed him by the back of his collar, jerked him backwards, and rapped him on the back of his head with the butt of the cue so hard that I winced.

"Call me 'honey' one more time and I'll shove this thing up your ass!" His head rolled and for a moment I thought she'd knocked him out. Then his eyes focused. He couldn't turn to look at her, but he nodded to me and swallowed. "Yes, ma'am."

She kept her grip on the back of his collar so that the front dug into the fleshy part of his neck. "I've got one question for you. If you answer right, you walk. Tell me everything you know about the Chadwicks."

"Okay. I'm the guy you're looking for. I met her, like three, four years ago. We got a place in Indiana. I got my own rig now; I'm leased on with an outfit in Illinois. After we're together a while she tells me her folks are really loaded. I don't know whether she's kidding or not. I mean, she never sees them. Anyway, she decides she wants to buy a house. We've got some money saved, but we need another ten grand—"

"Ten? Not forty?"

"No, lady. Ten. No bullshit."

Kate looked at me, but I still wasn't getting it. "Okay," she said. "Keep talking."

He swallowed again; it looked like Kate was choking him pretty tightly. "Work is real slow this time of year, and my truck needed a lot of work. So we dropped it off and came out here. I went to see her parents. She wasn't kidding; they really are her folks, and they're really rolling in it. I told them I could bring her to them for ten thousand. Her mom wanted to go for it, but her dad got pissed and throwed me out."

"But then her mom called you and said she'd get the money."

"Candy—that's the name she uses now—had to get on the phone and prove to her that she was her daughter. She fed her mom a line of b.s. about what she'd been doing. Anyway, once her mom was sure it was her, she agreed to pony up."

"Did you get it yet?"

"You think we'd be here if we did?"

"When did you talk to her last?"

"Couple of days ago. She said she'd have it real soon, but she wouldn't say when. When you guys came in I thought that you might be the bagmen, but you weren't."

"Do you know how to get hold of Mrs. Chadwick?"

He looked blank. "I could call her, I guess. But she said not to call the house."

Kate looked at me when she asked the next question. "Where do you think she is?"

"Home, I guess. She said she'd be the one to get in touch when she had the money."

"Last question. Where's Amy?"

He smiled a little. "You should know, lady; you laid her out yourself."

Kate let go of his collar and the two of us went back to the scene of the fight. The girl was wearing a black T-shirt with some kind of heavy-metal band logo, and blue jeans. Her hair was long, straight, and black. Somebody had propped her up against the pool table, but she was still out. I threw a half-empty glass of beer into her face, and her head began to move.

Kate picked up some of the girl's hair. "It's a dye job," she said. "The hair's black, but the eyebrows are blond. And look up at the roots; the blond is starting to come through again."

"I never could figure why a woman would want to keep it dark," Jack philosophized. Kate turned to him. "Beat it. We've got business with her."

"She's my wife. Common law, at least."

"We've got business with your wife then. So fuck

off.'' She raised the cue slightly. He vanished in the direction of the bar.

''I don't know,'' I said. ''This girl's hair is straight; Anne's is curly.''

''Anne has a perm, you idiot. And besides, look how light her skin is. It's her.''

I patted the girl on the cheek. ''Amy, wake up. We're from your parents.''

Her eyes opened. For a moment, until she fully woke up, they were perfectly ordinary dark eyes. Then they focused, and I knew she was Anne's daughter. They burned, just like her mother's.

''My name's Candy. Who are you?''

''My name is Dave and this is Kate.''

''But who are you?''

''We're not government. We're not here to give you any trouble.''

She looked at Kate. ''Ha. Except for knocking me out.''

By way of an answer, Kate stepped on Amy's hand. ''Ouch! Okay, okay, I guess I had it coming.'' Kate shifted her weight but kept the hand pinned.

I touched the side of her nose and turned her until she was facing me. ''The scam is dead. The only question is whether you and your boyfriend take a fall for attempt. Play ball with us and we walk out of here without you.''

''You can't make me do anything.''

''No, but there's a lot of shit going on around here; we throw enough of it at the wall, and something will stick. You clean with the IRS? Are you or your sweetie breaking parole by being in Pennsylvania? Any warrants out on either of you? Think that the Pennsylvania State Police would be interested in your little ploy? Your dad's got some political connections—maybe the FBI would decide that what you're doing is racketeering. You get the drift?''

She was made of sterner stuff than her boyfriend, or husband, or whatever he was. ''Twirl on it.''

''Let me talk to her,'' Kate said. She got down on her knees and put down the cue. ''Look, you think you're misunderstood? Not that it's any of your business, but I wrote the book. Do you remember me?''

''Remember you?'' Behind the dark eyes the wheels were turning. She didn't recognize Kate at all, but she was playing for time, trying to calculate if there was an advantage in saying that she did.

''It doesn't matter. I'll talk and you listen. Just tell me when I get too far off the beam.'' Amy just looked at her.

''You couldn't stand your dad. He never paid attention to you unless it was to get you out of trouble, and once you were in the clear he forgot about you again. Your mom just tried to stay out of the way. She spent her life waiting on him.''

''She didn't want to live the way she did; she just didn't have the guts to be bad.''

''But you did. You were smart enough to work the system and to get away with not studying because you could cram at the last minute and still get good grades. But every chance you got you cut school and forged excuses and shoplifted at the mall.''

Amy brushed the hair away from her face. ''Oh, man, you don't know the half of it.''

''Maybe not. So there were boys and dope and beer, too. Am I getting warmer?''

''Try truckers and quick tricks and you'd be there.''

''So talk to me.''

''School was the pits. I started cutting and hanging around pool halls, bowling alleys, anyplace grown up. I met men instead of boys, men who went out every day and made money and did whatever they pleased. Truckers. Construction workers. Men who didn't have to go to school for twenty years to know how to make a living, and who didn't have to kiss ass the way my father did. And if one of them liked me, he said so. If I told him to screw off, he did. And if I told him I liked him back, we knew where we stood. It was simple and not complicated and I liked it that way.

''I was dating this wimpy guy to please my parents. I talked him into taking me here. The minute we walked in I knew I'd made a mistake. One of the guys called him out and he went, like a jerk. He did pretty good, but the other guy was too tough. I watched him get beat up. And, you know, watching it, this biker beating up this straight-arrow high school guy, it turned me on. That's when I knew. I found a trucker heading west who was about my size. I traded him some dope for his change of clothes, then I cut up my stuff and burned it by the side of the road."

"Is that they guy you're with now?"

"Nah. I've hung with a bunch of different guys. Jack's lasted the longest, though. He's not the brightest, but he'll listen to a good idea."

"Like this with your parents?"

"Nah. He thought this was dumb; I had trouble getting him to go along with it. I mean about other things. Like, when I met him he was driving for somebody else. I hooked a little and hustled some pills to the other drivers and got together enough money for a down payment on his own rig. I made him go out in every weather and take every job he could get. But now it's nearly paid off. Then we start saving for the next one, and we're on our way to having a trucking company of our own."

"Is that what you wanted the ten thousand for?"

She shook her head. "When I need to, I can sell enough pills and tricks for that. The ten's for a down payment on a house. I explained to Jack how living in a trailer is bullshit. They cost like a house and depreciate like a car. It's just another way the rich fuck over the working class."

"You wouldn't consider borrowing the ten from your parents."

"No way. Take a penny, I owe him. He never knew me. He never cared about me. I busted my butt trying to be the daughter he thought he had and I'm glad I quit. I'm not going to get into that again. I'd rather hook or deal for it; at least then I'm earning it."

"What about your mom?"

"When it comes to fooling herself she's worse than he is. You know, he's closer to the truth than she is when he thinks I'm dead. The daughter he thought he had is dead. But Mom, wow, she's got this weird fantasy that explains how I could have lived away from them all these years without getting in touch. She just can't face that I had the guts to leave, and she didn't."

"Maybe she stayed because of you kids."

"Maybe. And if she did, that was up to her. I never asked her to bury herself. I never even asked to be born. Don't try to lay that on me."

"What was supposed to happen?"

"When she had the money Jack was to arrange a meeting. He would pick up the cash and I would spend some time with her. An hour or two. I was thinking we should split once we had it, but Jack said she was paying for it, I ought to see her."

"What were you going to tell her?"

She shrugged. "Go along with her fantasy. Whatever she's been kidding herself with, I'd listen and play along. If it was that I'd been abducted by bikers, or hit on the head and lost my memory, fine. The one thing I was sure to say was that I didn't think I'd be comfortable coming home, blah, blah. Maybe send her a Christmas card with no return address each year."

"Why do you hate her so much?"

"Because she didn't have the guts to admit what she was, and because she tried to break me, too. We're just the same, her and me, only I got out."

"You have any idea where she is?"

She smiled unpleasantly. "So she took off? No shit! When?"

"She disappeared a couple of days ago. We thought it was a kidnapping at first. We got a demand for a forty-thousand-dollar ransom, then after we paid it, they decided they wanted another two hundred."

She whistled. "Either she's in deep shit or she came up with a hell of a lot more nerve than I ever thought she had."

"What do you think?"

"Haven't seen the woman in years. You've got me. Except that I'm sure it's nothing to do with Jack and me. We never made any calls like that, and our deal was strictly ten. That was the only number Jack and I ever talked about.''

I looked at Kate, who shook her head and shrugged. There was nothing more for us here. We stood up and made our way to the door. No one tried to stop us.

Kate and I got into my car. ''Still thinking about having kids?'' she asked.

''Not like her.''

''No, not like her.''

I could tell she was thinking about her own kids. I drove in silence and let her.

19

Thursday, 5:00 P.M.

Ted Grigg's house was easy to find, once you found his parents' house, that is. The main house was invisible from the road, hidden by a hill and a tall stand of pines. The day was overcast, and the light was starting to fail by the time we found the address. Snowflakes, gray in the half-light, fell gently on the windshield and melted.

Ted and his family lived in the northern part of the county, just behind a ridge overlooking a series of shallow valleys and the city of Lancaster. As we drove through the property I couldn't help thinking that someday this would be carved up into a hundred building lots, and my old ambivalence about the prospect came back to me. I could never decide whether allowing the land to remain pristine and beautiful, for the benefit of a few, was better than allowing a lot of people to benefit from it a little.

Ted lived in a surprisingly small stone farmhouse. A BMW was parked out front and white smoke poured from the chimney. "Jesus, Kate, take a breath. This guy is burning applewood."

"No Presto-logs for him. God damn but it's cold up here. How can anybody live in winters like this?"

"It's okay, the summers are too hot, too."

We went up two stone steps to a porch and knocked on the door. It opened almost immediately.

"Can I help you?" It was an impossibly polite voice for the middle of a snowstorm.

"Mr. Grigg?"

"That's right."

"I'm David Garrett, Mr. Grigg, and this is Kate McMahan."

He looked at my face. "You look like you've been in some sort of fight."

"Actually, we have. And it concerns someone you know."

"It does?"

"Yes, sir. Can we talk?"

"Well, come in out of the snow, won't you?"

We followed him through a foyer into a sitting room with a fireplace. The sweet, spicy smell of apple was powerful. He motioned us into seats by the fire and pulled over a chair for himself.

When I got a good look I wondered if there could be two Ted Griggs. I had in mind someone who could sweep a woman like Anne Chadwick off her feet. This one was pudgy and well on his way toward baldness. His movements were fussy and awkward; he reminded me of a slightly obese aunt of mine from New York.

"Well, what can I do for you, Mr. Garrett?"

"Just answer a few questions for us. It won't take long."

"About what?"

"Anne Chadwick."

"Bruce's wife?"

"Yes, the one with the scar on one tit. I'm sure you remember."

Everything about him stopped, down to his breathing. When he finally spoke again, it was a quiet, hard voice.

"Exactly who are you?"

"I'm a private detective. Ms. McMahan is assisting me. We've been hired to find out what happened to Anne Chadwick."

"What *are* you talking about?"

"She's missing, and we have reason to think she's been kidnapped."

"Oh, come on."

"We've already paid a preliminary ransom demand, and we're on our way to make the big payoff tonight."

He came to a full stop again, this one lasting even longer than the first. "Ransom? Twice?"

I suddenly didn't feel much like sharing information with him. I just nodded.

He looked from me to Kate and back. "If there's ransom, and a kidnapping, where are the police?"

"We've been hired to work on the case, Mr. Grigg. We'd like you cooperation."

"Are you police, or not?"

"I'm a private detective. As I said."

"I imagine you have some proof of that."

I gave him a folder that contained my detective's license and some of my business cards. He looked at my license carefully and handed it back, after taking out one of my cards. "May I keep this?"

"Certainly."

He looked at the door like he was trying to will us through it and out of his life. "What can I do to help?"

"How well did you know Anne?"

"What do you mean?" I just glared at him. "All right, then," he said. "I suppose you know about our relationship."

"It's not much of a secret."

"It happened years ago, right after she moved here. I was one of the first people she met. We met at a tennis tournament, playing mixed doubles. I fell very much in love with her. Any man would. At first it was great, but I wanted more than she wanted to give. I asked her to leave Bruce and marry me; she refused. I persisted. So she broke it off. It all happened within a few months."

"How often have you seen her since?"

"Every couple of months. If you move in certain circles in this town, your paths just have to cross."

"It must have been hard," Kate said.

"The first few times, it was impossible. Especially seeing her with Bruce—"

"Did he know?" she asked.

"I don't know. I don't think so. But it wasn't that, anyway, it was that she was with him and I was alone because I'd failed, somehow. That if I'd done it right she'd be with me.'' He took a breath and looked at the ceiling like it was the sky. ''But that was a long time ago.''

''Feelings die hard,'' she said. I wondered whose feelings she was talking about.

''Yes, but they do die, eventually. At first when I saw them it was awkward, but it passed. She and I haven't referred to it in—God, it must be five years now. Sometimes it seems like a movie, like it happened to someone else. I read a short story in *The New Yorker* last year that said, if you can remember what it was like to be in love with someone, you still are, because you can't remember a feeling the way you can remember facts. You either have the feeling, right now, or you don't—you can't call it up.''

''And you?'' she persisted.

He shook his head. ''There was a time afterwards when I must have still been in love with her, by that definition, but that stopped a long time ago. Actually, tonight is the first time I've thought about those days in a while; there's been a lot of water under the bridge.''

I decided to take back control of the questioning. ''You say you've seen them frequently over the years.''

''Oh, yes. Anne and I have served on a United Way committee for years, coordinating private fund-raising. We make a very good team that way; I know the people and make introductions, and she takes over and solicits donations. So during the drive, and the planning of it, we see each other once a week or once very other week. And I see just as much of Bruce, because I persuaded my parents to invest in Uncle Chan's, and we have strategy sessions about the business. I saw him just last Tuesday. I'm trying to stay out of the way with all the work going on with the opening, but normally we're in pretty close touch.''

''You're an investor?''

''Oh, not me, my parents. And not a large part—they cosigned a note so he could buy the real estate on Columbia Avenue, and in return they get five percent of the net proceeds. It was an accommodation to Bruce and Anne more than anything else.''

''Do you participate in the business?''

He giggled once. ''Lord, no. I don't even like Chinese food. Give me northern Italian or Mexican any day. And he has all the managerial and finanicial help he needs.''

''You go to the site often?''

''You mean, on Columbia Avenue?''

''Yes.''

''My parents and I went to the groundbreaking and had our pictures taken with Bruce and a shovel. We had a bottle of champagne. I haven't been back since, except to go to the open house Monday. We were invited, and anyway, I thought it was the right thing to do, show our support and all that.'' He folded his arms across his chest. ''Now listen, I've been very patient with all these questions. You're going to have to tell me what is going on. Is she all right? Why hasn't this been in the papers?''

''Because my client doesn't want it there. And as to whether she's all right, I don't know. We have no evidence she's been harmed. May I use your bathroom?''

''Oh, Certainly. Through the kitchen and to the right.''

I didn't need to use the bathroom, although I was careful to turn on the light and flush the toilet; mainly I wanted a couple of minutes for a quick tour of the downstairs. It yielded nothing of interest except that Ted kept a water pitcher full of vodka on the kitchen counter. Dinner was on the stove; unless he was a very light eater, which I doubted, there was only enough for one. No purses on the counter or lipsticks next to the sink.

''Mr. Grigg, where were you late Tuesday afternoon?''

''How late do you mean?''

''Just tell me what you did after noon on Tuesday, till six.''

''Tuesday? That was a busy day.''

"It's important you give me every bit of detail you can."

"Let me see. I went to the Hamilton Club and had lunch with my accountant—or the family accountant, actually. It's getting near tax time and we had business to discuss, about selling some stocks and realizing gain. That must have lasted till about one-thirty or two. Then I went to our travel agency and asked about flights to Aspen. We go every year for two weeks in early April. I don't know how long that took, perhaps half an hour or an hour. I did some shopping; it was Tuesday, and Central Market was open, so I bought fruit and vegetables and meat for dinner, then I went home and started dinner. I was up at the main house, and the dinner was for Mom and Dad and me. They came home around five-thirty or six, and we ate. I cleaned up the kitchen a bit and came back down here. That was probably about eight."

"So, we've got your accountant verifying where you were until one-thirty and your parents after six. Who can cover the time in between?"

He looked at me with new eyes. "You mean, I'm suspected?"

"You're not excluded, yet."

"Shouldn't I have my attorney advise me?"

I sidestepped the question. "We're not the police. If you have nothing to hide you should open up."

"Well, I certainly don't. Have anything to hide, I mean. All right, then, The travel agent has known me for ten years, and I always use the same standholders at the market; they've known me even longer." He gave me the names and I jotted them down.

"That takes us to three-thirty or four at the latest," I said.

"That's when I went home. I got gas at my regular station in Neffsville and I spoke to the owner. I remember that was a little after four. We talked about how it was an hour before five and yet the traffic was already getting heavy."

"Where is Neffsville?"

"About four miles from Lancaster. In winter, it's about ten minutes, give or take."

"And how far from there to your house?"

"At this time of the year, with some snow and ice, five to ten minutes."

"What did you make for dinner?" Kate asked.

"*Ropa vieja*. It's Cuban."

"So you got home at four-fifteen or so and then made dinner?"

"It was a rush job. My parents are old, and pretty set in their ways about eating. You know, anytime for dinner is fine, as long as it's between five-forty-five and six."

"Your parents like to eat pretty early."

"For years I've tried to talk them into a more reasonable hour, like seven or eight. But Dad always wanted to eat soon after he got home."

"Will they be home tonight?"I asked. "We'd like to be able talk to them and exclude you as a suspect."

"I'm not sure where Mom is, on errands, somewhere. You can reach Dad at the office right now if you want. But as soon as he and Mom get back they're going away for a few days to New York. They're part of a group that goes up to see plays every year. I'll be house-sitting at the main house while they're gone." He gave me his father's work number and the name of his secretary. "Is there anything more you need?"

"Yes, as a matter of fact. You wouldn't happen to know who killed Nancy Saunders, would you?"

"What's that got to do with Anne?"

"What do you know about it?"

"Just what I read in the papers. Are you investigating that, too?"

"We're interested in it, let's just say that."

"From what I read it sounded like a robbery."

"But nothing was taken."

"I just assumed that whoever did it got scared and ran. But she was nice. Who would want to hurt her?"

"How well did you know her?"

"Not very well. I'd see her at the country club in the summer, and the Hamilton Club once in a while;

they let her stay on under her husband's membership. I knew her daughter better, though.''

''Karen?''

''That's right. We went to Country Day together. We even dated back then, a while. I'll be going to the funeral, of course. It's tomorrow afternoon.''

''How well do you know Karen these days?''

''Oh, I see her once in a while. I saw more of her and her husband before the kids came along. It's been a long time since I've seen them.''

''Were you aware they were having marital troubles?''

''No. But I'm a little surprised to hear it. When they first got married they seemed very happy. Maybe having kids hasn't agreed with them.''

''How old are their kids?''

''I don't know, exactly. Their oldest daughter must be eight of ten by now. It's a girl, I remember because I went to pick out a present at Appel and Webber. There's another child, I don't know if it's a boy or a girl, a couple of years younger.''

''You know their names?''

''No. Is that important to solving Nancy's case?''

''The names, no. But your knowing might be. Do you know of a Larry Bonner?''

''Not that I can think of.''

''He works for Bruce's restaurant.''

He put his hand to his chin. ''A young fellow with blond hair?''

''That's him.''

''I think I remember someone named Bonner that Bruce introduced me to, an accountant or something. He wasn't from around here. I can't recall the first name at all.''

''Did you meet him more than once?''

''If I did I don't recall.'' His eyes narrowed. ''Say, is he the reason Karen is having trouble with her husband?''

''We don't know for sure. All we have is rumors. And we'd appreciate it if you'd keep it to yourself.''

''Well, all I can say is, I'm not surprised.''

My pulse quickened. Perhaps, after all the blind alleys, I was getting a bit of luck. "How do you mean? I thought you said they seemed happy."

"Yes, but—meeting Jack, you always had a feeling about him."

"What?"

"That—well, that he swung both ways. So I can't say I'm surprised if he's taken up with another man."

I shut my eyes. The case was slipping away from me, just one more piece of flotsam on an ocean of small-town society. Could this possibly have a connection to Anne's kidnapping and Nancy's murder? Was I sure that it didn't?

"Did her husband ever make a pass at you?"

"No, not at all. I'm perfectly straight, personally. It was just a feeling I had about him, that he would have been receptive."

"Did Karen ever say anything to you?"

"No, hardly. If you asked me to guess, I'd say that she was interested in gardening, horses, big outdoor parties, going to the shore, and sex, strictly in that order."

"We've heard some rumors that she doesn't put sex so far down the list."

He shrugged and gestured at the window. "Well, one has to do *something* in the winter."

We thanked him for his time, and left.

20

Thursday, 7:00 P.M.

I drove away from Grigg's house slowly. Neither of us spoke until we were back on the main road.

"Well," I said, "whatever else we learned, or didn't learn, at least we can be sure that he's not a suspect."

"I was just thinking the opposite."

"Ted? He's halfway to fat, and nearly bald. He probably wears plastic shoes so he won't be responsible for any cows suffering. Not exactly my idea of a murderous kidnapper."

"One step at a time."

"I'm listening."

"Let's assume the kidnapping is staged."

"Why, exactly?"

"Because Anne needed money."

"She needed ten, not forty."

"Well, it's a reason."

"If she wanted out so much she could have divorced him and taken him for half of what he's worth. That would be a quarter of a million, half a million."

"Maybe that's the long-range plan," Kate said. "But it would take time; she wants it right now. You're assuming she doesn't intend to do both. Maybe a disappearance for a while now and a divorce later."

"You get any sense from Bruce, or her, that she could hate him that much?"

"No, but let's assume, all right?"

"Go on."

"She has to have an accomplice. To make the phone calls and pick up the ransom, maybe do other things. Maybe the accomplice did everything at the restaurant, too—"

"You think they're connected?" I asked.

"I'm guessing they are, that everything at Uncle Chan's was a preliminary."

"Why?"

"Well, they want the police kept out. If they tied the whole thing to the possibility of adverse publicity to the business, Bruce would be less likely to tell anyone. And they were right."

"Okay, so get back to the accomplice," I said.

"Ted isn't anyone Anne would run off with. I have trouble imagining her having an affair with him, except that it was years ago and maybe he was more attractive then. But anyway, he was in love with her; she could have manipulated him into helping her."

" 'Could have' and a quarter gets you a cup of coffee. And anyway, he's got an alibi for the ransom pickup. He was home cooking. And he wouldn't have given me his father's number if he didn't know Dad would back him up on the time they eat."

"Maybe he wasn't home cooking."

"Go on."

"I'm from Miami. That dish he mentioned, *ropa vieja*? It's spicy Cuban beef stew. You can make it hours ahead of time and let it simmer. You can make it the day before and reheat it—and it's better that way, to tell the truth."

"But he said he bought the food at market late in the afternoon, and that he was still ten minutes from home a little after four."

"We have no way of knowing if the food from the market went into the *ropa vieja* they ate that night. He could have made it the day before, bought the food for a second batch, and trashed it."

"So after he gets gas in his car at four he rolls back into town in time to make the pickup, then goes home, heats up the stew, and he's in business."

"You got it," she said.

"I'll give you a maybe. But all we really have is that his alibi isn't tight. What's yours for four-thirty Tuesday, by the way?"

"Uh—I was reading in my room."

"Anybody see you?"

"I got a book from the library after lunch and read straight through till dinner."

"So, did anybody see you?"

"Jeremy stopped by to see if I wanted a drink."

"What time?" I persisted.

"Actually, it was around four-thirty. I remember 'cause I told him I didn't drink before five. We made a little joke of it. So he brought me a big gin and tonic right at five."

"So either you're in the clear, or you and Jeremy are in this up to your necks."

"I see what you mean."

"If I were Anne, and I needed muscle, I wouldn't go to Ted."

"Muscle?"

"Think about it. The more we think that everything that's happened is the work of one person, the more it points away from Ted. Do you see him pulling off all of the sabotage at Uncle Chan's, and shooting at me, let alone the ransom demands and the pickups?"

"Then do you think Bonner's involved?" she asked.

"You know that old saw about once you have motive and opportunity, you have the criminal? Well, I tried criminal cases for ten years, and it's nonsense. Lots of people have opportunity to commit crimes, and lots of people have motive. What separates the ones who go on to do it from those who don't is—well, I'll call it attitude. Not just that they have some reason to kill their spouse—everybody does, but most of us don't do it. It's how they feel, what's important to them."

"Isn't motive and attitude the same thing?"

"No. Motive just means you did something for a reason, instead of at random. If I steal from my employer they say I had a motive: I wanted the money so I'd be richer. But, hell, that only explains why I stole money instead of stealing used toilet paper. Finding motive is backward looking. They look at the crime, say there must have been a motive, look around till they find a logical reason, and call that a motive."

"Okay. And what's attitude, then?"

"Attitude is the reason most employees don't steal from their employers, given the opportunity, every day. Most of the time it's the reason crimes *aren't* committed. I work for somebody for six months and each day I have a chance to palm a twenty out of the register, but I don't. Then one day I'm pissed at the boss or even at somebody else, and I do it. The twenty isn't worth any more or less than the day before. So why that day?"

"So how does that help us right now?"

"If I knew where to look, this case is ready to be solved."

"You mean, whose attitude you need to look at?"

"Right."

"My guess would be Bonner," she said.

"And why do you say that?"

"Because the victim is a woman, and Bonner hates women. He's just enough of a cold SOB to do it, too."

But Bonner wasn't at Chadwick's when we got back; Jeremy said he'd left about five-thirty. We tried calling his apartment but there was no answer.

We learned from Jeremy that his father and Mosier were out. He didn't say, but I assumed it had to do with the ransom money. The three of us fixed ourselves some sandwiches and settled down to wait.

"Are you going to get her back safe this time, Mr. Garrett?"

"I hope so. We have no reason to think she's been harmed."

"That wouldn't be very smart of them, would it?"

"No. Your mother is safe if she can't identify them. She's not a threat. If they're smart, they have her blindfolded, or in a dark room, or they wear ski masks. If they do any of those things they can safely let her go."

"But if by accident she saw their faces—"

"That's right. I'm counting on these people not making any mistakes."

"Why?"

"Because they haven't made any so far. Not a one."

"You really think so?"

"If they've made any, I've missed them."

Jeremy got up to clear the dishes, and Kate leaned closer to me. "That kid gives me the creeps," she whispered.

"How so?"

"I've got two kids around his age; he acts closer to fifteen than twenty-one."

"He doesn't get much attention."

"Are you agreeing with me or offering an excuse?"

"Both. And who gives you the creeps more, him or Bonner?"

"Bonner," she admitted. "Jeremy's just a little screwed up."

Before I could answer, Chadwick came through the door. Mosier was trailing behind him, carrying a briefcase. The look on his face told me what was in it. He set it down on the kitchen table but kept his hand on the grip.

Chadwick stood to one side, looking uncomfortable. "Hi, Dave, Kate." His voice was thin. He was dying to know about Amy.

"We have some new information," I said. "It's family stuff, and I'm not sure it has any bearing on Anne's case. Could we speak to you alone, Bruce?"

"None of that," Mosier said. "Anything that could possibly have to do with this"—he hefted the case—"is said in front of me."

I don't know what I was about to say, but Kate kicked me under the table and gave me a shut up look. "What we found," she said, "confirmed what you told us about Ted. There was an affair, years ago, when the two of you first moved here. She broke it off when he started getting serious." Mosier looked uncomfortable, which made me feel just fine. "He says there's been nothing physical between them in a long time."

Hearing Kate tell the story made me think about what Ted had said. Something about it sounded funny. Not wrong, just . . . funny, and I couldn't put my finger on it. "He has an alibi for the first ransom pickup, but it's not airtight."

"Well, it happened a long time ago," Bruce tried to sound matter-of-fact and fell very short. When he was under stress, I noticed, his voice faded to almost nothing. "Well, what about Amy?"

He was looking at me, but I caught Kate mouthing "no" at me. I lifted an empty cup to my lips to gain time, and Kate jumped in. "We asked around at the bar; it was quiet. The bartender said the weekend would be the best time to get information. So we didn't learn anything new."

"I didn't think you would, but thanks for trying."

I stood up, not so much at the time as to get out of there before he started asking questions that would trip us up. "You'll have to excuse me now; I have to get ready to deliver the money."

Chadwick looked at me. He said, "Dave," and stopped, but I knew what was coming.

I tried not to let my feelings show. "Yes?"

"I've given this a lot of thought." He looked at Mosier, who looked blank. "I don't want you to think I don't have every confidence in you, because I do. But I want to come along. What's happening tonight is important. It might make the difference in whether I ever see Anne again. I couldn't live with myself if I just stayed home at the phone. You've done a great job, both of you, in handling my problems for me. Now it's time for me to pull my own load."

"I know how you feel. Anybody would. But this is going to be . . . unpredictable. I don't know how it's going to go down. The one thing I'm sure of is that somebody out there wants serious money, and they're playing rough."

"All the more reason I should be in on this."

"I need someone here at the phones I can trust."

He shook his head. "Sorry, Dave, I don't buy that. Jeremy will be home if you want."

"I wanted somebody a little more responsible holding the fort."

"Kate will be home, and besides, the action is going to be downtown. There is no fort. Whatever the message will be, it will be."

"If there's a message at all," said Mosier, looking at his hands. "This may be another way to string us along some more."

This time is was even harder to keep my feelings out of my voice. "Mr. Mosier, I'm trying not to get your favorite franchisee killed. Who's side are you on?"

"Alone is not the way to do this. You almost got killed walking around the backyard by yourself in broad daylight," Mosier pointed out. "If Bruce wants to go, I say we go."

"You, too?"

"I've got to explain to corporate exactly what happened to their two hundred grand. If the shit hits the fan I'd rather be able to say that I was on the spot instead of home jerking off in front of the TV."

"They were pretty cooperative about the money."

"He is their favorite franchisee. And this is big business. Putting up, say, a half-dozen restaurants runs eight million bucks, including soft costs. The two hundred is more of a cash flow problem than anything else."

Knowing where the money came from, I couldn't help thinking that Mosier's words were more true than he realized. I looked around to make sure Jeremy hadn't drifted back into the room. "Do you realize how dangerous this is? We have no assurance that they'll let her go, or that they haven't killed her already. We're walking up to a bunch of felons in the dark with two hundred thousand dollars and no police backup."

It was Chadwick who spoke next. "Well, then, how about there being safety in numbers?" His voice was brittle and I could see a tremor in his right hand.

"The more people they see the more threatened they'll feel, and the more dangerous they'll be."

"So we take a van and Bob and I stay in the back."

"I recommend against it. Very strongly."

"Fine. We appreciate your concern. But we're going."

I looked from one to the other. "You don't have to prove anything to me, either one of you."

Neither one of them answered.

"Shit. Okay, then, here are the ground rules. You two stay in the back. When we get close, you get down on the floor. No lights, no cigarettes, no talking. Stay put unless I call for help. If I do call, don't get out. Stay in the van. Does it have a car phone?"

"All our cars do," Chadwick said.

"Then just dial nine-one-one and tell them it's a police emergency. Stay inside till they get there. Got it?"

Mosier nodded at once; Chadwick looked glum, but gave his assent.

I went back to my room for my own preparations. I stripped off my suit and changed into jeans and tennis shoes. My feet would be cold, but I wanted to move as quietly as possible. I pulled out a Kevlar vest from my luggage and slipped it on. I didn't have a lot of faith in the things. They didn't help against a shot to the head, and they could be defeated by Teflon bullets. They needed special care, and they wore out gradually, just like clothes. Even though they were supposed to perform better than the flak jackets we'd used in Nam, I missed the bulky reassurance of the old ones. My own vest was a used one. I could never remember if the brand name was Second Chance or Second Choice. Something like that, anyway.

I put on an oversize sweatshirt to hide the outline of the vest, and then a shoulder holster. I'd never worn the holster over the vest before, and I couldn't get the adjustments right. Finally I threw it down on the bed and put my gun in a holster on my left hip. I put on my parka and checked in the mirror; there was a slight bulge, but the gun itself was hidden. I stuffed an extra pair of gloves into the right pocket to make it about equally bulky.

We went back to Chadwick's office, where Mosier had the briefcase waiting. The two hundred thousand dollars was in hundred-dollar bills, neat rows of them tightly packed. I picked up the case and turned it upside down, showering packets of bills over the desk top.

"Hey," Mosier said. "What're you doing?"

I shook the case until it was empty, then felt around the inside pockets. "Just taking care. I wanted to be sure that somebody didn't decide to get cute and put some kind of gimmick inside. Like a smoke bomb, or an alarm, or one of those things that explodes dye. The kind of clever little thing that would wind up getting me killed if they want me to open the case for them." I looked at the two of them as I said it, and both of them gave me the same startled, dumb look. Either I'd given them way too much or way too little credit.

I repacked the case, not bothering to count the bundles. The count would be close enough for my purposes, even if it wasn't exact.

We went back to the kitchen. Kate was sitting at the table with a book in front of her, but she didn't seem to be paying much attention. Then I noticed that she was sitting facing the window and all the outside floodlights were on. "Kate, we're going now."

"You've got almost half an hour." She didn't bother to look at her watch.

"I'd just as soon be there first, if I can."

"I'd like to be in on this."

Finally I'd found someone I could say no to. "Sorry, I need someone responsible back here. Call the police if there's any trouble. Don't mention Anne and us unless you have to. You have the number of the phone in the van?"

"Sure do."

I tried one last time to ditch my companions. "Feel like you'd like to have someone with you?"

"Once you go I'll kill the inside lights and wait. I'll be fine. Can I talk to you a minute, Dave?"

"Sure."

She led me around the corner, down the hall, and put her arms around me. "David, please be careful," she whispered.

"I'll do my best."

"Don't take any chances, all right? I want you back here in one piece."

I kissed her. "I'll keep that in mind."

The van was out front; under the glare of the floodlights I could see that it was painted the green and yellow of the franchise, with UNCLE CHAN'S CHINESE in foot-high letters on the sides. A yellow fiberglass takeout food box, two feet high and three feet long, was on the roof.

"I'm glad I'm not driving anything conspicuous." They both looked at me blankly. "Get into the back and sit on the floor."

21

Thursday, 10:00 P.M.

As we neared the garage I checked my watch; we had almost twenty minutes to go. I drove slowly down North Duke Street, passing by the library, the city hall, and the courthouse. When we crossed over King Street the road became South Duke. One the left was a church with a shallow front lawn, well lit by streetlights, and a fairly tall iron fence. No one hiding there. On the right was a series of row houses converted to offices. I counted half a dozen doorways, but as I rolled past, each one was empty. The last one was the law office Kate and I had visited the day before.

Just past the lawyers' was a brick-and-concrete square, at least four stories high. "That's it," Chadwick whispered. "That's the entrance ramp for the garage."

There was a traffic light in the middle of the block, just before the turn-in to the garage, and fortunately for me it was red. I sat there, thinking about my next move. The entrance was dark, and the ramp sloped steeply up. If I took the van up the ramp, getting out would be tough if someone disabled it or blocked us in. Two men with cars could make prisoners of all of us without firing a shot. I didn't like it. When the light changed I pulled to the curb and stopped. The sign said NO PARKING. I tried not to let it bother me.

I turned to Chadwick. "Is there any other way up into this garage?"

"There's another ramp on the King Street side, but they both meet on the second floor."

I looked at the blackness beyond the start of the

ramp. It bothered me in a way I couldn't put my finger on. "What about lighting?"

"There's lots of light on the inside once you get upstairs. At least there is when they're open. They close at seven."

For nearly ten minutes I waited. Only a few cars went past, and no pedestrians at all. Seeing a Lancaster city police cruiser, I couldn't decide whether to feel better or worse. I didn't have to decide; he made the light at the end of the block and disappeared up a hill.

After telling them yet again to stay put and keep out of sight, I got out and walked slowly around the block. It was absolutely quiet, except at the rare moments when a car went by. Once I heard a siren, faint and far away, but it didn't come any closer. Somebody else's trouble, going on somewhere else.

I kept my hands out of my pockets and tried to be as inconspicuous as a man can be in the middle of a freezing night on a deserted street. I couldn't be sure the kidnappers knew me by sight, although my romp in the backyard the day before made it a safe bet. Still, it was dark, and perhaps the lookouts might not make me. I studied the store windows, all dark, and watched for tracks in the snow. The city, or whoever did the sidewalks, was too damned efficient; the concrete was bare except for the garage entrance, where it was several inches deep in ruts that had frozen over.

The garage covered a quarter of the block. I found the other vehicle ramp Chadwick had mentioned, and two fire exits. Both were locked from the outside. I assumed they would open from the inside—but then again, since the garage was closed, maybe Labor & Industry allowed everything to be locked tight. There were times when you wished you knew the damndest little things, especially when they might save your life.

The first floor was solid block, but above that, the walls were pierced by many dim lights. After a moment I realized what it was; either the masonry blocks were hollow core, or the bricks were arranged in a staggered pattern. Either way, the walls were pierced with hundreds of holes. Ventilation for the car exhausts, I figured. I didn't like that part of it, either. Someone inside had a thousand windows to look out, or shoot out, and from the outside I couldn't see a damned thing.

I got back to the van and walked around the street side, away from the garage. Chadwick popped a side window. "You okay, Dave?"

"Fine. Didn't see a thing, though. The garage could be empty or the First Airborne could be up there."

"This is the place, you know."

I stifled an impulse to say the first thing that came to mind; his nerves were as bad as mine. Instead, I opened the driver's door and took out the briefcase. I hesitated before coming out from behind the van. I knew why. I was postponing the start of it. When I was a kid, at the end of the high dive, I did the same thing. Looking for something more to do, something to say to someone, that would put off the moment when I had to jump off into nothing. Combat was the same way, and trials, too. *Right now I'm safe. But not if I move.* Then I made the connection. The ramp, the entrance to the path. The black hole I'd been avoiding for twenty years, and now it was time to stick my head into it.

I held the briefcase in my left hand and stepped around the front of the van. No one was in sight, but that meant nothing. I crossed the sidewalk and stood at the bottom of the ramp. A streetlight reflecting off the snow gave me enough light to see the slope of the ramp, but no more.

I unbuttoned my coat and shook it so it hung freely. Reaching inside, I unsnapped the fastener on my holster and made sure I could make a clean grab for the gun if I needed to. Then I started up, slowly, keeping near the left-hand wall, away from the light. All I could hear was my own breathing and an occasional soft noise when I stepped on a piece of slush.

The ramp was steep, and long, I was sweating when I reached the top, but not all of it was from the climb. Ahead of me the ramp cut left and broadened into the first parking level of the garage. A few banks of fluorescent lights were on, but many more were out. Directly in front of me was a darkened ticket booth. I didn't waste much time looking there; it wasn't much of a place to hide. The door was padlocked, and it was directly under a bank of lights.

I looked to my left, down the rows of empty parking spaces to the ramp that led up to the second level. I started walking, keeping to the left and staying in the shadows as much as possible. My feet crackled on the road salt, and the thin, brittle sound echoed off the concrete walls.

I turned the corner and looked up at the second level. It was sloped upwards, with the same intermittent lighting as the first level. A car was parked about thirty yards away, in the shadows between two banks of lights. I ducked back behind the corner pillar.

"Come out where I can see you." The voice was amplified, but not loud. And it didn't seem to be coming from the car.

"Where is she?" I yelled back.

"Where's the money?"

"I've got it. Let's see her."

"She's not here."

"How do I know you've got her?"

"Come out from there."

"Bullshit," I yelled back. "Tell me where she is."

"Come out," the voice repeated.

We had to talk, and trusting each other has to start somewhere. After all, if he was looking to pick me off, he could have done it earlier just as easy. I stepped out into view and held the briefcase away from my side. My right hand was clear of my body; but if he was looking closely he would have seen that I kept it at waist level, ready to move.

"Put down the briefcase."

"Tell me where to find her. Or when you'll let her go."

"She'll be home tomorrow morning." I looked to the source of the sound and saw a small dark box on the concrete over against the far wall. A wire ran back to the car. A speaker.

"How do I know that?"

"You don't"

"No deal. We've been jerked around before."

A harsh, broken noise came from the speaker; after a moment I realized it was a laugh. "Don't tell me about deals. What do you think he's going to say if you go back down and tell him you brought back the money?"

I bluffed. "That's just what I'm going to do if you don't give me some assurance she's safe."

"Oh, she is, believe me. Safe as safe can be. That's as much as you're getting. Now put it down and back off."

If it was my own money, I wouldn't have left it for someone else's wife on nothing more than a kidnapper's promise. But it wasn't my money, or my wife. I put the case down and backed up till I was nearly to the corner.

"Stop there," he said.

A bulky figure wearing dark clothes and a ski mask emerged from behind the car. It was a man, and he had a pistol in his hand, but that was all I could tell. "Get your hands up."

I raised them slightly, spread wide apart but not high, just a little above my waist."

"Get them up, goddammit!" he yelled. The noise echoed around the garage. His voice was cracking, and even at twenty yards I could see the tremor in his gun hand. I raised them all the way, touching the low ceiling.

For a moment he didn't move; then he came toward me in a sudden, awkward rush. I thought he was coming for me, but then he stopped at the briefcase, kept the gun on me with one hand, and snapped the briefcase up with the other. The gun was steady now, and pointed right at my face. It looked like a .45 automatic. At that range, even a graze would floor me, and a solid hit would blow out the back of my head. I fought the urge to close my eyes and looked at him instead, trying to make eye contact. Even with his features obscured by the ski mask, I could see his fear. He was more frightened than I was, which made him all the more dangerous. And as I looked at him, a thought, a connection, began forming. Some part of my mind knew who it was.

The roar of a gunshot close by struck my ears and reverberated off the walls. For a crazy second I thought I was dead; then I saw that he hadn't fired at all. He swung his gun to my left, fired once blindly, and started running back toward his car. I hit the floor hard, rolled to my right, and kept on rolling until I fetched up against a concrete pillar. As quickly as I could I twisted around to the far side and drew my gun.

The kidnapper was nowhere in sight. Possibly he was behind the car, maybe farther away. Maybe in the shadow of any of the dozens of pillars. Wherever he was, he had a gun and wasn't afraid to use it. I pulled back to the far side of the pillar and looked to my left. Huddled behind a steel guardrail at the turn between the first and second floors was Chadwick, holding a nickel-plated revolver. It glittered foolishly under the fluorescent lights.

"Bruce! Get back from there! The gun he's got will go right through that railing!"

"Where is she?"

"He hasn't said yet. Just that she's safe."

"When will we get her back?"

"I don't know! We didn't get that far before you started shooting."

"I thought he was going to shoot you."

"I thought you were going to stay in the van."

"I can't leave this alone."

"You're not helping. He wasn't going to shoot."

"It looked that way to me."

"I could see his eyes. And anyway, he could have dropped me anything he wanted to. Now get out of there. Every surface in this place will make ricochets. If you're gut shot by a flattened round it's not going to be pretty."

He stood up, but only to shield himself behind a pillar. "You up there!" he yelled. "Tell me where she is! You can keep the money."

I heard a soft sound from behind the car, then footsteps moving rapidly away. I looked at Chadwick, gesturing for him to stay down, but it was no use. He was already swinging around the corner and running after the kidnapper. I had no choice but to cover him, but when I stuck out my head, all I could see was a glimpse of the kidnapper rounding the turn onto the next level up. I stepped out and began to run.

"Bruce, let me do this!" But he paid no attention. I was faster, but his head start allowed him to beat me to the car. I caught up to him before we got to the turn to the next level and pulled him to a stop. Then I dragged him back into a far corner and put my face near his. "Bruce," I whispered. "You're going to get us both killed! Now do this my way."

"We've got to get him. He may be the only one who knows where she is."

"Bruce, for the last time, you do this my way or I'm going to shoot you in the fucking leg, right here."

His eyes widened at the words, and then even further when he saw that I wasn't kidding. "Okay."

"I'll go after him if you insist. You can back me up. But if we're going to do this, let me go first. I'll tell you when I want you to move. Just stay behind me."

"Got it."

I crawled up to the turn for the third floor and peered around the corner. There were two cars on this level, but both were to my right, almost directly across from me, under a panel of lights. No one was hiding behind them.

"I think he kept going and went right up to the next floor," I whispered. "Come up here and cover me while I move out."

I stood up, keeping my back flat against the wall, and began to move. All of the shadows cast by the pillars were uniform; either he wasn't behind any of them, or he was very careful. But somehow I didn't think he'd stop here. If he'd wanted to stand his ground, he could have done that back at the car.

It took twenty minutes to cover the levels of the garage until we came to the last ramp, the one that led to the roof. The wind was stronger, and there were no lights past the curve. I motioned for Chadwick to join me, and we crouched in the shadow of the elevators.

"Looks like we got him cornered, Dave. He can't run anymore."

"Looks like he's got us right where he wants us."

"Huh?"

"We go up that ramp, he's in the dark, we're in the light. It's a sucker play. He'll have us in silhouette and we won't be able to see a thing."

"You're not going to walk away from it now, are you?"

"No. I can't make it light up there, but I can even the odds. What kind of a weapon you got there?"

He held it up and looked at it, pointing it at me in the process. "A thirty-two, I think."

"Plenty for what I need it for. Give it to me." He handed it over and I shoved it into a pocket. My own gun went back in its holster.

I walked to the corner, just below the turn of the ramp, and cupped my hands to my mouth.

"Hey!" I yelled. "Can you hear me?"

No response. Just a cold wind and the faint noise of traffic far away.

I took a deep breath and shouted as loud as I could. "You can keep the money. We just want to know where she is. You have to know that. Come on."

I counted to ten. Nothing.

"Nobody needs to get hurt."

A car honked somewhere. No sound came from the roof.

I pulled out Chadwick's .32 and took aim at the bank of lights nearest the ramp. I took no chances; even though the lights were only ten feet away I used a two-hand grip and fired single action. A brief flash from the muzzle and the lights went out. I shifted to the left and shot out the next nearest lights, and then the next. When I was done, the half of the garage nearest the ramp was in darkness.

I dropped Chadwick's gun in my pocket and pulled out my own .357. It was time to hurry; even if no one had paid attention to earlier shots, these three were sure to bring the police running. Crouching down, I rushed the base of the ramp, then stopped. I counted to ten, listening closely, but there was nothing, not even the wind. It was as if the world was holding its breath.

I ran up the ramp on a diagonal and dropped down on one knee, my gun arm fully extended, but my eyes weren't night adapted and I couldn't see a thing. There was no time to wait. I took out my flashlight, held it out to my side as far away from me as I could, and turned it on.

It didn't draw fire, but suddenly I heard running footsteps again, far away and to my right. They were heading for a dark bulk I dimly saw in the far corner of the garage. There was a light burning over a doorway. It had to be a stair tower. Maybe this one wasn't locked. Dropping my flashlight, I ran toward the footsteps, zigzagging as I went. I heard Chadwick's footsteps behind me, on the ramp, but I didn't bother to look back. I slipped once on a patch of ice, but my other foot landed firmly and I kept going.

I dodged around a snow-covered car that I only saw at the last moment, and there he was, only a few yards away. The light over the door was a fair distance away, but I could see a little in the reflected light off the snow. He was slumped against the wall that went around the perimeter of the roof level, about three and half feet high. The briefcase was beside him. His hands were at his sides. I could see that footsteps led up to the door, and away again, in the fresh snow. So it was locked, after all.

I knew Chadwick wasn't far behind. "You can keep the damn money. Just tell us where she is."

He looked over my shoulder at Chadwick. And before I could reach him he rolled over the edge and was gone.

It's true what they say, that everyone screams on the way down.

22

Thursday, 11:00 P.M.

Chadwick ran to the rail and looked over, then back at me. When he opened his mouth I could barely hear him. "Jesus, Dave, why—did he do that?"

I closed my eyes, trying to find the right way to say it. "He was in a corner. He didn't want to shoot his way out, and he didn't know where she was. No, he didn't have to jump. But he did."

"He didn't know? Then this was another hoax?"

"I think so. I'm not sure yet."

He was rapidly getting his composure. There was a hint of impatience in his voice. "Well, what about Anne, then?"

I started back toward the ramp. I set a brisk pace, hoping he wouldn't be able to keep up. "When we get to the bottom, go and fill in Mosier. I'm going to check on the body. We don't have much time to get our stories straight. The police are going to be here any minute. It's going to take them awhile to figure out where that scream came from, and the shots, but half the city must be phoning in reports right now."

When we reached the second floor I stopped long enough to pick up the gunman's speaker and microphone set and jam them into a trash can. Chadwick stared at me. "Isn't that disposing of evidence?"

"You're damned right it is. And this is evidence, too." As quickly as I could I stripped to the waist and gave my holster and vest to Chadwick, along with my .357. I was pulling my sweatshirt back on before I began to really feel the cold. "Tell Mosier to hide all this in the van. Under a blanket or something. Be sure it's out of sight from the outside. If they're going to find it, at least it's not going to be a plain-view search."

"What's going on?" he asked as we walked.

"For three days you've been telling me you want to keep the kidnapping private, and I've been telling you to tell the police. Well, Bruce, the chickens have come home to roost. Unless you want to spend the next two years explaining yourself to a bunch of lawyers and a jury, we're going to stick with the program."

"I haven't done anything wrong."

"A man jumps off a building while you and your confederate have him cornered with guns. And there's a briefcase with two hundred grand found in your possession right afterwards."

"That's not the way is happened."

"Literally, yes, it is. But the thing is not what really happened, but what a DA can make it appear happened. But let's assume that eventually the charges of robbery and murder are dropped, after a couple of months of publicity—you like the scenario?"

"Not much."

"Then get ready to lie. Because I'm going to get to the bottom of this case tonight, and I have to be out on the street to do it, not answering detectives' questions."

Mosier was waiting for us at the van. "What the hell is going on?" But he sounded more frightened than belligerent.

I pointed to Chadwick. "All this stuff here, hide it good, so no one can see it from the outside of the van. And if somebody asks to search the van, tell them no. Keep it locked."

Mosier shoved everything into a cooler in the rear and threw a blanket loosely over it. "Who's coming?"

"Probably every cruiser on duty in the city. Now come on."

We hurried down the sidewalk and around the corner. The light was poor, but I knew when I first saw him that he was dead. The head hung completely over on one shoulder, and one arm was twisted underneath. The fall had ripped off the ski mask. Jeremy's eyes were still open, and a trickle of blood came from the corner of his mouth.

Chadwick reached the body a moment after me and sank down on his knees in the snow. "Oh, my God, no."

I put my hand on his shoulder and squeezed it. Mosier helped him to his feet and the three of us moved away to the wall. Across the street, porch lights were on and people were starting to come out of their homes. "Bruce," I said, "I'm sorry about Jeremy. I can't believe he would do anything to hurt his own mother. But he must have thought he could pull this off. The—"

"But why? It makes no sense. I gave him everything he wanted."

"I'm sure you did. But somehow he didn't have something he needed, something he thought the money would give him. Independence. Maybe he didn't want to live by just taking what you were willing to give him. Maybe it was proving to himself he could do it. Getting out from under. I don't know. I barely knew your son. I don't know if he knew why, exactly; he just had the need to do it."

"This can't be happening—"

"Look, Bruce. Here's what we have to say; the police will be here any second. Jeremy had run away from home a week ago after an argument and took the gun with him. You hired me to find him. The three of us came here tonight to meet him and bring him home. Mosier stayed with the van. You and I met Jeremy at his car on the second floor. We talked to him but he ran away, up to the roof. He shot his gun a few times, mostly at the lights. We followed him up to the roof, trying to talk to him, but he jumped. We ran downstairs and got Mosier and ran over here, but he was already dead."

Chadwick just looked at me; it was Mosier who spoke. "Sounds dangerous to mention you were on the roof at all."

"We have to tell a story that's consistent with the facts. There are footprints in the snow that put Chadwick and me up there. The story we're going to tell, they can't shake.'' I wiped the .32 as carefully as I could and wrapped Jeremy's fingers around the grip. I checked his pockets, found the .45, and dropped it down a storm drain.

''They're going to be all over your ass, you being at the scene of another dead body.''

''If we stick to it, they can't touch me. But I have to be in the clear tonight to wrap this case up. And if any of the truth gets out, the whole thing is going to unravel.''

Mosier was as blank as Chadwick. ''Huh?''

''They can't hang the Saunders murder on me. But if they knew to look, they could put it on Jeremy.''

Chadwick had lost all capacity for surprise. He just looked at me and asked, ''What?''

''If the police check his movements, I'll bet dollars to doughnuts he visited her Tuesday afternoon, after I was there the first time. He could have seen me leave the house on foot and figured out where I was going. He waited till I was on my way to the first ransom delivery and went over himself.''

Chadwick's first reaction was anger. ''Goddam you, Garrett. You chase my son off the roof and then you try and blame a murder on him—''

Mosier put his arm around Chadwick. ''Hear him out, Bruce. Just hear the man out, will you? Besides, he's right about Jeremy being gone. When Garrett left, he went right out the front door himself. Remember, I told you I was mad because he hadn't finished with the mail?''

Chadwick nodded and I went on. ''Saunders knew something about the kidnapping. She didn't tell me. I don't know if she told Jeremy or whether he was better at figuring it out. I don't think she told him anything. But it doesn't matter. The important thing is that Jeremy figured she was in on it. That meant she was in his way. So he killed her.''

Chadwick was indignant. ''Jeremy wouldn't hurt a fly.''

"He took a shot at his own father five minutes ago. And I'm almost certain he was the sniper."

"You said yourself, you don't think he was trying to hurt you."

"I have that feeling, but I don't know. Now we never will. But anyway, I don't think he set out to kill her. I think he was scared and desperate and saw his big chance slipping away. He may have meant to scare her and didn't realize how hard he'd hit her. Or they may have struggled—she was a pretty feisty lady. The—"

"Big chance? What big chance?"

"To collect two hundred thousand dollars."

"He would do that?"

"Look what he did tonight. Either he kidnapped his own mother, which I don't believe, or he was trying to pull off a scam. He was the one who sent the second ransom demand. The first one came in by phone, remember? But the second one was in writing."

"So?"

"There was a reason for that. He wanted it to appear as authentic as possible, but he didn't dare call it in. Anyone who answered might have recognized his voice. And he didn't have any accomplices to do it for him, at least not anyone whose voice might not be recognized, too."

"But why would he do it? I'm his father. We gave him everything he wanted. Why would he want to do that to me?"

"I barely knew your son. Mr. Chadwick. And not well enough to spot this, evidently. I don't think any of us knew him. Listen, I don't like having to lie to the police. It's stupid and it's dangerous. But if I'm going to get to the bottom of this thing without any more delay, I can't let the police get their fingers into it now."

Two police cruisers skidded around the corner behind us, their red and blue lights casting shadows on the buildings. Two officers got out of each car; one stayed back, a radio in his hand, while the other three approached.

"Over here, Officers," I shouted needlessly. "He's over here."

One of the officers knelt down, shined his light in Jeremy's face, and felt his throat for a pulse. "Call for an ambulance," he said after a moment, but there was no urgency in his voice.

"What about advanced life support?" his partner asked.

"Don't bother."

We handled the officer's questions as smoothly as we could, with me doing most of the talking. Just about the time the patrolman was finished I became conscious of someone in a trench coat standing alongside me. It was the same detective who'd been grilling me Tuesday evening.

"Evening, Detective."

He looked at me warily. "You seem to keep popping up at homicides, Garrett."

"This one's a suicide."

He took me by the upper arm and led me out of earshot of the others. "Fill me in, right now, or we go to the station."

I made a show of looking at Chadwick and Mosier, both of whom stared blankly at me. "Well, I'm afraid it's got to come out now," I said.

"I'm waiting."

"Well, now that it's all over, I can talk about it. I was hired by the Chadwick family to find Jeremy. He ran off on Monday—no, it was Sunday—and no one had seen him since. I was asking around, of course, and Nancy Saunders was one of the people I checked out. She said she didn't know anything, but her answers were kind of evasive and I decided to stop back and reinterview her. In the meantime Jeremy had been there and killed her."

"Why bring in a private detective just because their son decided to take off?" He looked at the body. "Was he a minor?"

"No, he wasn't. This is the reason." I pointed at the gun in Jeremy's hand. "It belongs to his father. When he left he was pretty upset, I'm told. He didn't threaten anyone in particular, but his parents were worried anyway.''

''What makes you think he killed Saunders?''

''I can't be sure, but in the absence of any other suspect, I suggest you at least look into it. I've got ten bucks that says your forensics will match him.''

He wasn't convinced. ''So what was he doing there?''

''She was very close to his family. He must have gone there for some advice, or to try and get her to take his side against his parents.''

''What was his motive?''

''I don't think there was one. He was very wrought up. I think she was trying to talk him into going home, he wouldn't, and they argued. I'm sure it wasn't premeditated. If you get physical with a woman of her age when you're mad, things can happen by accident.''

He looked up at the sheer brick face of the parking garage. ''So what about tonight?''

''I was trying to get him to come home, me and his father. He had arranged to meet us here. When we got here he ran to the roof and jumped. It all happened too fast, before we could get close enough to him to stop him.''

''Drugs?''

''I don't think so. Just a real unhappy kid.''

''You knew about his sister.''

''Some people just aren't lucky with their kids.''

''I feel damned sorry for them.'' He paused, then said, ''A red Fiero was seen parked across the street from the Saunders residence in the late afternoon.''

''The Chadwicks have one. Check it out.''

He asked me some more questions, then went over to interrogate Mosier and Chadwick. It seemed like he talked to them a long time, but maybe when a homicide charge hangs in the balance, everything seems longer. At last he came back to me, his feet kicking at the snow.

''The stories all hang together,'' he admitted grudgingly. ''But the forensics on Saunders will take another day. There weren't any usable prints on the murder weapon, so we're trying to match some hairs and clothing fibers. There wasn't much of a struggle, but there are some threads that aren't from the victim. Anyway, remember what I said about leaving town."

I smiled, nodded, said "Thank you, Detective," and got my people out of there before it occurred to anyone to search the van. By the time we got back to the house, Bruce was beginning to realize what had happened. Mosier and I helped him through the door and into a chair while Kate gaped at us.

"Is it bad?" she asked.

"Very bad. Now get your coat. I'll explain as we go. We have a long night ahead of us."

23

Friday, 2:00 A.M.

Kate knocked, and after several minutes a light came on and the front door opened. Ted was properly dressed even at that godforsaken hour of the night. Brown slippers, white silk pajamas with subtle red pinstripes, and a navy blue bathrobe with a belt and some kind of white crested design on the breast pocket. Not even his hair was mussed. I wondered if he slept standing up in the closet.

"Oh. It's you two again."

"You should be happier to see us than that," I said. "It could just as well have been the police."

"Police?" He had trouble saying the word without stammering. I didn't care what he thought of my manners; I pushed the door wider and we stepped inside. He shut it behind me and waited.

"You and I are going to have a talk. Right now. Not after you have a chance to talk to your lawyer, or Anne, or anybody else."

"I don't know what you mean."

'The hell you don't. This isn't a game anymore. Two people are dead. You've been lying like a rug. I'm willing to forget about that if you come clean right now."

"I've told you all I know." But the last word ended on a rising note, and it sounded like a whine.

"You know, you're not a very good liar. Poor people are usually much better. You don't have much practice at really needing to fool people."

"I don't need your insults at this hour of the night."

"Fine. Then you can have insults from the police. I don't care how much you pay in taxes; when capital crimes are involved they take off the kid gloves. Ever been in an interrogation room?"

"You said just a few hours ago the police weren't involved."

I wasn't going to give away any more than I had to. "They were called to the scene of Jeremy's death. It was necessary to explain the circumstances."

"Jeremy Chadwick? Dead? What circumstances?"

"I'm asking the questions. For the moment, that is. The police will be next. You can't keep a lid on this. Either Anne is dead, in which case a body will turn up, or she's alive. My money is she's alive and that you know where. If you won't tell me I'll put the police on you. Come clean and I'll see if I can keep you out. Now decide."

He tried hard to rally his nerve. "My family is very prominent in this town. You'd better be careful about your accusations."

"I saw you pick up the ransom money in Penn Square."

"Describe how this person was dressed."

"A ski mask over his face and a heavy jacket."

"Then you can't identify me."

"I know it was you."

In his own way he was plenty tough. He smiled at me slightly and shook his head. He was looking at me the way he probably regarded pushy door-to-door salesmen. "My dear man, Descartes proved quite clearly that a person can't *know* something that is false. There's a great difference between mere belief and knowledge."

"You and Nancy Saunders and Anne got together and came up with your story."

"And what story was that?"

"That your affair was a long time ago, all over, no hard feelings, nothing to do with the present."

"Well, that's just what I told you."

"But you used exactly the same words as Nancy did. I've thought about it—no two people will tell something like that the same way, word for word. Anne coached you two together. Or maybe she did it separately and because her memory is so damned good she got you both repeating it exactly the same."

Kate spoke up. "Loyalty's a great thing. But when it goes too far it's silly, even dangerous. With a kidnapping and two people dead you and Anne can't just slip away somewhere. The police will be looking for her. Hard. She's not just one of the thousands of spouses who take off every year; she's the key to a suicide and probably a homicide."

"Well, assuming the police want to talk to Bruce's wife, what's it to me? And I'm getting tired of this police bogeyman every time the two of you open your mouths."

"What you were counting on just isn't going to happen, and you'd better face it," Kate said. "You read Descartes. You're a rational man. You ought to know the difference between real possibilities and fantasies. It's hard, but you'd better face it."

His voice was very soft. "I am so very damned tired of accepting things."

We stood facing each other for several seconds. Faintly I heard a grandfather's clock ticking off to my right. At last he dropped his eyes to the floor.

"I don't have any choice, do I?"

I knew he was going to tell. It wasn't just the words, it was the slump of his shoulders and the way he looked at the floor. I could afford to ease up.

"No," I said. "Your choice is only how to bear it."

"Then—can I interest you in a drink?"

"Nothing for us. But help yourself."

He led us to a room that was a cross between a den and a library, with a fireplace at one end, a piano at the other, and bookcases lining all the walls. He poured himself a large glass of some golden liquid from a crystal decanter on the piano, tossed in some ice, and sat down in a wing chair.

"There's a lot of wisdom in this room," he said. "I just wish that more of it was between my ears instead of on the shelves."

"It's not always a matter of wisdom."

"Are you married, David?"

"Not now."

"How many times have you really been in love?"

"Once, at least."

"But at least the once."

"Yes."

He took a long swallow and then looked at the glass. The ice cubes spun around lazily. "I promised her I wouldn't tell."

"That was before two people died," Kate said. "You never bargained on that."

"And you know something, miss? I don't care about the two dead people. Even if they're people I know. I can't bring them back. I told her it was crazy; we didn't need the money that badly."

"You'd better start at the beginning," I said.

"I told you that I met her and her husband not long after they came to Lancaster. They both played bridge and tennis. All that part was true. The version Nancy and I told. Have you seen a picture?"

"Yes, and I've met her, too."

"Then you'll know what I mean when I say that there's never been a photograph that does her justice. She just takes your breath away, and it's not just her looks. There's something inside her that's so alive, it makes the rest of us seem like corpses. And she's smart, and funny, and so self-assured."

He took a pull at his drink and looked at it before he went on. "Our group took a trip to the British Virgins about ten years ago. It was right after they'd moved here and I'd only met her a couple of times before. We were all staying in bungalows near the beach. One night, it must have been about two in the morning, there was a knock at my door. It was Anne, in a bathrobe and bare feet. Her hair was wet and she smelled of the sea. She asked me if I wanted to go down to the beach. There was a wild look in her eye, almost like an animal. I was so surprised, I mumbled something about it being late for a swim. She just laughed and dropped her robe; she was naked underneath. She turned and ran toward the beach and I followed. That's how it all began."

"Did Bruce know?"

"I worried that he had to know. She didn't take pains to be discreet, not by a long shot. That night we were on the beach Bruce was in their bungalow; she was hoping that he wouldn't wake up and wonder where she was. But if he suspected I never had any sign. She said that she was the one taking the risk, but that wasn't so, not entirely, anyway."

"Go on."

He sipped at his drink and gestured around the room. "None of this is mine, none at all. Everything belongs to my parents. I have credit cards, accounts, a checking account with money put in from the family trust automatically every month, but no money of my own. And my parents are very strict about scandal. Years ago, when I was a teenager, my father went to his father and said he wanted to divorce my mother. They sat in this very room, as a matter of fact. He said he'd found someone else he was deeply in love with. What's more, she was pregnant. They were going to marry as soon as the divorce came through. My mother knew about the girl; she was agreeable to a divorce, too. She may have had someone of her own, for all I know. My grandfather looked at him and said, 'The Grigg family may have their quiet indiscretions, but they never, never divorce. If you do you'll have to make your way in the world without anything from Mother or myself. And this is the only time this subject will ever be mentioned.' And it was. Now that my father has reached that age he's come round to the same point of view. An open affair with a married woman in their social set would have been very displeasing."

"But you almost ran away with her, years ago," I said.

"Yes, it very nearly happened."

"Let's hear it."

"Our affair kept becoming more intense. Neither of us had any job responsibilities, so we saw each other every day. She used to joke that she saw much more of me than her husband. Then one day she told me she was ready to leave him. Jeremy was sixteen, old enough to drive, old enough to be on his own. She told me to pack a couple of bags and pick her up; we'd drive to Philadelphia, take a flight to Mexico, and arrange for one of those instant divorces. We knew what it would mean as far as my inheritance was concerned, and at the time I was resolved. But when it came time to pack, I found I *couldn't do it.* I'd start writing a note to my parents, explaining myself—then I'd say the hell with the note, and start to pack. Then I'd go back to the note. After a while I'd decide it was hopeless and I'd start to unpack. About the time I had everything put away again I'd realize what a wonderful woman I was throwing away and I'd start packing and writing all over again. It went on for three hours that way. My head was pounding and my stomach was in knots. Finally I called her and said I couldn't. No more than I could have deliberately put my hand on a hot stove."

"That was years ago."

"That was the end of the affair, of course. We saw each other, we still moved in the same circles, but neither of us ever mentioned it. Sometimes I would think that the whole thing was a dream. When I remembered it, it was like remembering a movie."

"Until a few weeks ago."

"I came home one evening and I saw a light upstairs. It was dim, like a night-light. Then I heard a noise, like splashing. I went upstairs." He paused for a moment, savoring the memory. "Outside the bathroom door was a woman's dress, stockings, and a pair of shoes, nothing else. I knew it was her. No one I knew would be so bold; and anyway, she never wore any underwear, she said it spoiled the lines of her clothes. I went in. The room smelled of jasmine. She was in the tub, with bubble bath, and candles all around the room."

"She was ready to give you a second chance."

"I'd had a long time to think it over. I'd made the wrong choice, back then, and I knew it. This time I was ready to see it through. I really was." He looked at me and I avoided his eyes. I was afraid that if I looked in his pathetic, irresolute face, I'd see myself.

"What was the plan?"

"She told me about how her daughter wanted ten thousand dollars, and how her husband had turned her down. As for that I didn't know what to think. She'd paid money before for nothing. I was dubious that this was anything more than good money after bad."

"For what it's worth, Anne was right. It really was her daughter."

"That's good. At least someone got clear of this mess."

It was too complicated to explain, and I wasn't sure what to think of it myself. Kate spoke next. "Couldn't you have borrowed ten thousand from your parents?"

"That was my first thought. As long as I had a reasonable story I could get that much. Actually I only would have needed about seven; I have a little bit saved up. But Anne said no—she said that if we were going to break away for good, we needed to burn our bridges."

"Keep going," I said.

"It was Anne's idea, as you might expect. She would leave the house, meet me, and we would leave her car by the side of the road. Mary didn't work for them when I was seeing her the last time, so I could call in the ransom demand without being recognized as long as she answered. Or any of Bruce's staff, for that matter. I picked up the money, just as you said. Anne helped. She was sitting in a car with a cellular phone, watching you. I had a portable phone."

"Why didn't you clear town right away? You had the money."

"Ten thousand of it was for Amy. Anne was supposed to call her Tuesday evening. By then we heard about Nancy on the TV. We were shocked, of course. We didn't know how it could be connected with us, but Nancy was the only other person who knew, so we were frightened. Whoever killed Nancy might somehow find us. We decided to sit tight for a day or two, or until they arrested Nancy's killer."

"They never will."

"The police here are very thorough."

"He's dead. I don't have any more time to talk. The game's up. Tell me where she is."

"After we heard about Nancy's death we decided that trying to stay here was too risky. She's at Mary's."

"You're kidding."

"No. She said it was the last place anyone would look. If the police were brought in they might check the motels, and if Bruce knew about our old affair he could come around here."

"What did she tell Mary to get her to be a part of this?"

"Mary doesn't know anything of this. Anne told her that after the sabotage she was afraid to be in the house till the restaurant was officially open. So she was just going to be there for a few days."

"Let me guess. Anne told her not to let anyone know she was there."

"I suppose so."

"Where's the money?"

"Anne has it with her."

"As far as Anne—we need to get her, you know."

He nodded. His body in the wing chair was completely limp. "Do I have to come along?"

"I think it would be better if you didn't."

"Then I'll give you directions."

"We know where Mary lives."

"And now, having betrayed the love of my life and my best chance for happiness, I'll have another drink and toddle off to bed. I think this calls for another drink, don't you?"

"You've done the right thing," I said.

"Icarus," Kate said. We both looked at her, but she was paying attention only to Ted. She was looking at him as if for the first time. "You flew too close to the sun and your wings melted. She was too much for you—maybe she's too much for anybody. I've met her daughter. You and Bruce are alike, you know. You've both allowed her to fool you about what she is—and what you are."

"I wasn't good enough, then or now."

"You're not good enough to surf a tidal wave, either, or survive being struck by lightning. If she's anything like her daughter she's that kind of force. All you can do is stay clear of it."

"I'll give that some thought."

"But put that damn bottle away and put on some coffee. Stay up and watch the dawn. It will do you good."

We got into the car and pulled away. "God, I can barely keep my eyes open," I said.

"My vision is starting to get blurry."

"Been a long time since you pulled an all-nighter?"

"So long I can't remember when."

"What did you think of Ted?" I asked.

"Like I said, Icarus. I feel very sorry for him."

"He'd have been better off never knowing her. Or at least not having an affair with her."

"After such knowledge, what forgiveness?"

"I haven't known very many people who were forgiven for anything, regardless of how much or little they knew."

"It's too late, or too early, to talk about it. Where are we going now?"

"To Mary's."

"It's getting close to four in the morning."

"Then they'll be up soon."

"Really?"

"Yes. With all the animals to tend, water to heat, they're up long before dawn."

"It doesn't look like anybody's up anywhere. All the houses are dark."

"We're still not out to the Amish area."

She looked out at the blackness. "How could he do it?"

We both knew she was talking about Jeremy. "What do you think?"

"As a parent it scares me to death. Okay, so his father worked too hard and maybe drank too hard, but he was home every night, he was a good provider, he didn't hit the boy, he had a lot of advantages. And whatever's wrong with Anne I can't imagine that she ever took it out on him. Where did they go wrong?"

"Maybe they didn't. Maybe there was nothing they could have done."

"You don't really mean that," she said.

"Why do you say that?"

"They have to have done something wrong. This doesn't just happen."

I took her hand. "The older I get the less I understand the explanations of things. Especially why people do things. Let's say, for the sake of argument, that all juvenile delinquents come from broken homes, or that all child abusers were abused themselves as children. But that doesn't explain delinquency, or abuse. It's just knowing your meaningless social science fact for the day. Because there are lots of kids from broken who don't become delinquent, and kids who were abused who don't become child abusers. Figure out why, and then you now something."

"So what does that mean?"

"It means that I don't know."

We drove on in silence for a few minutes as the suburbs turned into farm country. We began to see dim lights in some of the houses.

"We're almost there. You might want to put your jacket back on."

"Where's Intercourse?"

"To the west. We came down from the north this time."

"Looks like people are up, after all."

"Either they're Amish, or they have a dairy operation, or both."

I stopped in the Fisher driveway and we got out. Even though it was hours till dawn, a rooster was crowing from the direction of the barn. I could see lights in the barn, and in the house as well. I rapped heavily on the front door and stood back.

It wasn't long before Mary answered the door. She wasn't wearing her glasses, and it took her a moment to focus on us. Even after she recognized us, though, she kept her silence.

"Sorry to trouble you so early," I said. "We're here to get Anne." She hesitated, and I decided to make it easy for her. "We know all about it. Ted Grigg told me she was here."

Her face showed no emotion. "I'll get my husband," she said, and disappeared.

"Should we go in?" Kate asked. "What if they try to warn her?"

I shook my head. I didn't bother to explain because I didn't have any good reason for trusting them. As a matter of fact, the only thing I knew about them was that they'd concealed her from us. It wasn't much of a track record. But at four in the morning I was too damned tired to be suspicious.

Luck was with me. After a couple of minutes her husband came to the door, smelling of fresh milk and manure. His hair was mussed and he didn't look very happy to see us. But he jerked his head in the direction of the rear and said, "She's out back in the daughdie house." Then he shut the door in our faces.

24

Friday, 4:00 A.M.

Kate looked at me. "What did he say?"

"Daughdie house. It's Dutch, the small house that the old people live in, the word I couldn't remember last time. It's the building around back we saw the other day. She was right here all along."

We walked around the house. Directly in front of us was a low dark rectangle. There was no moon, and the stars were obscured by clouds. Except for a dim glow at one window, the little house was just one more piece of black against the night sky. Feeling my way long, I found the first porch step with my foot, and then a wooden handrail.

The door wasn't locked. Inside was a large room with a high ceiling. The only light was a faint red glow from a dying fire in the corner. I sensed bulky furniture, sofas and overstuffed chairs. The smells told their own story: mildew, cleanser, bleach, paint, tomato sauce with lots of garlic, and pine smoke. The progression was hopeful, and I was at the end.

"Mrs. Chadwick?"

There was no answer, and I stepped further into the room. Dimly I saw a wide doorway to my left, and beyond it white countertops and cabinets. A corridor led off to the right. Despite the silence I felt I wasn't alone. Someone was in the room, and knew that I was there, too. I stepped into the center of the room and saw a wing chair with its back to me, facing the remains of the fire. An empty wineglass was on the floor next to the chair. Next to it was an overflowing ashtray.

"Anne? It's Dave Garrett."

Still there was no reply. I moved to my left, circling around till I was to one side of the chair, only a few feet away. It was her, all right. Her hair, naturally red, burned with a dark golden fire in the light cast by the last embers. It was tousled, and fell down on both sides of her face. She was wrapped in a silk robe with a paisley pattern that fell down to her bare feet. She was staring straight ahead, whether at the fire or at nothing at all I couldn't tell.

She didn't look at me. She spoke slowly, and her voice was barely above a whisper. "I knew it was you as soon as I saw the car. Ted wasn't supposed to come until I sent word. Do you feel the silence here, Mr. Garrett?"

I found myself matching her quiet tone. "Yes, I do."

She waited before she answered, as if the words cost an effort. "It is the silence of defeat. The silence in between the words of the Moor when he said, 'Farewell the plumed troop/And the big wars/That make ambition virtue/Oh, farewell.' Do you know the play?"

"Not as well as I should."

She smiled, but there was no warmth to it. "None of us is as good as we should be."

"No. But we're usually not as bad as we think we are."

"What a comforting thought. Do you have an inspirational program on cable on Sunday mornings, by any chance?"

"I've got a camera, a tape recorder, a gun, a rice burner that's full of body rust, and some scars. And that about exhausts my personal inventory."

She acted as if she hadn't heard me. "I never gave any thought to the expression before. 'Blood on your hands.' But it's really true. Nancy's blood is there. I can almost see it." Without any change of expression, tears began streaming down her face. She didn't even blink.

I retreated into my lawyer bedside manner. "In the law, we say that a person is only responsible for things that are reasonably foreseeable."

"Nancy would still be alive if I hadn't played this stupid game."

"She'd still be alive if she'd gone to Florida on Saturday instead of hanging around. Or maybe her plane would have gone down. Let it be. You'll drive yourself crazy for nothing."

"What I did was pretty crazy."

"You'd better fill me in on the details."

For the first time she looked at me. "You have to understand, I'm not an evil person."

"I didn't say you were. Or even think it."

"Bruce and I were a mistake from the beginning. From the very, very beginning. I had just had a fight with my regular boyfriend and slept with Bruce to get even with him. His condom broke and I got pregnant. This was before legalized abortion. You needed money to get out of the country or for a doctor. I went to him for help; that was my second mistake. He told both our families and they pressured me into marrying him instead. I hated him for that and I never got over it.

"When our daughter was a year old, I left him. He didn't tell you that, did he?"

"No."

"Bruce was always good at denying things that didn't fit in with his view of things. Anyway, I had a letter from my school saying they'd take me back once the fall semester started. I had tuition and day care and my own apartment, just off campus. Bruce would come by to visit Amy. I didn't love him, but I felt guilty about having left him, and I was alone. He told me he'd had a vasectomy after I left. I was twenty years old and dumb about sex. And about him. It didn't occur that he would lie to me. He deliberately got me pregnant again. That was Jeremy."

A spark flew out of the fire. We watched it go from orange to red and then fade out.

"I can still remember the day I found out, sitting on the bed in my new place. I really tried to get an abortion that time, but it was still illegal, I didn't know any doctors, and all my money was tied up in school. And it was an awful pregnancy, physically. I was sick as a dog the whole time. I don't think he liked being in there any more than I liked him there. My parents wouldn't help, of course. After all, I was a married woman. Having babies is what's supposed to happen. You know, they've never really forgiven me even for asking. Finally I dragged myself home, to Bruce."

She looked down in her lap. "I don't know if I'm responsible for what happened to Nancy. But I am for how Jeremy turned out. I hated him from the moment he was conceived. Most mothers will tell you, if they're honest, that there're moments they hate their babies. Well, it wasn't just moments with me. I always resented him. I wouldn't even breast-feed him; I made Bruce hire a housekeeper so I didn't have to deal with him."

It was my turn to do something I wasn't proud of. I was more concerned with getting the whole story than letting a woman know her only son was dead. "Go on."

"I tried to accept my life, but I wound up just feeling resigned. Bruce wasn't a bad man, and he loved me. I didn't love him back, that's all. So as the years went by I had affairs. For the same reason other women do charity work or throw ceramic pots—it was my hobby. Bless him, Bruce never suspected a thing."

"And then Ted came along."

She didn't react to his name. "If he was as good at guiding himself as he was at guiding you, we wouldn't be having this conversation."

"He told me about trying to leave his life for you."

"I loved him. As much as I've ever loved anyone, anyway. But if he couldn't leave on his own I didn't want him." She looked back at the fire. "Whatever my sins may be, they don't include lack of resolution, Mr. Garrett."

"It's none of my business, but he doesn't seem like your type, exactly."

"You mean that he's soft and weak and indecisive?"

"Well, yes."

She laughed a little and shook her head. "Well, as far as he is physically now, he used to be better looking. But that's not important, anyway. The way he is now is my fault, and I admit it. If I'd told him, years ago, 'Damn it, you're going to leave your mother and father and that's that,' given him an order, taken charge, dragged him out of there, built him up, told him he could do anything, he could have been a hell of a man. He's smart and sensitive. All he needed was someone to give him some stiffening."

She reached for the wineglass, found it empty, and set it down again. "Want to hear a little theory of mine?"

"Go ahead."

"As much as men think that they pattern themselves after their fathers, men are really molded by the women in their lives. Their mothers first—what child doesn't see ten hours of its mother for every hour of its father? Later on it's his wife who takes over, pushing and prodding and maneuvering him. Ted's mother wanted him weak, and she got what she wanted. I could have made him strong, back then, but I didn't."

"Why not?"

"Because I was the worst kind of idiot. A high-minded idiot. When I told him I was ready to leave Bruce, I just announced my availability and waited for him to make the move to come to me. I should have driven over there in a dress cut down to my navel and just told him to get in the car and go, right now, without taking time to think. I knew, deep down, he might not be able to make the break."

She stopped for a minute, reliving that bit of the past. "I say I was high-minded—what I meant was, I wanted him to make his own decision to come to me. Now, looking back, I can see that I was just being selfish. I wanted him to share my guilt for the end of my marriage, which was silly. And I'm not sure if I was being honest with myself, either. I knew I could take him away if I wanted to. And if I did that, I was certain to have him, certain to be launched into a new life of my own. Letting him make the decision meant I accepted the chance nothing would happen. You see, I was afraid. By leaving it to him I could go all the way to the brink and not be sure I had to jump. And of course I didn't."

"And if you had it to do all over?"

She considered this. "I'd probably do exactly the same thing again. Whatever my reasons were, they seemed strong enough at the time."

"So bring me up to date."

"I knew that Amy was alive, somehow. Not that I'd heard from her, or that any of the ghastly people that showed up seemed very reliable. I knew because she'd done what I wanted to do, what I should have done. It's in the blood, you see. Our wildness is just under the surface. It doesn't take much to set us off."

"She got in touch with you."

"Her boyfriend did. I'm sure it was at her instigation. I thought it was nice of her to come up with the ridiculous story about being held hostage all these years—it was calculated to spare our feelings."

"She thinks it fooled you."

"Why do children always think their parents are stupid?"

"But the idea of a phony ransom started you thinking."

"Exactly. With Bruce, our argument about Amy was the last straw. I think the guilt of how I let her be raised finally caught up with me. He'd refused to face the fact that she'd run away to get out of a miserable home, because he refused to accept that the home was miserable in the first place. He puts a lot of energy into denial. I suppose that's why he's so successful. Anyway, after she disappeared he became impossible. He retreated into his office and never came out. The more he worked the more he was promoted, the more responsibility he had, and the more he had to work. He'd never been much of a family man, but after Amy it became a joke. I'd always avoided Jeremy; now Bruce and I avoided each other, too."

"The ransom."

"I took up with Ted again. I told him I'd run away with him. It was better than going by myself. But before we left I wanted to get Amy her money, and get back at Bruce. So I added thirty thousand on top of Amy's ten. I had Ted disable your car and pick me up by the side of the road. The two of us handled it from there."

"It was Ted who picked up the ransom in Lancaster."

"It's amazing how bold a timid man can be with a woman backing him up. Did you know that's why the barbarians fought so well against the Romans? If the men retreated, their own women killed them."

"What were you going to do with the thirty thousand?"

"It wasn't so much that I really needed it. Getting the money to Amy had to be done right away, but that was the only money I needed immediately. The thirty thousand—I just wanted to enjoy spending it. He'd taken my life away from me; whatever that's worth, it has to be more than thirty thousand dollars."

"So why not just get it as part of your divorce settlement?"

"Because Bruce would never let me be, if I just left him. The way it was with Jeremy, it would be again. He's so full of denial about who I really am and what our marriage is. Stealing his money would have forced him to see things for what they were."

"So what was the plan from there, once you had the money?"

"The plan was not to have a plan. Travel. Go somewhere we could live cheap. Just to get away. When we really needed money, in a year or two, I would come back and get a divorce settlement."

"What about Bruce?"

"I've sweated out him being missing from our marriage for twenty-three years. He could handle a year or two till I was good and ready to see him again."

"You didn't get the ten thousand to Amy."

"No. Once we heard about Nancy's death we decided to sit tight till her killer was caught. We were afraid whoever killed Nancy might be after the money."

"Did Nancy know everything?"

"Oh, yes."

"I assume you know why I'm here."

"Not only that, I know how you got here. Ted broke down and led you straight to my door. It's the only way it could have happened."

"I was hired by Uncle Chan's to solve the kidnapping and see you home."

"I know all about Uncle Chan's."

"I didn't when I took on this case, but I found out along the way. I would never have taken it on if I'd known who I was really working for."

Her voice was harsh. "So why did you stay with it?"

"Because of you. And Nancy Saunders."

"Did Nancy tell you I was good at math?"

"She was very proud of that."

"She treated me so much like a mother. Better than my real mother. But the math is how I figured it out. I would sit with Bonner at the kitchen table when he had financial information spread out. He wouldn't talk about it, of course, but he didn't mind that I could see everything, upside down. He must have thought that even if he'd shown me everything right side up, since I was a woman, I was too stupid to understand."

She looked up, and for the first time her voice became animated. "You know how I figured it out? The rice. Reading the numbers upside down and totaling them in my head, they were showing a ridiculously high cost of goods. But the rice really caught my eye. You can go to a convenience store and buy a pound of rice for a dollar. They were buying it by the truckload, in five-pound prepackaged bags, at five dollars a pound. Not a bag, a pound. I worked the numbers in my head, and there was no way the costs could be real unless they were selling their lunches for eight dollars a plate, which they weren't."

"Did you ever tell Bruce?"

"I tried once; he shrugged it off. After that I kept it to myself."

"It was you who sabotaged the restaurant."

"Ted and I. It was my idea, of course, and it worked

damned well. Too damned well—it brought you in. Ted shot out the windows with a pellet gun of Jeremy's, and I did the rest myself. You never know how invisible you are until you're the boss's wife showing up at the business. No one paid me the slightest attention, no one even asked me what I was doing."

"You did it as a diversion."

"Of course. If there was nothing else going on, even Bruce might suspect the ransom was phony. But with a threat to his precious business, he just stopped thinking clearly."

"You're a very talented woman."

"You look a little old for this, Mr. Garrett, but I'll give you some free advice anyway. If you ever find yourself in bed with someone who has her whole life ahead of her, don't do anything to take it away from her."

I thought about the Chadwicks and their lives and what had happened in the last four days. It seemed like a good piece of advice.

"Is it time to go now?" she asked.

"There're are two things I have to tell you. First, about you. My job is to bring you back to the house. You're an adult; if you want to leave again I'm not going to stop you. But I am going to take you back there. The people behind Uncle Chan's want their instructions obeyed. If I have to take you back there against your will, technically that's kidnapping and you can go to the police about it. And that's fine, because I'd rather have that to deal with than have those people after me."

"No. I'll come with you. As far as the house, anyway."

"There's one more thing. I have some very bad news. I'm sorry to be the one to tell you. Jeremy's dead." There was no reaction. "He knew about the forty-thousand demand, and he must have figured out that it was phony. He was planning to make a demand of his own, for two hundred thousand. I don't know what he wanted the money for—I think he wanted to get out on his own, away from the house. He must have thought it would be easy money, because he didn't have to actually kidnap anybody—all he had to do was be sure that no one found out it was a hoax. But Nancy knew. He must have stopped in and asked for her help. She refused and said she was going to call your husband. Or you. Whatever she said, it was a threat to his plan. So he killed her. I suspect it was an accident, but I really don't know."

She didn't say anything for a long time. "But . . . he seemed to like her so much. She was like a grandmother to him."

I wanted to say that people who grow up without love are capable of anything, especially if they see money as a substitute, but I kept it to myself. "From there he delivered the ransom note and waited. He shot at me to discourage my poking around; I don't know if he was trying to kill me or not. I like to think he wasn't. Anyway, when Bruce and I went to deliver the ransom, Bruce started a gunfight. Jeremy killed himself rather than be found out."

"The poor soul." But there were no tears, not even then. "He could have done so much if he hadn't been born to us."

"I'm sorry to have to tell you this."

I don't think she heard me. "Do you think people know when they're going to die? Or that they're going to die young?"

"I don't know, Anne."

"He was always such an unhappy child. When he was five we bought him a puppy. He loved that little dog so much. He'd sneak it into his room at night so it could sleep with him. He'd hug the dog by the hour. Do you know what he used to whisper to it?"

"No, I don't."

"He'd be hugging the dog, his face against the dog's, and he'd say, 'I know you won't be here forever. But you'll be here a while yet. And I'll make things good for you while you're here.' Can you imagine a little child already worrying about their dog dying? It used to frighten me to hear that. It was so strange and sad."

I had a brief flash of Jeremy as a child, saying that.

It was like looking into madness itself. I shut my eyes and shook my head to drive out the image.

"It's time to go. Is there anything here you need?"

She gave a harsh and ragged laugh. "No, there's nothing here I need. Or anywhere else for that matter. I'll get dressed and be right with you. The money's still in the bag." She stood up slowly. "Just go outside and tell Ted to go home. Please."

"He's not here. He didn't want to come himself."

"Well, I'm not surprised."

She went into the other room to change and I was alone in front of the fire, in the dark. Nancy Saunders, Ted Grigg, Jeremy, Bruce, and now Anne—a lot of people to feel sorry for. Maybe even Amy qualified, too. A lot of harm had been done by basically good people. I thought of a friend who'd said that the Bible should have been rewritten for God to say, You have before you the choice between good and evil. Choose good. But if you must choose evil, be damned careful.

25

Friday, 6:00 A.M.

I brought my Honda to a stop in Chadwick's driveway. The sun was starting to rise, and the eastern sky was dappled with a few gold and red and yellow clouds. It had all the makings of a fine, clear winter's day.

Anne had been riding in the back, with Kate. In the rearview mirror I could see that Kate had her arm around her, but no one said a word.

I opened the door gently, even though I was sure neither of them was sleeping. "Kate and I are going to go in and talk to Bruce. We'll be out in a few minutes."

"All right."

The front door was locked and the porch light was out. But Kate had a key. In the faint sunlight I could see her face was pale with fatigue. "How are you feeling?"

"I'm on pure adrenaline, and I'm running low."

"It's been a very . . . wearing day." I turned my head slightly toward the car. "God, what can you say to someone who's lost both of her children, plus her best friend and her lover, within a few hours?"

"Nothing at all. The most you can do is just be there, I think."

"I wonder how Bruce is doing. With the news about the kids, I mean."

"He's had Bob with him."

"I underestimated Bob. He was such a turkey—but give him a crisis and he's fine."

"You have him just right. He's a jerk except when there's a big enough crisis to soak up all his energy."

The house was dark inside. We tiptoed down the

silent hallways and checked the bedrooms. His bed hadn't been slept in. Downstairs again, we worked our way to his office. The door was shut but a sliver of light came from underneath.

I knocked. No response.

"Bruce, it's Dave Garret. Kate's with me. We need to talk."

Again, no response. I tried the knob, found it unlocked, and pushed the door open.

Bruce was behind his desk, which was bare except for a stack of computer printouts and a half-full bottle of Johnnie Walker Black. I didn't see a glass anywhere. The only light was from a reading lamp on one corner of the desk. "Morning, Dave. Kate." He spoke slowly, but I couldn't detect any slurring.

"Morning, Bruce." We sat down. "Has Bob gone home?"

"He left about three. I've been trying to make some decisions about staffing patterns after sixty days, once we get through the initial opening rush. But . . . it's hard to concentrate."

"We have Anne with us. She's fine."

"Where is she?"

"Out in my car."

"Why?"

"I thought it was best to tell you some things myself, first. I was right about the forty-thousand-dollar demand being suspicious. There was no kidnapping. Anne faked the whole thing. She's responsible for the stuff at Uncle Chan's, too. There never was anyone out to hurt the restaurant. It was all part of her plan to keep you from thinking too carefully about whether the kidnapping was phony. She wanted forty thousand dollars to leave town on, and this was her way of getting it."

"I can't believe that. She loves me."

"You can ask her yourself."

"Where did you find her?"

"At Mary's. Ted Grigg was in with her on some of this. It was all her idea, though."

"No. You're wrong. If that's true she would have

been gone Tuesday afternoon, once she had the money. It doesn't make sense."

I looked over at Kate. She leaned close to me. "It's time now," she whispered.

I was careful to keep my own voice low. "You didn't want me to tell him last night."

"He needed a clear head more than he needed the truth. We're not doing him any good helping him kid himself any longer."

"Bruce, this is going to be hard to take." I spoke slowly, giving the words time to sink in. "Anne had a good reason not to leave right away. Your daughter Amy. She's alive. Kate and I saw her yesterday afternoon. She's in good health, she's married, and they live in Indiana. She and her husband have a little trucking business, long hauls." His expression was shock, with a wild, desperate grin starting to form at the corners of his mouth. I decided to press on before I lost him. "But there's something else. She didn't want to see you or her mother. She wants to be left alone—"

"Then they're holding her, still. Or they've brainwashed her."

"Nobody's brainwashed anybody." Except maybe themselves, I thought to myself. "She ran away of her own free will. She could have returned anytime she wanted, she just doesn't want to."

"They must be holding her. They took her clothes and burned them."

"She did that herself, so you would think she was dead and not look for her."

"Do you expect me to believe that?"

"We both heard it right from her," Kate said.

He turned to her sharply. "And where was that?"

"The bar you told us about."

"And who else was there? That scum who came to the house last month?"

"He was there," Kate admitted.

"And I bet some of his friends were there, too. How can you believe that what she said was her own free will?"

"Bruce, if you were there, if you'd seen what we saw, you wouldn't be asking these questions," she said, "She pushes him around, not the other way. She runs things. You should see it for yourself—"

"You're damned right I'm going to see it for myself! I refuse to accept that Amy could say such things unless she was forced. Who knows what they did to her. And I'm surprised at both of you for falling for it so easily."

"Bruce, the reason Anne didn't leave on Tuesday was Amy, at least in part. Your daughter wanted ten thousand dollars as the price of meeting with her mother. The guy who came to see you, his offer was genuine. Anne believed it and followed up. She must have dug the name out of the trash. The forty thousand—ten was for Amy."

He shook his head stubbornly. "Then don't believe us," I said. "Ask your wife. She knows more about it than we do."

He put his head down and turned a little away from me. I couldn't see his expression, but Kate reached across the desk and took hold of his hand. It was awhile before he started to speak.

"When you start out," he said, "life is so full, there are so many choices. You can live anywhere and marry anyone and do what you want and be a fireman or an engineer or a pilot or president. Then it starts. You go to college and you find you can't learn all that stuff, you have to pick some little corner of some major, and that's all you know when you get out. So you can only do things in that one field. You go to graduate school, thinking it will help, but it just gets you deeper into your own hole. Now you really *have* to work in that field, you've got something invested. And all the other things you found so interesting, you don't have time for them. You find a girl and settle on her and it doesn't really work out, but you're married, and you've got kids, and all the other women you could have been with just pass by. You do your job and it bores the shit out of you and by the time you know it well, you're too old to drop everything and start over. And the day comes when it tires you out to climb the stairs, and you start forgetting things, and it doesn't get as hard anymore. You try to keep going and pretend that everything is okay but you know that your family hates your and you hate them right back and you know *that your life has narrowed down to nothing at all.*"

Kate held his hand while he cried.

At last, he leaned back in his chair and looked at me. It was the first time I'd really seen him, and it wasn't pretty.

"My job is done here, Bruce. I'm going to pick up my things and leave now. I'm going to send Anne in. You two can get divorced tomorrow or put it back together or whatever you want. But whatever happens in the future, right now, today, the two of you are parents and the worst thing in the world has happened to you. I want you to think about that when you see her."

We shook hands and I left the house for the last time.

Anne was still in the car. "I've talked to Bruce about Amy."

"How is he?"

"He's had a bit to drink, but he's doing as well as anyone could. He's in his office."

She got out. "You've treated me better than I deserve."

"The only crime you've committed is theft by deception. And you've made full restitution."

"I don't mean legally."

"No, but it's a starting point for thinking about things. Listen, you gave me a good piece of advice. Let me return the favor. I'm not a marriage counselor, and I can't do divorce work anymore. But you and Bruce are back where you started; there are no kids, just the two of you. Whether you stay with him or not, he's feeling a lot of guilt. And some of it's deserved. No one has the right to blind themselves to everything going on around them. But he's not a bad man, and right now he really needs you."

Kate hugged her. "Hey, I know I'm not exactly your

long-lost sister, but I am family. If you want me to go in with you, I will.''

Anne shook her head. ''It's something I have to face alone.'' She walked to the front door and stood there for a long moment; then she pushed open the door and shut it behind her. The sound echoed against the trees and snowbanks, a hard, final sound. I thought about Nancy Saunders.

I threw my bag into the backseat and turned to Kate. ''And what about you?''

She rubbed her eyes. ''I want some sleep but I don't want it here. I've had enough of this place.''

''I'm going to find a motel for the rest of the morning and sleep. Then I want to go to Nancy's funeral.''

''You only met her once, and she lied to you,'' Kate said.

''She was standing by her friend the best way she knew how.''

''I'll come with you.''

''You never met her at all.''

''My flight back to Miami is first thing Saturday morning, out of Philadelphia. Today's my last chance to see you.'' She touched the side of my face. ''Have you ever made love after a funeral?''

''Too damned many times already.''

''All the more reason you should.''

Don't miss the next
Dave Garrett mystery,
BURNING MARCH,
Coming from Dutton
in March 1994

Tuesday 10:00 A.M.

I didn't know the receptionist, which was a relief. It was difficult enough being back at my old firm without seeing someone right away who remembered me. When I'd left, we'd been using a stout mother of five who spoke with a South Philadelphia accent and transposed phone numbers. I wondered if she'd been one of the hundreds of thousands of Philadelphians who'd fled to the suburbs in the last couple of years. The woman behind the desk was one of the new breed of city office workers—young, black, probably single, and very likely still living with her parents. The clothes and jewelry didn't look like they came out of a budget that included a rent check.

"My name is David Garrett. I'm here to see Emily Voss."

I didn't get the reaction I expected. She just looked at me, her mouth slightly open. She started to say something, but it trickled away after a couple of syllables. Then she recovered enough to put some words together. "Uh . . . do you have an appointment, sir?"

"Yes, I do."

"Please—just have a set for a minute." She picked up the phone, but hesitated long time before punching the buttons.

The room was just the same as when I'd last seen it more than two years ago. Dark wood paneling, scarred by contact with the backs and armrests of the wooden chairs. A couple of dim lamps. A low table with magazines. I noticed that they were still making the same mistakes with the reading material—what kind of impression did *Law Office Economics* make on the clients? I remember telling Emily it gave me a funny feeling that we set out *Condé Nast Traveler* for a clientele that included shabbily dressed young couples filing bankruptcy. ''It'll give the kids something to shoot for,'' she said in a voice that left no room for disagreement, and I'd let it drop.

The last time I'd been in this room was the day my disbarrment took effect, the day before Thanksgiving. Somebody at the Pennsylvania Supreme Court had a hell of a sense of humor, picking that date. The next day I couldn't think of much to be thankful for. I remember boxing up my things with the help of my secretary and carting them down to my car. It was an awkward day, and the strain showed in everyone's face. Attorneys clogged the hallways and the door to my office, mostly being silent, sometimes offering help or encouragement. The partners I'd been closest to took me out for a last lunch. If we'd been daytime drinkers we might have achieved the atmosphere of a good Irish wake, but we weren't. One of them, not thinking through his words very well, suggested that since I wasn't a lawyer anymore I could go ahead and get as drunk as I wanted, which didn't help the atmosphere much. There was simply nothing useful to be said, and by the end of lunch our table was completely silent. People were afraid to face me. When we returned we saw that Tom Richardson, the senior partner, had signed himself out to ''Legal Research—Law Library.'' We all knew that he hadn't been to the law library in twenty years. He never came back the rest of the afternoon.

''Dave, I'm glad to see you again.''

The voice was warm and rich, and a little scarred by forty years of smoking. I looked up; Tom was standing at the doorway that led back to the private offices. He was stout and short, with just a dark wisp of hair at the temples.

''Tom, you haven't changed a bit.'' I offered him my hand, but he came forward and embraced me instead.

''We've missed you, Dave.''

"It's good to see you again, Tom" We released each other and I got a good, close look. He was wearing trifocals now instead of just bifocals, and his skin looked a little more flushed, but the most important thing was his eyes, which were baggy and almost glazed over with fatigue. I was looking at a very tired man. I lied a little. "You look just the same as ever."

"That's the advantage of being bald and fat, not much more can go wrong." But his tone was flat and he didn't even try to smile.

"I was here to see Emily, actually."

"That's what Denise told me." His tone became more clipped. "Dave, we have to talk. In my office. Coffee?

"Thanks. Black, no sugar."

I had some time to look around while he ordered coffee. It was an old man's office, full of the smells of pipe smoke and furniture oil. His desk was an immense oak affair, darkened by the years and covered with books and piles of legal documents. In one corner was a photograph of his wife, dead before I'd ever joined the firm. One wall was taken up with a decaying set of nineteenth-century Pennsylvania Supreme Court decisions, which gave off a faintly musty smell. The leather chairs smelled of sweat, from the days before offices were air conditioned. A state-of-the-art dictating machine sat on a table across the room, still in its factory plastic.

"Still dictating to Margaret?" I asked.

He glanced at the machine briefly as if he was surprised it was there. "Never could figure out what was supposed to be the advantage of those damned things. It takes me the same amount of time to dictate no matter if she's here or not. And if I make a mistake or leave something out, she's right there to ask me about it."

"And if she takes it down herself you know that she'll do the typing herself and not the office pool." It was an argument that had gone on the whole time I'd been a partner.

"And so what? Being the managing partner ought to have some perks, shouldn't it?"

An unfamiliar secretary brought in coffee—evidently Margaret had reached the stage in life where she could delegate such things—and quickly disappeared. "You won that fight a long time ago, Tom." The dictation system had been my idea, five years before, and before I'd ever presented it I had known that an exception would have to be made for him.

I saw him looking at my ringless left hand as I held the cup of coffee. "Things didn't work out with Terry, I suppose," he said.

"They'd been rocky for a long time anyway. She lost her license, too, you know."

"You're a generous man to look at it that way. She's the reason you're not a lawyer now."

I sipped my coffee. I appreciated his concern, but talking about it didn't help. "So what's going on with Emily? Isn't she in yet?"

He avoided my question. "When did she call you?"

"Last Friday. She wanted me to come down to talk about something. Monday was bad for me, so we set it for this morning."

"What did she say she wanted to see you about?"

"What's going on here, Tom?"

"Do you know what happened to Emily?"

"Happened?"

"She's dead."

"When?"

"Late last night or early this morning. There was a fire in her apartment."

"Jesus, I didn't know anything about this. When did you find out?"

"The police called the firm's answering service about four this morning. I've been up since then."

"I liked her. She sent me a nice note after I left."

"We're all going to miss her. The reason you don't see Margaret is because she's taken the day off. She came in and left right away when she heard the news. They were close, you know."

"You look like you could stand to bag it, too."

"There's too much to do." His voice was worn and thin. He'd never looked younger than his age, but now he looked a lot older.

"When's the funeral?"

He shook his head. "She left instructions she didn't want a burial, just a memorial service, and cremation, and the ashes scattered on the ocean. I'll be taking care of that, since there's really no family. She wasn't close with her sister, and the woman's all the way across the country."

Neither of us said anything for a moment, and I had a feeling where the conversation was going to go next. But I wanted to let him take the lead.

"What did she want to talk to you about?" he asked.

"I wish I knew, Tom. She just said that she wanted a consultation to decide whether or not the firm needed an investigator."

"To investigate what?"

"She didn't give me any idea. It wasn't a long conversation. The main points were that it involved the firm, and that she hadn't made a decision to hire me, she was just checking out options."

"She was an employee. What gave her the idea she could make a decision like that?"

"I don't know." But I had a hunch that whatever she wanted to talk to me about, she didn't feel comfortable sharing it with any of the partners, at least without talking to me first.

He drummed his fingers on his desk. "Her calling you." This is very . . . disquieting, Dave."

"Did she say anything to you last week?"

"Just the usual day-to-day things. She certainly didn't mention you. Or why we'd need an investigator."

"What about yesterday?"

"She wasn't here."

"Oh?"

"She called in first thing Monday morning and said she was ill, that she wouldn't be in the rest of the day. The fire took place late last evening or very early this morning." He frowned. "She was hardly ever sick. I can't remember the last time she'd taken a day off, except for vacations."

"You sound like you've already done some checking."

"Well, the illness was real enough. I saw her on Friday, and she had a cold. I talked to her family doctor, got him out of bed at six this morning. He saw her late Friday afternoon and gave her some pills. I talked to her briefly on Saturday afternoon and she said her throat was sore, that she was feeling worse."

"Did she mention whether she'd be in Monday?"

"No, it wasn't discussed."

"What did she say when she called in Monday morning?"

"She left a message with the answering service; no one here talked to her. The message was just that she would be out Monday but would be in Tuesday. This may be none of my business, Dave, but had Emily ever called you before last Friday for anything?"

"No. And I'll save you the trouble of saying it. The call to me and her death—it may be a coincidence, but I'm not convinced. I'd like you to fill me in on what you've learned."

"I haven't seen the report myself, but the medical examiner's office read me the highlights over the phone just a few minutes ago. They say that the fire was accidental."

"Hold on a minute. How does the M.E. get to that conclusion? That's the fire marshal's job."

"I'm sorry. This isn't my field and I'm getting things a little confused. The fire marshal said that it was a kitchen fire. They said that they would be suspicious only if it was shown that she died before the fire. In other words, that she was killed and then the fire was set to cover up a homicide. And the medical examiner says she was definitely alive at the time of the fire."

"How did they determine that?"

He swallowed. "They said they found smoke and soot particles in her bronchial tubes. It shows she was still breathing during the fire. Does that sound right to you?"

"Sounds plausible to me, but this is a little out of my field."

"I thought you were the fire expert."

I shrugged. "I handled some fire cases when we used to do subrogation work for Prudential, but I don't know about cause-of-death issues. The fire marshal's theory is that she put something on the stove and forgot about it?"

"Basically, yes."

"As I recall from Christmas parties, she drank, didn't she?"

"Not heavily."

"The pills the doctor gave her, were they some kind of antihistamine, that she shouldn't have taken with alcohol?"

"I have the names from her doctor; I haven't had time to look them up yet."

"What if she took her pills, put something on the stove, had a nightcap or two while waiting for her dinner, and just went out?"

"And what if she didn't?" It wasn't really a question.

"Tom, come on. You should hear yourself."

He turned away from me and looked at the rows of books on the far wall. He chose his words carefully. "I knew this woman very well. She was as methodical and careful as anyone you'd ever meet. In twenty years the books were never off by a penny. Do you think she'd ignore a warning about mixing alcohol and medication? And what would she be doing up in the middle of the night, cooking a meal? She practically never cooked—she lived where she did because there were enough all-night restaurants and take-out places around that she didn't need to. And even if she took a day off, can you imagine her not checking in to see if everything was all right?"

"There's nothing in what you've said that isn't explained by her illness, except the cooking. And as far as that goes, we don't have to assume she had an urge to play Julia Child at midnight. She could have been just heating up some take-out, or a doggie bag. You said yourself she had no great experience in the kitchen; maybe with some pills and a couple of drinks in her she didn't realize the danger of leaving food unattended."

"So explain why she was cooking in the middle of the night."

"She'd slept all day and her sleep patterns were screwed up."

"He sighed. "You're giving me quite a hard time."

"That's because you're a friend."

He looked at me impatiently. "So do something other than cross-examine me."

"Assuming, just assuming, that her death is suspicious, do you think there could be any connection to the firm?"

"What do you mean?"

"A lot of money passed through her hands."

"So?"

"Perhaps she was diverting funds."

"I don't believe it, not for a second."

"Just assume."

He moved uncomfortably in his seat. "All right. I'll entertain the idea. How does that explain a murder?"

"Maybe she was stealing on instructions from someone, or to pay a blackmailer, and they leaned on her too hard."

He snorted. "Emily being blackmailed? What on earth for? That sounds pretty silly."

"Can you think of anyone who meant her harm?"

"Not a soul."

"Do you know anything about her life out of the office?"

He thought for a moment. "Mmm. Not really."

I sighed. "Are the books being checked?"

He looked across the room at the Supreme Court opinions for a while before he answered. "I decided to do that after I got the news this morning."

"Why?"

He seemed surprised at the question. "Well, when I made the decision I was just thinking that whoever is going to take over needs to be sure everything is in order. We're having a review done by the accountants. It should be getting underway later this morning."

It was an interesting step for someone who said he had no reason to think her death had anything to do with the firm, but I kept that to myself. "You've been busy."

"I've been up since four. You can get a lot done in six hours if you don't have any distractions."

"What do you have in the way of documents at this point?"

"I'll give you what I have." He handed me a slim folder. It was an office file, with "Thomas H. Richardson" as the client and "Emily Voss" as the file name. Tom was nothing if not organized. I opened it and found myself looking at her picture. There's a Jewish superstition about pictures of the dead, and seeing the photo sent a tingle up my spine. She didn't look like a person who ought to be dead—she was smiling at the camera, and her head was turned a little to one side. Her hair was gray, and I'd never seen her hair in anything but a bun, but in this picture it was down to her shoulders. From the background, it looked like she was sitting at a table in a sidewalk café. She was wearing slacks and a loose-fitting scooped neck top that did a better job of minimizing her middle age spread than the suits that she wore to the office. I corrected myself—that she *used* to wear.

I put down the picture. I'd known her only as the person who kept the books in order, not as someone who let her hair down and smiled in the sunshine. . . . It depressed me that we'd worked closely for years and how little I really knew about her. I realized that she was fifty—only six years older than me.

Next was her personnel file, in its own folder, which I put aside for the moment. Last was Tom's notes from his conversation with the medical examiner's office, written on a yellow legal pad. His handwriting was clear and precise, and it read as easily as a typed memo. I reviewed it carefully and looked up at him.

"Tom, you said she didn't drink heavily."

"No, she didn't."

"What makes you so sure?"

"She was here for every Christmas party for nearly thirty years, plus the employees' annual dinner. I never knew her to have more than two glasses of wine."

"Could she have been a weekend binger?"

"No." He was annoyed by my questions. "She was in the office most Saturdays and sometimes on Sundays, and I never had a hint she was hung-over, not once. And I keep an eye out for that kind of thing, you know." I nodded; he had been the first to suspect that one of our associates was addicted to cocaine when none of the younger partners had a clue. He could be a surprisingly modern man when he wanted to be.

"What if she just didn't come in on the weekends she was loaded?"

"She was in a lot more weekends than she wasn't. And even when she was at home, sometimes I'd need to talk to her about finances. I never found her drunk, or even drinking."

"Sometimes alcoholics can fool the rest of us pretty well. They can act sober even when their blood alcohol is high."

"Answer me this—even if someone drunk could pull off an act, she wouldn't be able to do things that alcohol impairs, like complicated calculations, would she?"

"That's right."

"Even on the weekends she wasn't in she took work home, and it was always done by Monday. Always."

I thought about what he'd said for a minute, looking for flaws. Then I held out one of the yellow note pages to him. "Tom, right here, you have written "point-three-three-seven. You see where I mean?"

He leaned toward me and moved his head up and down, hunting for the proper angle out of his trifocals. "Yes, I see it."

"What does that mean?"

"That was what they said her blood-alcohol level was."

"That's what I thought. Are you sure you got it down

right? I mean, could it have been point oh-three-three-seven?"

"No, I'm sure of it. I made him repeat it for me. Does it mean anything?"

"How much did she weigh?"

"What? How would I know?"

"I'm guessing around a hundred and forty."

"I suppose. But what does that mean?"

"If she died before she ate the food that was on the stove, then her stomach was probably empty."

"What are you talking about?"

"Someone of her weight, on an empty stomach, would have to drink the better part of a fifth of hard liquor to get that kind of a reading. In Pennsylvania, you're guilty of drunk driving if you're caught with point one percent blood alcohol—she was more than three times the legal limit. It's more than enough to make someone pass out who wasn't a heavy drinker."

"I'm not sure I'm following you."

"Maybe she drank that much herself—you know, you have a drink and a cold pill, and you forget what you've done, and you keep drinking till you've gone too far. People die that way from barbiturates and alcohol accidentally all the time. But maybe she didn't drink it, at least not voluntarily."

"What are you saying?"

"Maybe, just maybe, someone forced her to drink it and set the fire after she passed out."

He gave no reaction. For a moment I thought he hadn't heard me or hadn't understood. Then I saw that he'd dropped his eyes and was staring at an empty space on his desk. A full ten seconds went by before he raised his face. "That's horrible!" he said softly. "How could anyone want to do that to poor Emily?"

"I don't know that they did, Tom. It's just a possibility."

He shivered and pushed himself back from the desk. Suddenly he didn't seem to know what to do with his hands. "Emily being gone is bad enough, but this . . ." His hands made an aimless gesture and collapsed into his lap.

"It's worse than that."

"How could it be?"

"She wanted to see me about something to do with the firm—I don't know exactly what about, but I'm sure it wasn't a personal matter. If her phone call to me is tied in with her death, the killer could be someone in this firm."